ALL OUR YESTERDAYS

LYRA LAVENDER

Copyright © 2020 Lyra Lavender
All rights reserved
First Edition

PAGE PUBLISHING, INC.
Conneaut Lake, PA

First originally published by Page Publishing 2020

ISBN 978-1-64701-912-9 (pbk)
ISBN 978-1-64701-913-6 (digital)

Printed in the United States of America

Acknowledgments

There are so many people who help and influence us in our lives and in the stories we weave. It's impossible to officially remember them all, but I would like to mention a few who did.

I want to thank my wonderful parents, Sara and Sam, for giving me love, for teaching me to respect others and myself, and for fostering in me a deep appreciation of knowledge, humor, the arts and the English language. Thanks to my dear and brilliant sister (and partner in many childhood fantasies and stories) Carol, her ever-entertaining and helpful husband and their beautiful and exceptional children and grandchildren (whom I have always thought of as mine) for their encouragement and good times through the years. To my marvelous husband, Charles (my Charlie), for giving me love when we were young and for finding me again many years later (a true romance) and for making me a part of his own great family. And to my friends, present and past—you were all very special to me. We shared many good times, and you taught me a lot about friendship and about myself, and I'd like to raise a glass to you.

And I'd like to recognize the staff of Page Publishing for their invaluable help in bringing this book to fruition. Thank you all, especially Matt Johnson and Nicole Reefer.

Also, I'd like to acknowledge some of the many authors who have inspired me through my life. Thanks to many fascinating historical novelists I've enjoyed, such as Georgette Heyer, Elizabeth Mansfield, Mary Balough, and especially Maud Hart Lovelace. And I also appreciate the writers of fantasy, particularly Elsworth Thane (*Tryst*), Robert Nathan (*A Portrait of Jenny*), and Jack Finney (*Time After Time*), who showed me that supernatural stories can sometimes seem pleasant, comforting, and romantic, and even both super and natural!

Chapter 1

"I'll be thrilled if I look half that good when I'm eighty." Serena Cassidy sighed, studying the final portrait of her namesake, Serena Longworth.

Serena wasn't exaggerating. The picture, which bore a plaque, dated 1885–1974 showed a truly lovely woman. Her rose dress hugged a still-tiny waist, the gray hair piled on her head appeared thick and lively, the skin smooth and firm, and the hazel eyes, which seemed to stare into Serena Cassidy's own hazel ones, looked clear and enthusiastic.

"One of the many reasons my parents wanted to name me after Mrs. Longworth was that she was such a vibrant attractive woman," Serena continued.

"Oh gosh, yeah," said the woman beside her. "I knew her when I was a kid. I'm Martha Whitter, by the way. You can call me Martha. You see, my family has lived next door to the Longworth's for generations. My great grandfather was the first school administrator when it was just a boy's prep school. Anyway"—she pointed to the picture—"she was about that age when I knew her and she was a great old gal! Downright beautiful for her age and just so energetic and up-to-the-minute at the same time that she was sort of old-fashioned. She had a knack for knowing what was going to come in style, almost what was going to happen before it did."

"My parents thought she was remarkable," said Serena, a little amused at the woman's loquaciousness.

"And funny too," Mrs. Whitter continued her story. "She was such a lady, but sometimes she'd whisper cusswords that I didn't really even know the meanings of 'til years after! But I think the thing that I remember most about her was that she was so happy! I asked her once what made her so happy and she said it was love! She said she had had the greatest and most remarkable love with the most wonderful husband in the world and that she'd had the best parents and children in the world and that she knew she would see them all again someday—and you know, she even said she'd see me again someday, which I thought was so sweet of her to say—so I guess her faith must have been really strong too—" Mrs. Whitter paused for a breath of air and looked directly at Serena for the first time in several minutes. "You know," she said, "I think you may look very much like her, when you're that age. Are you a relative?"

"No. My parents went to school here in the seventies. And Mrs. Longworth introduced them."

"Oh, how lovely!" trilled Martha Whitter. "Are your parents here too?"

"No," said Serena, slowly. "They, uh, were killed in a train wreck recently."

"Oh, you poor dear," said Martha, putting a hand over Serena's.

"B-but they really loved Longworth College," Serena hurried on, hoping to get past the awkward moment and the tears she felt threatening, "and…and Mrs. Longworth. So they always contributed to the alumnae association—and I've continued it in their names—though I didn't attend college here. And they were so excited to attend the centennial celebration ten years ago, so I really wanted to come to this event in their names."

"Well, of course, you did," said Mrs. Whitter soothingly. "So sweet of you to represent them. Is this your first visit to the college?" she prompted, when Serena seemed about to give in to sadness.

"No," said Serena. "My parents brought me up here when I was thirteen. Of course, the house wasn't open for tours then, but," she added, a bit shakily, "they showed me all sorts of things, including the rhododendron bush where they stole their first kiss.

"What fun," said Martha Whitter, leading the younger woman to a comfortable wicker settee on the side porch. "And Serena Longworth introduced them?"

"Yes," Serena answered. "Here in this very house, back in 1972."

ALL OUR YESTERDAYS

Martha Whitter smiled encouragingly and somehow it seemed natural to continue. For such a vociferous talker, Martha was a surprisingly good listener. So as they sipped their cocktails and waited for the next tour to begin, Serena related the story of how her parents had come to know each other and Serena Longworth.

Early in their senior year in high school, in 1971, Carolyn Niels and Michael Cassidy had both sent for several college catalogs, picking the schools mostly on the advice of their school counselors. Both were somewhat surprised to receive correspondence from Longworth College, which neither had requested.

Included in each packet was a catalog which showed beautiful photos of the small, but prestigious college nestled in the foothills of the Virginia mountains, application forms and a letter stating that each recipient of the packet had been picked specifically as an outstanding student and promising future addition to Longworth College and offering the strong possibility of a scholarship.

The receipt of an unsolicited catalog wasn't really unusual for Michael. He was salutatorian of his large graduating class and had scored 1,500 on his college boards, but he did live rather far away from the school—in Lincoln, Nebraska. He knew, however, that the college's founder, Trenton Longworth had served as a US senator and the letter stressed the school's strong history and political science departments, so he supposed his having been one of that year's winners of the World Peace Essay Contest for civics students might have influenced the school to recruit him.

On the other hand, having lived her whole life in Greenville, South Carolina, Carolyn was closer to the school, but she was still amazed to be chosen for special notice by a college. Though her college boards were well above average, most of her grades had always been mediocre, since she wasn't particularly interested in academic subjects.

Of course, she had won art awards all through school and the letter touted the college's fine arts department. Still, she was curious, if flattered, about being singled out.

However, since the college application process could become expensive, both Michael and Carolyn decided to follow their counselors' advice and applied first to the schools the counselors had originally recommended. But Longworth College did not give up. When Carolyn and Michael did not immediately respond to the initial packets, they received second letters, including further inducements and encouragement, including offers to wave the application fees. Both then decided to apply and were quickly offered generous scholarships, which both eventually accepted and both of them began to eagerly anticipate their freshman year.

They were not disappointed. Not only was Longworth College a bounty of graceful colonial architecture and spectacular scenery, but also their reception seemed extraordinary. Their accommodations were more than adequate; their assigned roommates seemed chosen precisely to complement their personalities and each staff member appeared anxious to meet them personally.

"It was like I'd come home," Carolyn said later.

At the end of orientation week, Michael and Carolyn, along with other selected students and dignitaries from the school and surrounding areas, were invited to a reception at the home of Serena Longworth, widow of the college's founder.

Michael often told of being graciously accosted by the beautiful old woman, who asked him "a million" questions, enthusiastically presented him to VIPs and, finally, with much fanfare, introduced him to Miss Carolyn Niels, as soon as Carolyn came through the door.

For the rest of the evening, Michael and Carolyn were together, often accompanied by Serena Longworth.

"We already sort of wanted it to be just the two of us," Carolyn told her daughter. "And Serena realized it too. She kept saying, 'Well, I'll leave you two alone,' but then she'd always come back. But we didn't really mind. She was such a dear. And she seemed to think we were so special. I'd never been treated quite that way before—maybe not even since."

The very next night, Carolyn and Michael had their first date and by their second, they were stealing kisses behind the famous rhododendron bush.

"Which was pretty fast for the early 1970s!" Michael said.

From then on, all the couple's free time was spent together. Much of it was also spent with Serena, who seemed to dote on them. "She kept up with all our activities. She even teased us about the rhododendron bush—we never figured out how she knew about that—it wasn't close to her house. Really, you would almost think she didn't have any children of her own," mused Carolyn, "but she did—children and grandchildren and she was very close to all of them. So, of course, we met all of them too."

In addition, Michael and Carolyn were introduced to all the many famous and fascinating people who came to visit the great old lady.

At the end of their sophomore year, Michael Cassidy and Carolyn Niels became officially engaged. Serena Longworth lived long enough to effusively congratulate them ("It's just as it should be!") and then died, smiling in her sleep, a few weeks later.

It wasn't too surprising, given her intense interest in them, that Mrs. Longworth would leave Serena's parents something in her will, but they were amazed to learn that their bequests were nearly equal to the widow's children's portions of the large estate. Serena's children didn't appear to mind, however, and seemed to find the settlement fair.

With this money, Michael and Carolyn were easily able to marry just after graduation, without any financial help from their own parents and to leisurely establish themselves in their chosen careers.

Michael eventually joined the diplomatic corps, and as she traveled with him, Carolyn began to make a name for herself as an artist, painting vivid watercolors, mostly of flowers, from unusual points of view.

They were having so much fun, it was several years before Carolyn and Michael decided it was time for children. When their only child, a daughter, was born in 1984 it seemed the most natural thing in the world to name her after their benefactress.

Throughout their lives, the Cassidys continued to feel Serena Longworth's influence. With nearly every opportunity offered them, they found that their friend had laid the groundwork years before, giving a word here and a hint there with influential acquaintances "just in case."

"How did she know just what we'd need?" Michael often asked.

"So I spent most of my life traveling with my parents," Serena told Martha. "I went to school all over the world, I even had summer art classes at the Sorbonne. And we all had so much fun!"

"I guess you have friends everywhere!" said Martha.

"Oh, of course, or at least very dear acquaintances, fascinating people!" answered Serena. "But if you mean really close friends—the soul mate sort—not really, I'm afraid. I was always so close to my parents, especially my mother—she was always my best friend. Of course, I had buddies when I was a kid, but we moved so much, those relationships didn't amount to much. I didn't feel like I needed anyone else but my parents. Looking back, I guess it was a mistake, but then it seemed like we had all the time in the world."

"Oh, I know," said Martha Whitter. "It always seems like that. I felt the same way when my husband passed away and we'd been together for thirty-seven years!"

"But I'm sure your parents were wonderful people," added Martha, evidently sensing Serena needed to spend more time on the subject.

"Oh, they were!" Serena smiled. "Mom was tiny. She always seemed so much younger than she was like my age, you know. We were always being silly together. Even after all those years, she loved to travel and see everything in each place we visited. And she had nicknames for everyone. She called Dad everything from 'Mickey Mouse' to 'Michelangelo,' because of his name. But her favorite was 'Ol' Brown Eyes,' because his eyes were so remarkable. She said she thought the main reason he was so successful as a diplomat was because his eyes mesmerized people.

"A-and he—I don't know—he just took care of everything. Mom and I were modern women, I think—I mean, we could take care of ourselves if we had to, but we really didn't need to. He was such a whiz with finances and reservations and schedules. You hardly thought about it—it was just done for you with no fuss. And he was funny too—always quoting Mark Twain—and W. C. Fields.

"And then that train in France…," she whispered, her eyes glistening with tears.

"Were you with them at the time?" asked Martha gently.

"No. I was in my senior year in college in England. My parents loved this school so much and it's so beautiful up here, I always sort of intended to study here. But then I got this offer to study commercial art in England and that way, I could still see my parents some on weekends."

Martha Whitter patted Serena's hand. "That must have been a very hard time for you."

"Yes, it was terribly hard," admitted Serena. "Somehow, I managed to finish college, but then I wanted a complete change. So for a little more than a year, I've been working for an advertising agency in New York."

"How's that going?" asked Martha.

"Well, not great. Actually, I've had some success, but I just don't feel comfortable. It's a cliché, but it's true, advertising is a dog-eat-dog world. Ethics and aesthetics aren't really concerns, just profit margins. And it's so aggressively modern. I guess I'm a child of the computer age, but I've never really liked them.

"To tell you the truth, I'm on a leave of absence now. I have some money from my parents, so I'm just going travel around in this area for a while! I seem to need peace and beauty and…and old stuff like this. And New York can be pretty lonely too."

"But you must have lots of boyfriends," said Martha. "A pretty girl like you."

"Well, no," sighed Serena. "Oh, I date and I've even been engaged a couple of times, once since the—uh, wreck, but it never seems to work. It just doesn't seem right. I'd love to have someone, and I really try, but I just never find guys on the same wavelength I am."

"Don't worry, sweetie," crooned Martha. "Your other half is out there somewhere."

"I hope so," said Serena. "But sometimes, I feel like the man for me is not in this world. But listen to me, monopolizing the conversation with my problems," said Serena, her natural buoyancy surfacing. "I'm sorry. You mentioned your husband, but you're not just sitting around bemoaning your fate."

"Well, it's been a while," said Martha, easily. "But speaking of Arnie," she continued quickly. "You know, Serena Longworth helped me get ready for my first date with him? Like I said, she had such a knack for that sort of thing. Loved clothes. She would have been crazy about that dress you have on," she said, assessing Serena's crocheted lace with its ice-blue lining.

"Really?" asked Serena. "Thanks. I had it made from antique tablecloths. That was one of the things that attracted me to this celebration, the fact that they encouraged the 1908 costumes. I love clothes from that era."

"Well, it looks great on you," said Martha. "And that cameo really sets it off."

"I bought that after I got here, in a little antique store in Belle Vieux," said Serena, fingering the broach at her throat. The pin's oval center was intricately carved, showing three elegant Greek ladies, each holding a musical instrument and standing under an archway of flowers and it was bordered by delicate gold filigree and pearls.

"The guy there didn't know much about it—just that it came from an estate sale from somewhere around here. But it doesn't seem to be a genuine cameo—I mean, this isn't shell it's carved in. We thought it might be an early Wedgwood design, though this aqua background isn't typical for them either, is it?"

"I don't think so," said Martha. "It's quite unusual, but the color is perfect for your dress."

Serena thanked Martha again and was complimenting her on her long navy skirt and middy blouse when the door to the main house opened and a woman in a black lace dress stepped out.

"Ladies and gentlemen," she called to the people grouped around the entrance hall, lawns, and porches. "I'm Grace Pierson, president of the Friends of Longworth College Society. If you'll just gather round me, our tour of the house will now begin."

Chapter 2

"This house was opened to the public in 1999, after being restored to its original condition. It has been called one of the best surviving examples of Victorian architecture in the country, one of the 'grand old ladies,' as we sometimes call them," said Miss Pierson, with a bit of a simper. "It was built in 1890's, after the original house was burned.

"Trenton Longworth acquired the services of one of the era's leading architects, but the basic design for the house was Senator Longworth's. Of course." she laughed, "he wasn't a senator then. He was a young man. Very young when you consider that he had already, in 1898—as you know—affected the transition from the Longworth Preparatory School for Young Men (which was established in 1884, by his father, Nigel Longworth) to Longworth College.

"Yes," continued Miss Pierson. "Trenton Longworth was truly a Renaissance man—educator, statesman, architect, author—very much like his fellow Virginian of a different era, Thomas Jefferson.

"I'm sure most of you have observed these portraits," she said, with a grand gesture around the foyer. "This, of course, was Trenton Longworth. This was the last portrait painted of him, done in 1954, four years before his death of a heart attack. At that time, he had retired from his long-held senatorial seat and, as professor emeritus, was lecturing only occasionally at the college. He said that he retired so that he could travel and spend more time with his wife. He was said to be healthy and vigorous 'til the end."

Serena stared once again at the picture of the handsome old man with the iron-gray hair. Through the years, she had read as much as she could about her namesake and her husband. She had always admired Trenton Longworth and had seen many pictures of him in the past, including reproductions of this one. However, tonight, the deep gray eyes seemed to be communicating with her in a way they never had before.

When she had finished the long list of Trenton Longworth's accomplishments, the society's president turned, with a sweeping gesture to the portrait on the other side of the hall.

"And this lovely lady is Serena Longworth, Trenton's second wife, actually, but they were married for nearly fifty years and she was definitely the love of his life and the great lady of this great man!

"Serena Longworth was also a person of great accomplishment, in her own right. As a volunteer, she worked extensively with programs for the handicapped, was instrumental in bringing the arts to this area, and even to more isolated mountain regions. With Dr. Margaret Sanger, whom Serena traveled to consult in 1910, she fought to bring birth control to the women of Appalachia. Mrs. Longworth also collaborated with her sister-in-law, Constance, to establish a needlework pattern company, which is still in existence and family-owned today. But perhaps her greatest accomplishment was Longworth Women's College (now consolidated with the men's school) which, as Trenton Longworth admitted, was opened due to her influence.

"In addition, she was the mother of two children—a son who was an award-winning artist and architect, and a daughter who was an outstanding educator. And," Miss Pierson finished proudly, "one of her granddaughters Rebecca Marshall is presently one of our state senators!"

Serena shook her head admiringly. "Wow, she really was something!" she whispered to Martha, as Grace Pierson ushered them into the front parlor.

"If you'll direct your attention to the Chippendale drum table," said Miss Pierson. "You'll see photographs of Anne Drayton Longworth, first wife of Trenton," she told them, pointing to a picture of a pretty, delicate-looking woman with a high ruff around her neck, "and Trenton Longworth, age twenty-three, at the time of their marriage."

Serena looked at the sepia photograph of Trenton Longworth. Even in the stiff style of the daguerreotype, his youth and vitality fairly burst from the frame. Trenton looked handsome, happy and confident, as if he could take on the world.

With many arch smiles and game show hostess gestures, Grace Pierson continued to point out various furniture styles and Longworth family mementos.

"The portrait over the fireplace," she said, "is of Trenton Longworth in about 1905 or 1906. He had facilitated the school's becoming a college in 1898, and his first wife, Anne Longworth, after a long illness, had passed away in 1904. As you can see, these things must have weighed quite heavily on him then."

Serena turned to look at the portrait, which she hadn't noticed before. Miss Pierson was certainly right that something appeared to weigh heavily on him. It was amazing to think that only ten or twelve years had passed since the photograph on the table. If she hadn't known, she would have thought she was looking at a man of almost fifty, rather than one in his early thirties. Lines had begun to form between his nose and mouth, his dark hair showed gray at the temples, and his expression—though determined—also revealed bitterness and resignation.

He must have loved Anne Drayton very much, thought Serena, romantically.

Yet later pictures always portrayed a man young for his years. Had Serena Longworth given him back his spark?

"Now," said Miss Pierson. "If you'll just step—"

A short, gray-haired woman in a long flowered dress rushed into the room. "Excuse me for interrupting, Mrs. Pierson?" she said breathlessly. "But Senator Marshall is here."

"Oh dear," said Miss Pierson, clutching her thick gold necklace. "I'm afraid I'm going to have to cut this tour short, but I will be conducting another one after the buffet, which we should be just about to serve in the side garden. Please enjoy yourselves and, uh, excuse me." Clearly flustered by the dignitary's arrival, she darted out of the room.

"Well, I never!" said Martha Whitter. "Kept us waiting in the foyer all that time and then cut us short after all. Oh well," she continued. "I guess it's about time to check on Mama, anyway."

"Your mother is with you?" asked Serena.

"Yeah, out in the garden with some friends. She's lived in the house next-door all her life. I moved back home with her after Arnie went. She's over a hundred years old, so she needs some looking after."

They passed from the right side porch to an elegant walled-in garden with a fountain in the middle. Around the spacious green lawns, buffet tables had been setup.

While Martha went to fetch her mother, Serena got a glass of champagne and perused the sumptuous spread. There was everything from the usual "drummies," assorted fruits, cheeses, and vegetables to more exotic Beluga caviar and truffles, and heavy stuff like prime rib and vegetable casserole.

"What are the cherry tomatoes stuffed with?" she asked the young server at one of the tables.

"Um, mock crab," answered the girl.

"Are you sure it's 'mock'?" Serena emphasized.

The girl assured her it was, so Serena added a couple to her plate.

As she traversed the tables. Serena watched the other partygoers with interest. Most of the men were in traditional black-tie regalia.

Probably, for most of them, dressing up at all seemed like enough of a concession, much less dressing up in costume, Serena thought.

But the women's clothes were much more interesting. Except for the caterers, in their usual uniforms of black slacks and white blouses, all the women seemed to have attempted 1908 garb with varying degrees of success.

Many of the ladies simply wore ruffled blouses and long full skirts, but there were also perfect Gibson girl dresses and walking suits, some with the stamp of newness and others which must have been family heirlooms or antique shop finds. Accessories were plentiful. There many beaded bags and lots of antique jewelry. There were parasols and picture hats and several bustled skirts.

Serena was glad she hadn't let her dressmaker talk her into a bustle on her dress.

Beside the higher costs for fabric and labor, the addition of a bustle would have made the dress more cumbersome. Besides, her research indicated that bustles had pretty much gone out of fashion by the early 1890s.

Serena's lined crocheted dress with its flared skirt, tiny pointed front waist, and leg-of-mutton sleeves looked exactly like the fabric plates and catalog illustrations Serena had found at the library and on the internet. She had combined her favorite elements from all the pictures to design the dress and then had found three modern patterns which could be combined to make it. She had wanted to make the dress herself, but her job had kept her busy right up to the day she left New York, so she had found a talented dressmaker. Though the woman had tried to persuade her to make a few changes in the design, Serena had prevailed and had gotten just what she wanted. The dress even had tiny buttons down the back instead of a zipper, and Serena had bought a front-hook corset and petticoats to make sure the fit was authentic. She felt comfortable among the other woman.

Serena was glad she had come. A gentle breeze stirred the leaves of the big elms overhead and Scott Joplin's ragtime wafted over an outdoor sound system. She wasn't well acquainted with anyone here, but her travels had made her used to that. She enjoyed people watching at functions like this.

Grace Pierson, Serena noted, was speaking effusively with a very attractive woman in a long green linen dress with beautiful cutwork flowers, whom Serena assumed was Senator Marshall. Though she didn't look it, from her reading Serena knew that the senator was about sixty.

She might have been around here when my parents were, Serena thought, deciding she'd try to ask her about it later.

"Here you are," called Martha Whitter, coming up beside Serena with a tiny white-haired woman in tow.

"Mama," said Martha slowly, facing the little woman and also speaking with her hands. "Remember I was telling you about the young lady I met during the tour? I'd like you to meet her." She turned to Serena. "My mother is deaf, dear, has been since birth. 'Hard of hearing' or 'hearing-impaired,' if you prefer, but Mama thinks euphemisms like that are a waste of time."

The little woman beside Martha laughed.

"Well, anyway, as I was saying, just face her directly when you're speaking to her and she can read your lips."

Serena smiled, wondering as she turned, if the mother's handicap contributed to Martha's love of conversation.

"Mama," Martha was saying, "this is Serena Cassidy. Serena, my mother, Letitia Jenson."

Miss Jenson was looking at Serena with an intensity which seemed odd, even for someone reading lips. "Miz Rena," she said in a high, oddly pitched voice.

"I'm pleased to meet you, Miss Jenson," said Serena carefully.

"Miz Rena!" said Letitia Jenson, sounding even more quavery and beginning to communicate with her daughter in rapid hand signals.

"No, Mama," said Martha determinedly. "This is not Miz Rena! That's what we called Mrs. Longworth," she added in an aside to Serena. "This lady's name is Serena too, but it's Serena Cassidy."

"Miz Rena," the mother insisted. "I know! Miz Rena!" Her hand motions became more agitated and her daughter's answering ones were just as emphatic, but still, the older woman insisted, with lots of head shaking and nods, "Miz Rena!"

Martha turned so her mother couldn't read her lips. "I'm sorry," she said to Serena. "I've never seen her like this. I guess her age is finally catching up with her. Maybe this crowd has been too much."

"Miz Rena," said Letitia, almost crying with frustration.

"It's okay. Mama," Martha faced her mother again and put her arm around her. "I think you're a little tired now. Why don't we go home for a while and have some of your peppermint tea?"

Miss Jenson allowed herself to be led, but still looked back imploringly at Serena.

"I'm sorry!" said Serena.

"Oh, honey," called Martha, over her shoulder, "don't think a thing about it. We have a lady who stays with us and helps out. The two of us will get Mama calmed down and she'll be fine. It's just next door. I'm sure I'll see you later."

But as they were going through the gate, Serena could still hear the old lady saying, "Martha, Miz Rena," in a plaintive voice.

"What a pity! Miss Letitia's such a dear old thing," said someone at Serena's elbow.

She turned to find Grace Pierson beside her. She was there, Serena felt sure, to be certain her social event suffered no more rough waters.

"But you certainly shouldn't feel responsible," Grace added smoothly. "At her age, they just get confused. But I couldn't help hearing that your name is Serena Cassidy. Are you, by any chance, the daughter of Michael Cassidy and Carolyn, uh, Niels?"

Serena nodded.

"I went to school with them here. Such charming people!" said Miss Pierson. "Such a pity! We *heard*, you know. But so good of you to continue the donation in their name."

"Well they loved this school," said Serena. "And Serena Longworth was so good to them."

"Oh, she loved them!" effused Grace Pierson. "And who could blame her? Michael was so handsome! And, and Carolyn was—uh, such a good artist."

Serena smiled. Miss Pierson was actually blushing. Could it be that this august lady had had a schoolgirl crush on Pop?

Ol' Brown Eyes strikes again! She laughed to herself.

"Have you met the Bartletts?" asked Miss Pierson, changing the subject quickly.

Serena was glad to let Grace Pierson do the hostess bit for a while; she was still a little shaken from having unintentionally upset Miss Jenson. Also, seeing Martha and her mother together had made her wish for her own parents even stronger.

Miss Pierson saw that Serena got another glass of champagne and escorted her around the garden, praising Serena and her parents and introducing her to several pleasant groups of people, including the Ingersols, an energetic couple who were in charge of the next day's parade around the campus.

"We're putting people from the class of '58 in cars from that year," said Mr. Ingersol. "And we have people from other years—a few of 'em before '58—on a special float."

Eventually, Grace Pierson excused herself to go back to the podium area; the Ingersols began discussing last-minute arrangements with some of the alumnae, and Serena drifted back to the buffet tables.

She was selecting a couple more stuffed tomatoes when she noticed Senator Marshall at the next table, by the petit fours.

"Senator Marshall," Serena greeted her when she reached the older woman's side. "You don't know me, but I think you may have known my parents. I'm Serena Cassidy—"

"Oh!" Even from the side, Serena could see the woman's eyes widen in what appeared to be amazement. Senator Marshall put down her plate of decorated cakes and looked Serena up and down, in a disconcerting way. "It's true! Grand—"

"And so, without further ado"—Grace Pierson called over the loudspeaker—"let me present our own Senator Rebecca Marshall."

"Oh jeez!" The senator grimaced. "I really have to go on up there. But please," she took Serena's free hand in both of hers. "Please, let's talk as soon as I finish."

Senator Marshall didn't act very dignified for a politician, Serena thought, popping a cherry tomato into her mouth, *but at least she was eager to please.*

Still, Serena thought. *I've been getting some very odd reactions from people up here.* She felt a little breathless.

After a stammering beginning, Senator Marshall launched into a standard gracious speech, welcoming the alumnae and saying how important the college would always be to her family.

The speech was pleasant but unremarkable, but as she listened to the senator, Serena swallowed over a lump in her throat, a painful lump.

The lump quickly became a searing cramp. Serena threw her paper plate down on the tablecloth and supported herself against the table.

The cramps were coming in earnest now, through her abdomen and chest and her tongue felt thick. Desperately, Serena knocked on her chest with one fist and rubbed it in circular motions, at the same time, trying to take deep breaths.

"Miss Cassidy, are you all right?" Grace Pierson was, once again, at her side.

"N-not really, I'm afraid," Serena said, with difficulty. "It feels like I'm having an allergic reaction, but I don't know to what. I wondered about the tomatoes, but they said they were stuffed with mock crab—"

"Unh uh," said the head caterer, who had come over to see what was wrong. "We're not using the mock recipe this time. It really is crab meat in the tomatoes."

"And you're allergic to crab?" Grace Pierson assumed ominously. Serena nodded.

"Do we need to ask for emergency assistance?" asked Miss Pierson. "Maybe we have a doctor here tonight"

"I hope that won't be necessary," said Serena, between gasps. "I have some antihistamine pills with me."

"Then, a glass of cold water?" asked the hostess, directing the caterers to fetch it. "And maybe some soda crackers?"

"That might be good," said Serena, fishing in her purse for her pillbox. "Thanks. And," she felt the familiar bubble rising in her chest, "if you could just direct me to a ladies' room."

"Of course," said Miss Pierson, putting her arm around Serena and ushering her into the house. "Can you make it to the second floor? We've restored the powder room downstairs with 1899 fixtures, but the one next to our office upstairs has modern facilities and there's a sofa in the office to lie down on, for a while."

Serena attempted a smile. These social amenities weren't easy to maintain at the moment, but Miss Pierson was being very nice to her. Serena wondered if her solicitousness was due to the woman's old crush on Pop or to genuine concern. Or maybe that she didn't want the Longworth Association sued for poisoning a party guest.

Serena swallowed several times. "I seem to be causing a lot of trouble today."

"Don't be ridiculous," said Grace Pierson, ushering her into a room with a desk, modern office equipment, and the promised sofa. "Actually, it's other people who're causing you trouble. Where are you staying this weekend?" Grace added.

"I have a room in Belle Vieux," answered Serena, with effort, wishing just to be alone for a few minutes.

"Did you come up here on the alumnae bus?"

Serena nodded again.

"Oh dear," said Grace. "They'll be going back rather late, I'm afraid. But, you know, I think the Ingersols will be leaving early to get ready for the parade tomorrow. They live in Belle Vieux. If you don't feel up to staying, I'm sure they'd be glad to drive you back. Here's the powder room," she added, opening a door. "Mrs. Longworth had it done over in the sixties."

The room had peach fixtures and peach-and-light-green tile. Retro, compared to today's stark bathrooms, but very pretty, Serena thought fleetingly. They were the same colors she'd used to decorate her apartment in New York.

"Do you want me to stay with you?" asked Grace.

"No, th-thanks," Serena gasped. "Really, I'll be fine."

"All right," said Grace Pierson. "If you're sure. Here's a damp washcloth. I'll check on you later."

Ten minutes later, Serena was beginning to feel like herself again. Sitting at the vanity table in the tiny adjoining dressing room and munching on crackers, she surveyed herself in the mirror. Considering the evening she'd spent, she thought she looked pretty good. Her honey-colored hair, which had been styled in a perfect pompadour, finished with an ice-blue bow, looked almost as good as new, and her clothes had not been mussed at all. She had touched up her makeup (which she had kept very light to simulate the natural look of the early 1900s), and she had rinsed her mouth with some minty mouthwash she'd found in the cabinet. Too bad she didn't have any eye drops. Her eyes were still red, but she assumed they would soon get back to normal.

When Serena stood up, she realized she was still a little woozy and decided she'd avail herself, for a while, of the sofa in the room outside the powder room. She hoped she wouldn't have to leave early.

Serena opened the door into the office and was surprised to find the room in darkness. As she felt around for a light switch or lamp, her eyes adjusted to the lack of light and she realized she was in a bedroom with old-fashioned furniture.

"What the!" she whispered.

Oh well, she rationalized, she had been feeling really bad when Miss Pierson brought her in; the bathroom had two doors leading to adjoining rooms and, obviously, she had just gotten confused and come out the wrong one.

She felt along the wall 'til she got back to the bathroom door and opened it.

Inside, she found a closet. Panic began to grip her. Stupidly, she tapped the back wall of the closet for an exit, though she knew she hadn't stepped through long dresses and shoes to get out.

"Well, there's another door, then," she told herself.

But try as she would, Serena couldn't find any other door (except the one leading to the hall) in the large room. She opened the closet door again, as if expecting it to be like a magician's trick box, but the space remained a closet. Finally, after several moments of bruising her shins on the unseen furniture and nearly toppling over tables and shelves of knickknacks, Serena gave up and went into the hall.

The hall wasn't any better. Serena was sure that the lights in the hall had been mostly small chandeliers, with electric lights made to simulate flames. Now the walls held sconces, connected to one another by brass tubing and topped by fluted globes, which protected real, unmistakable fire.

Serena walked along the wall until she found a door, still expecting to find the mystery restroom from the other side. But instead of the office furniture she hoped to see, she found more massive and masculine furniture and she could see in the flickering light from the hallway, that there was no door at all on the wall shared with the other bedroom.

What in the hell is happening to me? Serena thought. *They may have to call 911, after all!*

From far away, she could hear the sounds of laughter and music and she knew the party was still going strong. Human contact would probably make her feel better, but on the other hand, she was afraid to let anyone know how disoriented she apparently was.

Well, the combination of food allergy, antihistamine, and the cocktail and champagne, plus everyone's peculiar reactions to me was bound to screw me up a little bit, she told herself, deciding to head toward the outside. *I'm sure things will seem back to normal soon.*

But instead of normalcy, she kept noticing subtle changes about the house. There was more chintz and more needlepoint covers on the furniture and there was a group of tintype pictures that she didn't remember, on the table close to the door leading to the side garden.

Still, she was reassured by the sounds of the party outside. Maybe Martha was back? If not, she'd talk to some of the other people. Surely seeing an even somewhat familiar face would put things back in perspective.

But when she walked through the door and down the stairs, she looked in vain for Martha or the Ingersols or even Senator Marshall or Grace Pierson. The guests laughed and talked and ate hors d'oeuvres just as they had before, but there wasn't one familiar face in the bunch.

The crowd was dressed in old-fashioned clothes, but none that Serena remembered. Nowhere did she catch a glimpse of Grace Pierson's shiny black lace or the glitter of her heavy gold jewelry or of Senator Marshall's green cutwork. There were no bustles at all and nothing as casual as a middy blouse and skirt. The men were still in evening clothes, but the cut of their suits seemed different and their collars were higher and looked much stiffer.

Serena began to feel short of breath, very much as she had earlier, from the allergic reaction. Clutching her chest, she walked farther into the group.

There was a string quartet playing light classics in one corner of the garden and Serena couldn't see a hint of the sound system that had been tacked to the trees earlier. Behind the tables, the caterers no longer wore their black slacks and white shirts, they were in long gray dresses with white pinafore-type aprons over them and they had little ruffled caps perched on their heads.

Could this be some colossal practical joke? But these people hardly knew her. Why would they play a joke on her? Or maybe she had walked into a gag for someone else.

Then, as she tried unsuccessfully to convince herself that it was all a trick, Serena noticed the banner stretched between the trees over the tables. Emblazoned in gold on white satin, it read: Longworth College, 1898–1908, Ten Years of Quality in Education.

"Oh god!" said Serena, just above a whisper, turning feverishly to take everything in. "Oh jeez!" And then in the street French she had learned from the students at the Sorbonne, "Oh merde!"

"Is something wrong, miss?"

Serena turned to find a tiny, dark-haired woman in a peach dress looking at her with concern.

"Everything's different!" said Serena. "I don't understand."

"Different?"

Hold on, kid, Serena told herself. *Don't say anything too irrational. You really don't know what your situation is here.*

"I'm sorry," she said aloud. "I'm still not feeling too well. I, uh, got sick from eating the crab, you know. I'm allergic to it and—"

"Crab?" said the young woman. "I'm sure we're not serving any crab. I know, I supervised the whole menu. It's really too early in the season for shellfish. But I'm sorry you got ill," she continued sincerely. "Is there anything we can do for you now?"

"Well, I-I don't quite—" Serena stammered. *How in hell do I express this,* she wondered.

"Con, is there a problem here?" asked a deep voice, resonating with authority.

Serena turned. Finally, she saw a familiar face. The broad-shouldered man towering several inches over her had a mesmerizing presence. He exuded virility, but also a kind of menace! His features were strikingly handsome and aristocratic, but full of bitterness, with lines forming about his flared nostrils and his grim line of a mouth and a tightness around his strong square chin. His thick black hair showed strands of gray, where it waved over his forehead and temples and his slate-gray eyes were fierce and seemed to be boring into her. To say that he looked at her with distrust would be putting it in much to positive a light.

Serena had hoped to see a familiar face, but this face! She was standing close enough to him to know that he wasn't wearing stage makeup or anything that would change his appearance. Yet he was the exact image of Trenton Longworth, as he had appeared in the 1905 portrait.

For the first time in her twenty-four years, Serena fainted.

The blackness began to subside, tossing Serena into a frightening vacuum with disturbing flashes of color and sound. For some reason she didn't understand, her instinct was to yell, but a stronger instinct told her to be cautious. Serena didn't know where she was. And then, she remembered and decided her instinct for caution was very appropriate.

Serena became aware of voices and realized that the man and woman she had seen earlier were discussing her. There was something soft under her head, probably a pillow, though she assumed from the breeze and the noises around her that she was still in the garden. Also, there seemed to be a wet cloth on her head. She kept her eyes shut and pretended to still be unconscious, so she could listen for a while. She supposed it might be some form of eavesdropping, but at the moment it seemed like self-preservation.

"We don't know anything about her," said the man. "Suddenly, a young woman comes to our party, uninvited as far as I can tell and claims that something we served made her sick.

"If the truth were known, it was probably from too much champagne that she got sick. Her eyes were very red."

"Trennie," said the woman. "She didn't seem drunk, just confused."

"We have no idea how or why she got all the way up here," he continued, as if she hadn't spoken. "Then she promptly passes out on our lawn!"

"Oh, Trennie," said the woman, "don't be so dramatic. I'm sure she came up with Estey Wooten. I didn't really get to meet all the young ladies Estey brought with her this time."

"Oh, I've no doubt she was among Estey Wooten's horde come, at the drop of a hatpin, to descend on our poor students en masse!"

"Trennie, there's nothing wrong with Estey's girls. Estey Wooten runs a respectable boarding house. The way you talk, you'd think it was a bawdy house!"

"Connie!" the man exclaimed, but there was laughter in his voice. "You shouldn't know such terms, much less repeat them! I suppose there's nothing actually wrong with 'Estey's Girls', as you call them," he went on. "Still, I'm leery. She piles all those women into that contraption and carts them way up here every time we have any kind of event, just so they can meet eligible bachelors. And I think this girl might be wearing paint!"

"Oh, that's ridiculous," said the woman. "She isn't painted. And there's nothing wrong with men and women wanting to meet each other, either. It's not that easy when one lives way up in the mountains," said the young woman, sounding a little sad.

Serena felt her take the cloth off her forehead and replace it with a fresh cool one. "And that contraption is an automobile. Randy has one and you don't complain about that."

"It's not the automobile that worries me," he answered. "Though I doubt that Estey keeps it in good enough repair for these mountain roads. I think the shiny green finish is her main concern. But what really bothers me is that detachable phaeton seat she perches precariously in back and fills with cackling, giggling females. If one of them fell out of that thing and hurt herself, I'm sure she wouldn't hesitate to implicate the college."

"Trennie, what a cold thing to say! You sound as if you don't care about—"

"Of course, I don't want one of the young ladies to be hurt. But I also care about the college. We're still fairly new and can't afford to have any kind of taint on the good name that we—and Father—have established."

"Oh, do speak the truth," teased the young woman. "You're just upset because Estey Wooten has decided you've been a widower too long and has set a cap for you herself."

"I really have no idea what you're talking about," intoned the man, an affable sarcasm coloring his deep voice.

"Of course, you don't," giggled the girl. "That's why you run like a jackrabbit every time she comes up here twirling a parasol! You just have to accept it, dear, as long as Estey contributes as much as she does to the school, we have to invite her to all our public events."

"I suppose so," he agreed, grudgingly. "But do we have to give her carte blanche to bring so many others with her? Now here's one of her young ladies—if, that is what she is—" Serena hoped it was her status as one of Estey's group, rather than as a lady, he was questioning "—who's managed to get herself left behind, swooned on our lawn, and, from the looks of it, intends to take up residence in our garden!"

This last comment warned Serena that she had been "out" for about as long as she could risk. Not having had experience with a person susceptible to fainting spells, she hadn't known exactly what period of time she could get away with, but now, not wanting to raise more suspicion, she decided to "come to." She was both relieved and panicked by the conversation she'd overheard. She was relieved, because their mention of Estey Wooten's girls had given her a good excuse for being here. But even more, she was panicked because the simple comments between two people, who didn't know they were being overheard, told her more than anything else would have that, impossible as it seemed, she had somehow blundered into a different time.

No, it's got to be a dream, she told herself. Yet her senses said it wasn't.

The softness of the pillow under her head, the coolness of the damp cloth on her forehead, and the prickles of the grass against her body. The smell of the nearby roses and of the food kept warm in the braziers, drifting on the breeze. The music of the string quartet (including the occasional missed note), the distant tinkling silverware and the party conversation, and the way the man's voice struck some resonance within her. It was all too real, too visceral, somehow, to be in a dream.

Well, she thought. Dream or no, it was time to open her eyes. She moved her head back and forth on the pillow, the way she'd seen lots of movie heroines doing and moaned softly. But when she blinked and looked up into the faces of the young man and woman she had seen earlier, she didn't ask the usual "What happened?" and "Where am I?" She went directly to the questions that she really wanted answered.

"C-can you tell me who you are?" she asked. "And, excuse me, but I am rather disoriented right now, can you tell me the date?"

"Well," said the man, harshly. "I would hope you might know your host and hostess." All the humor he had shown to the other woman was gone from his voice now. "But I am Trenton Longworth and this is my sister, Constance Longworth. And the date, of course, is September 2, 1908."

Serena had been anticipating his words, and yet, actually hearing them took her breath away.

For the second time in her life, as well as the second time that night, Serena fainted.

Chapter 3

Serena's next conscious sensation was of the play of sunlight through her eyelids. Once again, she lay with her eyes closed, trying to acclimate herself to her surroundings. It felt as if she were in bed, but certainly not on the rock-hard mattress in her motel room. This bed was very soft, like some of the feather beds she had slept on in Europe. She could hear faint sounds like movement in a house around her, faraway voices, doors closing, a creak on stairs, and what could have been children playing in the vicinity.

When she opened her eyes, Serena found herself in a large square-canopy bed, with elegant white lace hangings and covers. The room surrounding her was appointed with every amenity of a 1908 bedroom, from the sterling silver brush set to the intricate pastel quilt to the washbowl and pitcher. It hadn't all been just a dream!

Deciding it was time to confront whatever was going on, Serena started to get out of bed and saw that she was wearing a white nightgown with ruffles at the throat and cuffs, but when she stood up, she noticed the deep ruffle at the hem ended in the middle of her calf.

It must be one of Constance Longworth's gowns, she decided.

Swallowing hard, Serena hesitantly ventured over to the window, hoping the magnificent view would calm her, but soon discovered she was still light-headed. This wasn't like her, she thought. But, of course, time travel, or whatever it was, wasn't your normal, everyday experience, either.

To steady herself a bit, she was just heading back to the bed when she heard a light knock on the door.

"Oh good. You are awake," said Constance Longworth, peeping around the door. She was dressed in more casual clothes today, but it

"Putting him on?"

"Pretending about her interest in the school and all."

"Yes," said Constance. "That is to say, her interest in the school's advancement was real enough, but only because she thought it would bring them more money and prestige. She was first attracted to Trenton because he was handsome and had such an important position for a man of his age. But she was unhappy when she realized that his interest in the school was second only to his interest in his family. She called him a boring old skinflint. And she hated it up here! Said it was provincial. She was from Charleston, South Carolina, and was used to lots of social life. She hated being snowed in, in the winter. She disliked the people, called the professors a bunch of stuffed shirts and the mountain people yokels. She constantly pouted and whined and manipulated.

"She always begged Trennie to take her to Richmond or somewhere and, if he couldn't, she'd go there on her own. She'd run up huge bills for clothes, hotels, jewelry, carriage rentals. Trennie's still paying out some of them. And you know, I…uh…think there were men too.

"I know I shouldn't be telling you all this, but somehow I just feel right talking to you."

"That's all right," said Serena. "Of course, you can talk to me. And I can tell how concerned you are that your brother had to go through all that."

"It was awful!" answered Constance. "And it only got worse when she got sick. She'd always had a weak heart, but she wouldn't really rest and when the doctor said she was killing herself, she just said, 'Oh pooh!' and continued to travel and dance and shop and—and goodness knows what else—well, you know, just gad about. But then, if she had nowhere to go, she'd just stay in bed. She refused to move an inch, even to adjust her own cover. She kept everyone running at her beck and call all the time, especially the servants. She was horrible to Malcolm (probably because she knew she didn't impress him) and to Trennie, who tried so hard to keep her happy. Even her last words were insulting to him. She said he must have never loved her, because he would never give her the things she really wanted."

"And those were her last words?"

"Her very last."

"How awful for him. No wonder he doesn't have much use for women these days. But at least it's good to know he'll get over it eventually."

"Well, I hope he will," said Constance, doubtfully.

"Oh yes," said Serena. "I, uh, feel sure he will someday. But, in the meantime, I do wish he trusted me more."

"Don't concern yourself," said Constance, patting Serena's hand. "He has already agreed to let you stay here until we're sure you're well. We've arranged for our doctor to come over this afternoon."

"Constance, I-I didn't bring much money up here with me," said Serena, thinking for the first time about the small beaded purse with the few bills, change, and completely useless credit cards. "Did you bring my handbag up here last night?"

"I don't think so," said Constance. "We'll look for it in the garden. But don't worry about the doctor. He's retired and moved up here so his son could go to school with us. He usually doesn't charge for his visits. But I'm sure you feel lost without your belongings. Malcolm has already put the word out, with his brigade, to get a message to Estey, about your staying up here until you're completely well. We can tell the boys to ask for any belongings you need too."

"Put the word out with his brigade?" asked Serena.

"He calls it his Dun Brigade. 'Dun' is Gaelic for 'hill.' It's just a group of boys who live between here and Belle Vieux that Malcolm has organized to relay messages, and sometimes even belongings, from the college to town. You see, we can't get the telephone up here. There are a few instruments in Belle Vieux, but they haven't brought the lines up this high as yet. So Malcolm came up with the idea of a boy's club. They meet every month, if the weather permits, and he reads them funny stories and plays games with them and awards them badges and prizes for outstanding service. He actually began it just to help us communicate with the town, but the boys love it. And I think he might enjoy it too."

"How ingenious! Malcolm sounds very resourceful," said Serena.

"Oh, he is!" answered Constance, her eyes bright. "A problem hardly presents itself before Malcolm has it solved. He's—Well, anyway, if you make up a list of the things you need from Mrs. Wooten's, the boys can pass it down to town and bring your belongings up here the same way, if there's not too much for them to handle."

"Oh, that probably won't be necessary," said Serena, wondering what Estey Wooten would say when told to turn over the belongings of a phantom guest. "I-I can retrieve it when I return to Belle Vieux. There's not much there, anyway."

"Really?" asked Constance, sympathetically.

"I had to sell a lot of my things before I left California," Serena improvised, "Because the shipping charges were so exorbitant. And-and then my trunk was lost somewhere on the train. They think it might have been stolen, so I only had what was in my carry-on, uh, carpet bag."

"Well, at least it won't be so much for the boys to carry that way," said Constance.

"No, please, don't bother," said Serena, quickly. "I don't, uh, want to upset Estey. You know how she is," she added, hoping some trait of Estey's would apply.

Constance nodded and Serena, deciding it was time to change the subject, said the first thing that came into her head. "It must be inconvenient to be up this far, with no phone service."

"Phone? Oh, you mean telephone. You do speak differently sometimes. But, of course, we're used to living without the modern conveniences. We do have running water though," she added proudly. "We have our own well and Trennie had a complete plumbing system installed in the entire college three years ago."

Thank God! thought Serena. "But you don't have electricity yet?" she asked, remembering the gas lamps in the hall.

"Goodness, no! Even Belle Vieux doesn't have electricity."

"But I thought I saw a Victrola downstairs."

"Of course, we have a Victrola, but they don't use electricity."

"That's right. They had a crank," Serena muttered, almost to herself. "That is, there are some, in California now, that run on electricity—gramophones, I think they're called. After California, it's, like, kind of hard for me to get used to things here. But"—she hastened to add—"I like it here."

"How long have you been in this area?"

"Oh, about a week," said Serena.

"And are you employed somewhere in Belle Vieux?"

"Not yet. I've been, uh, hoping for an opening in one of the shops, but so far, I'm just living on my savings, which are becoming pretty slim," admitted Serena. "I'm afraid I may be ill-prepared to work in this era, uh, area."

"But, if you'll forgive my presumption," said Constance, "you appear to be well-educated."

"Yes, I attended college."

"That's wonderful," said Constance. "Where did you go?"

"I-in California," said Serena. She regretted the huge framework of dishonesty she was building for these kind, decent people, but she knew of no other way to explain herself in this world. So she simply made up a name. "I went to—Berkley Seminary for Women, but I studied art and I'm afraid there's not much use for that around here."

"Art," said Constance. "That must have been wonderful. I studied English, which was fine, but I wish I could have studied art. But I'm probably tiring you," she went on. "I'd better let you get some rest for a while."

"Well," said Serena, "maybe, if you came back later." She really hated to see Constance go; it was easier to talk to her than to anyone she'd ever known, other than her parents. However, all the fabrication was beginning to be a strain.

"I just had a thought," said Constance, turning with her hand on the doorknob. "Since you lost most of your belongings on your trip, I have some clothes that you might be able to use. They're from my cousin Violet, who couldn't wear them after she had her baby. They look as if they're new and she has wonderful taste, but I decided that altering them to fit me would just be too much trouble. You're wearing one of my nightgowns now, and I think you're about Violet's height, so you can see the discrepancy. But I think they might fit you."

"Well, if you can't use them—" Serena began.

"Good!" said Constance. "You get some rest and maybe I can show you some of them later."

Damn, thought Serena, when Constance had gone. *I was hoping to ask her more about Trenton.*

She told herself that she shouldn't think so much about Trenton Longworth. He was a historical figure in the world in which she had always lived and, besides, last night he had acted very cold. And yet to her, he had seemed very real and had made her feel very warm and alive.

But when she considered actually leaving this room to go out and talk to Trenton Longworth, in his world of 1908, Serena's heart began to pound wildly.

In fact, the thought of leaving the room under any circumstances was frightening to her.

I'm just not ready yet, she told herself, settling back into the bed and pulling the cover up around her neck. *Constance is probably right about my needing rest.*

So deciding, Serena spent most of the remaining day in deep sleep, using sickness as an excuse to hide in bed.

In the early afternoon, the doctor, a comforting gray-haired man, came to examine Serena. He said she was in a weakened condition, possibly due to an allergic reaction to food and recommended bed rest.

Later, Constance returned, bringing one of Violet's nightgowns (which fit Serena to a T), a robe (which Constance called a "wrapper") and two easy-fitting, cotton housedresses.

Besides Constance and the doctor, the only person Serena saw was the maid, who came to bring her meals. Serena was sure she heard Trenton Longworth's resonate tones outside her door a couple of times, but he never came into the room.

Each time someone came in and woke her, Serena was amazed to find herself still in 1908. It really wasn't a dream. However it had happened, it had happened. But the phenomenon was very confusing and, even at the end of the day, she wasn't ready to deal with it. So she escaped once again into dreams, which, right now, actually seemed more realistic than her waking moments.

By the next morning, however, Serena decided it was time to face the outside world.

She rose, splashed water on her face from the pitcher and bowl on her dresser, donned the flowered housedress, and twisted her hair into a passable-looking topknot.

Looking at the mountains and drinking in the crisp morning air through the window, she was anxious to get outdoors for a few minutes. But when she got to her bedroom door, she felt the paralysis creep over her again.

Come on. You can't stay in this room forever, she told herself.

So squaring her shoulders and taking a deep breath, Serena opened the door and headed for the stairs.

Though she could hear sounds from the back of the house, Serena didn't see anyone until she passed through the parlor door and onto the side porch.

"Ready or not, here I come," piped a childish voice.

Through the open garden gate, Serena could see two small boys in knee socks and knickers, and a small collie, playing hide-and-seek in the yard next door.

These must have been the children she had heard the day before, she decided. Somehow, it was comforting to watch them. They acted just the same as children anywhere and at any time.

As Serena continued to watch, the side door of the neighboring house opened and a woman ushered a little girl out onto the porch. The child appeared to be about four or five years old. She was dressed in a crisp beige sailor dress with black braid and tie and a large black bow adorned her curls.

The woman wheeled a tiny wicker carriage holding two china dolls beside a chair into which she gently pushed the little girl. Then the woman sat momentarily in a chair beside the child's, her legs crossed at the ankle, her back straight, her hands clasped in her lap, her head tilted and a beautiful smile on her face, in an obvious and exaggerated imitation of "ladylike" behavior. The little girl mimicked her exactly and looked at the woman for approval. Satisfied, the woman rose, patted the child on the head and went back into the house.

The little girl leaned over to play with her dolls, but otherwise retained her ladylike behavior until the boys noticed her.

"Dumbelina's out," said the older boy.

"Mama said not to call her that," answered the other.

"It doesn't matter," his brother answered. "She can't hear us anyway." He began to clap his hands and yell, "Hey, dummy! Look here, dummy!" and then to jump up and down and imitate several animals, including an animated rooster, all of which made the collie yelp and dance in accompaniment. But the little girl continued to play with her dolls and didn't respond at all.

When both boys began to throw the tiny pebbles surrounding the shrubbery near the porch, the little girl still didn't respond, whether from ignorance or calculation, Serena couldn't decide. Even when a few pebbles landed in her lap, the child only brushed them off and gave the boys a bored glance. But when a pellet hit the fragile face of one of her china dolls (as far as Serena could tell, without damaging the toy), it was a different story. The little girl made a sort of growling sound, leapt off the porch, and lunged for the boys, who ran from her, giggling and shrieking. They all raced around the back of the house, with the dog following joyously behind.

Just then, Serena noticed a flash of light behind the Longworth's shrubbery and looked over to see her small evening bag, open, behind the bushes, the light glinting off the beading and some of its contents scattered around it.

It suddenly occurred to Serena how strange the contents of that little purse would seem to her present hosts. The makeup, compact, eyeliner, and lipstick. Besides being "paint," they were all in plastic containers. Everything seemed to be plastic or part plastic—the tag on the motel room key, the small vials of eye drops and cologne, the clear cover on her driver's license, and the credit cards. Credit cards! What would the Longworth household make of those thin rectangles of plastic, which she'd so recently and proudly acquired and which did her no good here, with their hologram pictures and embossed names and dates? Dates! She had thought she could offer the Longworths the few bills she had stuffed into the purse; she didn't think money had changed much since 1908, but the earliest date on them was 1981! Her driver's license said she'd been born on February 2, 1984. And all those expiration dates in the 2000s! She'd read that the 2000s were somehow a frightening concept for people in the 1990s. What would 1908 inhabitants think of it?

She couldn't let anyone see these things, thought Serena. But just as she was quickly stuffing everything back into the little bag, a shadow fell across her arms. Serena looked up into the eyes of the little girl from next door, who was staring quizzically from Serena's face to the contents of the purse.

Serena snapped the purse shut and dropped it into the pocket of the flowered housedress.

The child continued to stare at Serena and at her pocket.

She's very young, thought Serena. *Surely she won't place any significance on this stuff. And,* she decided, with a pang of guilt, *it appears that she's profoundly deaf, so she probably can't explain what she saw to anyone, anyway.*

She knew it was terrible to be glad that someone lacked communication skills, so to assuage her guilt, as well as to distract the child, Serena began to speak to the girl in gestures. She'd learned the deaf alphabet one year at summer camp and had renewed the knowledge in high school when she'd written a paper on the history of education for the deaf, and she thought she remembered almost all the letters.

She spelled out a few phrases with her fingers, but the child looked completely bewildered, so Serena settled for simply smiling broadly, thumping her own chest, pointing to the girl and forming the symbols for the word "hi," with her index and second fingers slanted to the left and then her little finger pointing up. The little girl began to giggle almost convulsively and then to imitate everything Serena did, including giving a silly and possibly derisive grin in answer to Serena's smile. But at least she wasn't looking at Serena's purse any longer.

Serena changed her tactics, looking the child earnestly in the eye and simply repeating the symbols for "hi." The little girl was soon echoing her motions and looking seriously at Serena, as if she might realize what Serena was trying to say.

"She doesn't know what that means," said a deep and sardonic voice behind Serena. "She imitates everything."

Trenton Longworth was standing on the sidewalk behind her, a mocking expression on his craggy face.

"I-I realize that," stammered Serena, wishing this man didn't make her so nervous. "But I, uh, figure if I repeat it enough, she'll know."

Trenton Longworth only raised his dark eyebrows.

"It's the Signing Alphabet. I'm sure it's already in use now, uh here. I mean, I know it started in France, but—"

"Yes, I am familiar with it," Trenton said, coldly. "But the Trices—the child's parents—have been told that it's too early to teach her. She's only four."

"But they realized later that"—began Serena—"That is, in-in France," she improvised, "they're using it with some younger kids now. I'm sure you know that, generally, the younger you learn a language, the better. I, uh, knew a girl in California, whose, uh, younger sister was hearing-impaired and she told me all about it and taught me to sign. She said—"

"Yes, well," Trenton interrupted. "Surely you can see that this child's mimicking is just a game to her, at this age."

"Yes, but isn't that how all children learn to speak at first?" asked Serena, her determination taking the place of nervousness.

"I suppose so," said Trenton Longworth.

"And she seems eager to learn and to communicate with me," continued Serena, "and intelligent."

"Possibly," conceded Trenton. "It's hard to tell."

"But her brothers don't think so. They call her 'Dumbelina'!"

"Yes, I've heard them," said Trenton, with asperity. "They received a Hans Christian Anderson anthology last year," he explained.

"So it seems like anything that would help to change their opinions would help her too," said Serena.

"If, in fact, it had that effect," said Trenton.

"Well, I could at least try," insisted Serena. "Just think how hard it would be to live in a world you didn't really understand and not be able to ask anyone to explain it to you," she added, thinking that, for different reasons, she was in much the same situation.

"Perhaps you're right," Trenton conceded, once again. His face became more relaxed. His expression wasn't exactly a smile, but it was pleasant. "In any event, it's good of you to be concerned. But," he added. "I really should take her home now. Her mother worries when she strays from the yard."

"Of course," said Serena.

"Come along, Lettie," said Trenton, smiling into her face. The little girl trustingly took the hand he offered (a strong but artistic-looking hand, Serena couldn't help noticing), and they started to walk toward the gateway, smiling at each other.

Lettie! thought Serena. *The old lady's name was Leticia.* But if this were a dream, it would be natural to people it with those she recently met.

"Oh, by the way," said Trenton, turning back. "I came out because we—Constance was wondering if you'd like some breakfast."

CHAPTER 4

Feeling more lighthearted than she'd thought she could only a few moments ago, Serena went in to the dining room, to find Constance presiding over a huge pre-"cholesterol-conscious" breakfast of scrambled eggs, bacon, biscuits with butter and apple jelly, grits, sliced tomatoes, coffee with real cream, tea, and milk.

The mountain air had brought back Serena's appetite. She ate generous amounts of everything but the grits, which was a Southern tradition she'd never quite gotten used to.

She also found conversation with Constance as easy as ever. They laughed and talked like old friends. Serena even stopped worrying about making "time" faux pas.

The only disappointment was that Trenton Longworth didn't join them at the table. In fact, she had only one or two other tantalizing glimpses of him all day. Serena didn't hide in her room today, but Trenton did retreat to his study, even taking his meals there. Constance said he was working on schedules for the coming school year, but Serena thought he was mostly avoiding her.

"You mustn't worry about it," said Constance. "He'll come around. And in the meantime, you can meet everybody else."

True to her word, Constance showed Serena around the entire house and introduced her to the staff. Serena met the family cook, Frances, a comfortably plump middle-aged Irish woman with twinkling eyes; Neva, an attractive young mountain woman, who said she had been to school "down to Charlottesville" to learn to be a proper housekeeper; and Elyn the parlor maid, a bubbly Welsh girl whom Constance said could double as a lady's maid, if Serena needed her. Also, there were Clara Lou and Pansy, two sturdy cheerful mountain girls, with decided mountain twangs, who served as maids.

Finally, Serena met the redoubtable Malcolm, presented by Constance with an unconscious little flourish. Shorter, but even broader of shoulder than Trenton, he seemed more like a lumberjack than a butler with his curly dark hair, Irish lilt and big hands. But he performed his duties with an air of dignity and he spoke to Serena with a serious look in his arresting brown eyes.

"Please let me know, Ma'am, if I can assist you in any way," he said, and Serena felt as if he really meant it.

Most of that afternoon was passed by Constance and Serena in a sunny attic room analyzing Cousin Violet's donated wardrobe. Serena felt as if she'd tried on hundreds of articles of clothing—blouses ("waists," Constance called them), skirts, and dresses of every description and even some accessories and lingerie. Some pieces had zippers, which Constance declared "very modern," but most fastened with an amazing assortment of hooks, snaps, and tiny decorative buttons.

Serena liked almost everything she tried on. Violet appeared to have nearly flawless taste and her color choices coincided with Serena's perfectly. Also (*Just like a dream,* thought Serena), most of the things fit like they were made for her. Only the flared skirts puckered a little across the back. Constance and Serena decided that Violet must have measured a little longer than Serena from waist to hip.

"But that's no problem," said Constance, fitting Serena in a stunning aqua walking skirt. "This one is long enough so that we can take it up vertically to the waistline. And a lot of the shorter ones have large enough seams, so that we can let out the width at the hip. My sewing machine is right up to the minute. We can have these done in no time!"

"But Constance, you're doing too much for me," protested Serena. "Of course, I appreciate it, but I'm a virtual stranger, and—"

"Oh no you're not!" insisted Constance. "Well, I-I suppose you actually are, but it doesn't feel like it. It's so easy to talk to you. It feels like you've been here forever. Almost like a sister."

"It's true," said Serena, feeling touched. "I've never talked this easily to anyone but my—mother."

"So it's settled then," said Constance. "And, by the way, call me Connie or even Canny or Uncanny or one of those other silly names Trennie gives me, if you like."

"Okay, Uncanny." laughed Serena, trying to imagine Trenton Longworth making up silly names. But she settled on "Connie" and Constance started calling her "Reenie," and soon they shortened it to "Con" and "Reen."

All afternoon, they talked nearly nonstop. Constance told Serena some of the funny things that had happened with the college and prep school boys through the years; about the people in the surrounding community; about Randy, the furniture manufacturer's son, whom Constance sometimes "saw socially"; and about Malcolm's adventures, working his way across the British Isles and the Atlantic. And with some prompting from Serena, she talked about Trenton and their childhood together.

For her part, Serena talked as much as she could about her own life, without referring to time. Also she didn't mention that she had traveled all over the world, being afraid that she would slip up, talking about modes of transportation. She told Constance about happy times with her parents and about the closeness they had shared.

When the sounds of the children playing next door came through the open dormer window, Serena told Constance about her encounter with Lettie that morning, minus the discovery of the purse.

"Oh, I think that's wonderful," said Constance, when Serena mentioned her attempts at sign language. "I'll take you over tomorrow and introduce you to her parents. (Her father is the school's treasurer and business manager.) They're very concerned about Lettie, and I'm sure they'd be thrilled for you to teach her!"

"I'm not sure I'm really qualified, Con," said Serena, hesitantly. "I only know a few words and I'm not even certain I remember all the letters."

"But wouldn't anything you could teach her be a head start for when she goes to school?" asked Constance.

"Well, I suppose so," agreed Serena. "I guess we can see what her parents say."

Serena's third full day in 1908 was even more eventful. Once again, she lay for a few moments, with her eyes closed, expecting when she opened them, to find that it had all been a dream. But the difference the third day was that finding herself still in the past didn't scare her anymore; she was filled with almost unadulterated delight. Somehow, she felt she was where she really belonged.

In the dining room, another sumptuous breakfast awaited her. "This food is too good," Serena complained. "If I don't get some exercise, I'm going to be big as a house!"

"We could go for a hike when we finish, if you'd like," suggested Constance. "The path to Butler's Peak is very pretty this time of year, and it's not too far away."

"Sounds perfect," agreed Serena.

So when they got up from the table, Serena and Constance changed into their oldest housedresses, Serena into Cousin Violet's checked one and taking the baskets, aprons, and gnarled walking sticks Constance had retrieved from the pantry, set out to climb Butler's Peak and pick some blackberries.

"Might as well, before the season ends," said Constance.

Serena thought she was in pretty good shape. In 2008, she had attended aerobics classes two or three times a week and worked out a little at home in between. She had also done a few exercises in her room the night before (though the long frilled 1908 nightgown had gotten in the way). However, she soon found the climb to Butler's Peak exhausting. While Constance trekked easily ahead, Serena had to stop several times to catch her breath and rivulets of perspiration were soon running down her face and neck and matting in her hair.

"It's the thin air," Constance consoled her. "It bothers everyone when they first visit the mountains."

As the incline leveled off, Serena's breathing became easier, but the path began to disappear into a tangle of branches, which caught at their ankle-length skirts.

"Since we're up here, where no one can see us," said Constance conspiratorially, "we can tie our skirts up."

Serena watched as Constance gathered her hem into tails and tied it into a knot on each side, bringing the bottom up a few inches from the ground and closer to the body, and then Serena copied her. The skirts still grazed some of the taller bushes and Serena wished they could tie them higher, but it did help some.

"There's a huge patch of blackberries just over here," said Constance, darting over and beginning to fill her basket and her mouth with fruit.

"This is my favorite fruit," she said, between berries, "and Malcolm's."

"They are delicious," said Serena. "And the view up here is spectacular."

Below them, the lush greens of the valley were dappled with sunlight and shadow. Quaint-looking houses dotted the landscape, a white church spire gleamed, and on a red-clay road, a tiny horse and cart moved slowly. To their left, Serena could see the elegant buildings of the college partially obscured by trees. On the other sides of the valley higher peaks soared into the clear blue sky.

"It truly is," answered Constance. "I suppose I take it too much for granted, having lived here all my life. But it is beautiful and there's a great echo up here too!" She suddenly amazed Serena by crowing like a rooster. Serena gasped as the sound reverberated through the valley.

"Oh, did I startle you?" Constance laughed. "Trennie and I used to have contests to see who could make the funniest sound. We loved to imitate the Trices's rooster. Then, we saw Maude Adams, in *Peter Pan*, in New York and she taught the children in the play to crow. Trennie and I swore they stole it from us and we dreamed up a really complicated story of how someone heard us up here and the sound traveled all around the world, 'til James Barrie finally heard it in England and decided he must put it in his play. Of course Anne said we were insufferably silly!" Constance continued.

"Anne?" asked Serena. "Trenton's wife?"

"Yes. She was very put out with us and so afraid her sophisticated New York acquaintances would hear us. Trennie said she was lucky we didn't crow along with Miss Adams the way the children in the audience did."

Serena stared unseeing into the beautiful valley. Just three or four years ago, Trenton Longworth still made up ridiculous stories and teased his wife with threats of even worse. How had he so completely changed in such a short time? Or did he just act that way because of a strong aversion to her?

"It's your turn," said Constance.

"What?"

"According to Trennie's and my rules, you have to repeat my sound and then come up with one of your own."

"Oh my god—uh—goodness!" said Serena. Feeling very self-conscious, she imitated the rooster crow and then, feeling even sillier, she made a chimpanzee sound.

"Very good!" said Constance, with a giggle. "Like the monkey at the zoo!" She repeated the sound and then gave a creditable horse whiney.

After a couple of false starts, due to laughter, Serena whinnied. "This is silly," she said. "But it's sort of fun. And I suppose it's very cathartic for the psyche."

Constance tilted her head quizzically.

"You know," said Serena. "Armchair analysis?" But Constance only furrowed her brow.

That's right, thought Serena. *Freud is not yet an accepted household name and pop psychology is years in the future.*

"Never mind. It's just California talk," she said, with some truthfulness. "I'm just saying it's probably a good way to let go of some emotions."

"That's true," said Constance, thoughtfully. "We have to be so careful about appearances, especially because of the college. But up here, no one can hear us. And it's still your turn," she added with a mischievous smile. "You can't change the subject that easily."

Serena cawed like a crow, which prompted Constance to do a whip-poor-will call.

More birdcalls followed and then more animals, all accompanied by gales of laughter, as they picked and ate and spilled blackberries down the fronts of their dresses. They were acting like a couple of six-year-olds and Serena hadn't had so much fun in years. Much of the tension of the last few days and even some of the sadness of the past year seemed to dissipate in those few moments on the mountain.

"It's you again," said Constance.

"I can't think of another," wailed Serena.

"One more," insisted Constance. "I started it, so you have to finish it."

"Okay," said Serena. "You asked for it." She threw her head back and gave a guttural Tarzan yell, which echoed over and over through the hills and valley.

"My goodness," laughed Constance. "What kind of animal is that?"

"It's not an animal. It's Tarzan. You know, from the…uh, novel…the boy who was raised by apes?"

"I missed that one," said Constance. "But it's wonderful. Trennie would love it!"

"Oh no, please," Serena begged. "Don't repeat it to Trenton. He'll think I'm crazy!"

"Oh, all right," Constance conceded. "But it's a pity." She glanced at the sky. "It's probably getting close to lunch time. Let's get a few more berries and then head down."

"Don't you think we have enough?" asked Serena. Their baskets were full to overflowing with the dark shiny berries.

"Just a few more," coaxed Constance. "Malcolm loves blackberry pie—and-and Frances enjoys indulging him. And of course, we'll put a lot of them in blackberry jam and Trennie might brew some in wine or brandy."

"Okay," agreed Serena. "If we can get any more in our baskets."

Ten minutes later, the two girls set off down Butler's Peak laden with blackberries and engulfed in merriment. The incline was such that it made them run much of the way and their conversation came out in bursts, between gasps and giggles.

For the third time that morning, Serena suddenly found herself on her bottom in the red clay.

"You've fallen again?" teased Constance, when she was sure Serena was all right. "Anyone would think we'd already had some blackberry wine."

"Well, you're the one with the deep purple mouth, from sneaking all those berries," jibbed Serena in the same childish tone.

"Yours isn't much lighter," said Constance. "And you have more stains on your dress!"

It was true, Serena thought, looking down at herself. To say nothing of what the seat of her dress must look like. For the hundredth time that day, she thought how convenient a pair of jeans and a T-shirt would be. She had always adored the fashions of this era and she hadn't changed her mind, but sometimes they were inconvenient.

"You're right," she told Constance, apologetically. "You no more than offer me Cousin Violet's wardrobe than I start to ruin it."

"Don't worry about that," said Constance. "A good soaking will take out a lot of those stains. Besides, that's what housedresses are for. One last prank before we return to civilization," she called over her shoulder. "Let's see if we can jump the stream."

The stream was shallow, but about a yard wide and they had used a footbridge to cross it on the way up the peak, but Constance was leaping over the water, so Serena threw caution to the winds and followed.

To her surprise, they both made it and they continued running and laughing toward the back of the house, until the sight of a stern-looking Trenton Longworth, watching them from the end of the side porch, brought Serena up short.

Serena shuddered to imagine what she must look like. Her hair was damp and matted with leaves and escaping from the inexpertly twisted knot in wisps and huge clumps all over her head. Though they had untied their skirts, her hem was left pulled and badly wrinkled. They had also tied up their aprons to hold extra blackberries and Serena's bulged around her waist and caused extra stains on her already-stained and dirty outfit. The heavy "everyday" half boots she wore were caked with mud. Her breath still came in ragged gasps and perspiration seeped from every pore.

Trenton Longworth, on the other hand, was immaculate—and devastating—in a pearl-gray suit and dark striped tie. He shook his head and, with a slight mocking smile on his lips, disappeared into the house.

All of a sudden, the fun went out of the day.

"Oh, don't mind him," Constance said again, pushing Serena through the back door. "As if he didn't jump the stream, himself, only a month ago. And as if we hadn't both fallen in the stream lots of times too," she went on, as they deposited their baskets and sticks in the storeroom and offered the blackberries to an appreciative Frances.

Serena left Constance and Frances, discussing how thrilled Malcolm would be with the blackberry pies, to race upstairs for a quick sponge bath, and change of clothing before lunch.

The sight that greeted her in the mirror over her dressing table was even worse than she'd suspected. Her face was shiny with perspiration and splotched with red and her stained cotton dress, chosen for the trek in the first place, because it was the least attractive of Cousin Violet's bequests, looked like she'd slept in it. Why must she always appear at a disadvantage with Trenton Longworth? And why did she care so much? Well, she decided, she would redeem herself at lunch, if possible.

She stripped off the offending checked dress and washed and dried and powdered thoroughly, brushed and re-twisted her hair, making sure it poufed becomingly on the top and sides, donned fresh lingerie ("unmentionables" Constance called them), and picked one of her most becoming new dresses (a mauve handkerchief linen with lace insets). To finish, she added her own pearl earrings, doused herself in lavender water, and even touched her nose up with the powder puff from her cache of makeup, hidden away in the little beaded purse, kept at the very bottom of her lingerie drawer.

And, of course, Trenton Longworth did not appear at lunch. Serena imagined him, in his elegant suit, eating from a tray in his office, rather than share a little conversation with her.

Constance, who was also neat and primped, suggested they go next door to the Trices, to talk about Lettie.

"Well, at least someone will see me looking decent today!" said Serena.

But she couldn't shake her disappointment, even though the Trices were charming people and seemed genuinely thrilled to meet her, insisting that she and Constance have refreshments (though they had just finished lunch) and bringing Lettie into the room as soon as they heard the reason for the call.

Seeing the feisty little girl did boost Serena's spirits somewhat. When her father first brought her into the room, the stubborn set of Lettie's jaw implied that she hadn't wanted to come, but when she saw Serena, the child broke into a grin and gave the gestures for the word "hi."

Seeing this, Lettie's parents were even more insistent that Serena start teaching their daughter right away.

"You have to realize that she doesn't know the meaning of the sign," said Serena, remembering Trenton Longworth's caustic comments, the day before. "I guess she just associates it with me."

"Of course," agreed Mrs. Trice. "But I'm sure that eventually she'll know what it means. And look how quickly you were able to teach her.

"A lot of people these days don't like sign language," she added. "They want them to learn only lip-reading. But I want Lettie to learn everything that might help her."

It was finally agreed that Serena would work with the child two or three times a week and that the Trices would pay her two dollars for each lesson. At first, Serena had objected to being paid anything, making sure that she emphasized to the Trices that she had no training in teaching the deaf. But the Trices were adamant and Serena finally decided it would be good to have a little something to give the Longworths for her board. She had no way of judging how much the fee was, compared to 2008 prices, but she imagined they were being very generous.

Serena and Constance left amid so much effusive thanks from the Trices and signing and giggling from Lettie that Serena was smiling when they entered the Longworth's front hall and nearly collided with Trenton, whose face looked like a thundercloud.

"Well, now I know why Prof. Rivers didn't arrive on the train yesterday," he told Constance. (At least she hadn't caused his frown this time, thought Serena with relief.) "One of Malcolm's boys brought up a telegram from Belle Vieux. Rivers fell from a train platform and has a compound fracture in his leg. It'll be several weeks before he's able to travel."

"What are you going to do about his classes?" asked Constance. "The boys will be arriving next week."

"I really have no choice," said Trenton. "We can't do without freshmen English. I'll have to give up the modern literature course for the time being and teach the freshmen myself."

"But you were so looking forward to teaching modern literature" said Constance.

Trenton's voice was irritable. "Well, it can't be helped. If these boys don't have a good foundation in the basics, we'll never be able to teach them anything else and all the rest of the faculty have full schedules."

"Maybe I could help," Serena heard herself saying. "I've taught English, not in college, but on secondary level and that can't be too different from freshmen study."

(Well, it wasn't a complete lie. She had been an English tutor for her fellow high school students, and she knew her command of English grammar was very good.)

"That's…uh…very nice of you, Miss Cassidy," said Trenton, "but I'm afraid we employ only men as teachers and only people with degrees."

"Oh, Trennie, it'd just be temporary," Constance interjected. "And besides, Reenie has a college degree."

"Do you?" Trenton raised his eyebrows. "From what institution?"

"Berkley Seminary for Women," answered Serena, hoping that was what she had told Constance. "In California."

"I see." Trenton looked doubtful. His gaze, as it swept over her, was anything but salacious, but Serena felt her color rise. "And you really feel you could handle classes of college-aged boys?"

Serena was amazed. Was he actually considering it?

"Yes, I think I could," she answered, hoping her doubts didn't show.

How did these 1908 teenagers differ from the tattooed, pierced, rap-deluged, cynical sophisticates of the twenty-first century? Surely they were more naive, but would they see through her composure, as she had always felt modern teenagers could?

"Well, it would just be temporary and Rivers did say he would forward lesson plans," Trenton was saying. "But still, a young woman—"

"Trennie, Mother used to take some of the prep school classes, when someone was sick."

"Yes," said Trenton, with a wave of his hand. "But those boys were younger and Mother did little more than babysitting."

"Well, Serena is a real teacher," Constance rallied. "The Trices certainly seem to think so!" She told him about their visit to the neighbors.

Trenton's mouth formed a moue. "Well, the Trices are so desperate to help Lettie that I'm afraid they'd clutch at straws."

Serena felt the color rising in her face. She was sure Trenton was implying she'd cheated the Trices in some way.

"I told the Trices I didn't have experience in teaching deaf children," she said emphatically. "But they wanted to try it anyway. However, I have taught English and my students always said they learned a lot from me," she added, with even more vehemence.

"Well." said Trenton, with a slight smile. "I guess it couldn't hurt to try it. It *is* only temporary." Serena's smile was brilliant. "We'll have to figure out a pro-rated salary—"

"Oh no," Serena rushed in. "I couldn't accept pay. You've been so good to me, letting me stay here as-as long as you have and-and everything else you've done for me. By teaching the class, perhaps I could begin to repay you in some way."

"That is generous of you," said Trenton slowly. "We'll have to come to some definite agreement, in any case. However, I hope you won't stammer so much in front of the classes," he added.

"I don't think I will. I doubt that they'll be as daunting as you are."

"You find me daunting?" Trenton asked. "I haven't intended to be. Well, uh," he continued, stammering some himself, "we'll see how it goes. If you'll excuse me, I have other dilemmas to solve before next week. We'll talk further when the lesson plans arrive."

Serena was engulfed in equal parts of joy and fear. Had she bitten off more than she could chew? She had never seriously considered going into education and yet, in one day, she had taken on two teaching jobs. And had she actually had the nerve to tell Trenton Longworth he was daunting? Not that he didn't deserve it. And she believed she'd even gotten to him a little.

She watched his back as he walked toward his office. He held his shoulders even straighter than usual, almost as if he knew he was being watched. Suddenly, he shrugged and turned back toward them.

"By the way," he said, as he confronted them. This time, there was definitely a smile playing about his lips. "When classes begin, it would probably be good for you two to keep such things as animal calls, yodeling—or whatever that was—and creek jumping to as much of a minimum as possible."

Serena and Constance reacted at once.

"Oh my god, you heard us!" gasped Serena.

"Trennie, you know very well we've said that everyone has to let his hair down, once in a while," his sister defended.

"Well," said Trenton, actually laughing now. "Please let that be all the, uh, coiffure dismantling you do for a while."

Chapter 5

The next few days saw a definite change in Trenton Longworth's attitude toward Serena. Serena was thrilled. She decided that the ice had finally been broken, or at least cracked.

The very evening of their conversation about the English class, Trenton surprised the two girls by joining them for dinner and, thereafter, for the majority of the meals.

Serena, taking her cue from Constance's attire, began to delve even more into Cousin Violet's wardrobe, enjoying the contrast of the more sophisticated darker silks and crepes to the daytime whites and pastels. Their dinners, lit by candlelight, under the beautiful painted pastoral scene on the domed ceiling were all that was romantic to Serena. And to actually be able to converse with Trenton was a dream come true.

Trenton seemed impressed with Serena's knowledge of the arts and she enjoyed hearing his opinions, most of which struck her as quite enlightened, though he did scoff at the fledgling motion picture business.

"You mark my words," said Serena, lifting her wine glass for emphasis. "One day, the movie industry will be a force to be reckoned with."

Serena saw Trenton and Constance exchange an odd little glance, but she told herself not to worry, that no matter what they thought, they couldn't possibly guess the truth.

But she usually didn't take chances or make predictions, however, trying to confine her discussions to artists, music, and authors from before the twentieth century. When she did slip up, she always said something like, "Well, I guess he's only known out on the west coast."

It was hard to talk about music without mentioning Gershwin or art without Picasso and not to bring in authors who were staples of literature courses, like Salinger or even Hemingway, but somehow their conversations were still lively. So lively, in fact, that Malcolm, standing straight and stalwart after serving the soup, forgot himself enough to make a comment during a discussion about Mark Twain. He immediately apologized, but Trenton and Constance told him not to be ridiculous and insisted that he sit down and complete his account of the frog-jumping story. When he finally did, Malcolm warmed to his tale so much that he even imitated the voices of the competitors, sending everyone into gales of laughter.

"I'm sorry," said Malcolm, suddenly rising from the table, his face ruddy. "I shouldna' be carryin' on like this, when there's the next course to call for."

"Oh no," said Constance, her eyes shining. "It was wonderful."

But Malcolm hurried off to the kitchen with the soup tureen.

The men around here are certainly protective of their dignity, Serena told herself.

On Friday, one of Malcolm's boys delivered several newspapers from Belle Vieux and everyone read them voraciously. Serena particularly devoured every word, hoping to get a better picture of the era in which she found herself.

At the dinner table that night, the subject of politics came up and Serena, armed with her newfound knowledge from the newspapers, felt free to express her opinions.

"You're not a suffragette, are you, Miss Cassidy?" asked Trenton with some of the old sarcasm in his voice.

"Well, I'm not going to chain myself to a cannon or anything," answered Serena. "But if you're asking if I think women should vote, then the answer is yes. Of course, not all women will make informed decisions, but neither do all men and, certainly, women like Constance and me are capable of casting our vote intelligently."

"Perhaps you're right," said Trenton, slowly, meeting her eyes with his silvery gaze. Serena felt a smile pass through her whole body and not just for having made her point.

Another thing which was better than expected was Serena's attempts at teaching. She had gone over to the Trices's on two afternoons during that first week and she was pleased with how fast Lettie seemed to be learning. The child made the sign for "hi" when Serena entered the room. (Of course she continued to do it intermittently throughout the lesson, but Serena hoped she soon would realize it was a greeting). Also Lettie eagerly copied other signs that she was shown. Serena had decided to concentrate on the letters A, B, C, and D for a while and planned that on the next visit, she would also show Lettie how to write the letters.

Then on Friday afternoon, she received what she felt was a high honor. Trenton told her that some of River's lesson plans had arrived and invited her into his study to discuss them.

Serena had never been in Trenton's office and felt that she was being ushered into the Inner Sanctum.

The small room smelled pleasantly of lemon oil. Its traditional paneled and book-lined decor was brightened by brass and jade figures, which reflected the afternoon sun. Family photographs and pictures of the school's graduating classes were on display on the walls and bookcase shelves. And on the walls with his diplomas were pictures of Trenton: the younger, happier Trenton from his own school days, one in the college glee club, another in an old-fashioned, sparsely padded football uniform and two in surprisingly silly costumes and poses.

"From fraternity lampoon nights," he said, with a sheepish smile.

Serena realized that what he chose to put on these walls and what he eliminated—nowhere in the family and school pictures was there a shot of Anne—could tell her a lot about Trenton Longworth. She would have loved to look longer. But Trenton pulled out the green-upholstered chair from behind his desk and Serena felt she must sit down and concentrate on Rivers' lesson plans, spread out before her on the desk.

As they looked at the various lessons, Trenton stood over her, leaning closer to turn a page or point out something.

"I'm sure you can see," he said, his voice resonating enticingly in her ear, "the beginning of the course is just a review of their secondary school grammar. I don't know how you can make that part especially interesting for them. Rivers has a way of sprinkling a few jokes into his lessons, but—"

"No, I can't see myself making that work," said Serena. "It's not that I don't have a sense of humor—"

"Of course not," said Trenton quickly.

"It's just that—"

"That you're a bit shy in some circumstances," he finished, perceptively. "And the students can sense if you don't feel comfortable with it. Of course—"

"Yes?" Serena said, looking up, when he didn't continue.

"I was going to…uh…say that they would certainly look at you, but that they might not hear what you say."

Serena didn't know how to answer. She felt a blush rise up to her hairline.

"I'm-I'm sorry," said Trenton. "I had no business saying something like that." He reached abruptly for a book.

"No, please," said Serena, involuntarily stopping his hand. "I'm glad. I—" but she couldn't finish because of the look in his eyes.

It was as if they existed together in a vacuum. Neither spoke or moved. Serena was acutely aware of everything: the prickle of the horsehair upholstery through the fabric of her dress; the sounds of the servants moving somewhere in the house: the particles of dust dancing between them in the sunbeam shining from the skylight overhead. But mostly, she was aware of the harsh but sensuous line of Trenton Longworth's lips.

The grandfather clock in the hall struck the quarter hour, but still neither of them stirred. Then, almost imperceptibly, Trenton began to move toward her. Serena held her breath.

Then, suddenly, it was over. Trenton straightened and shook his head as if to clear it. "I'm…it's getting late," he said, not acknowledging what had just happened between them. "I think we've done enough for now. Didn't Con mention you're going for a walk together?"

"Yes, but—" said Serena, pointing helplessly toward the lesson plans.

"It's okay," said Trenton, closing the folder. "You take this with you, go over it some more and then we can discuss it further, if we need to." His smile was strained, as he opened the door.

Standing in the hallway, clutching the brown leather folder, Serena felt a mixture of elation and disappointment. She was elated that Trenton appeared to be attracted to her, as she was to him. And no matter how much she told herself that he was probably a part of a dream and that, if he was real, he'd be meeting the *other* Serena soon, she couldn't stop feeling disappointed that he had cut short that tension-filled, enticing moment between them.

What a wonderful time and place to be alive, thought Serena, as she stopped with Constance to look at the view that afternoon.

The mountains stretched around them as far as she could see, the closest peaks shining bright green in the last rays of sun, with the farther summits appearing darker green and then purple, until they were so light and hazy they could have been mistaken for clouds. What could be more peaceful?

Since she had traveled so much in her lifetime, leaving the era of technology wasn't as much of a shock to her as it might have been to others. Serena had stayed in hotels in Europe, which had only basins and pitchers of water in the rooms and had the bathroom down the hall and where the modern conveniences hadn't been as advanced as they were in the 2000s US. If she never heard another chirp, whistle, or bleep from a computer, Serena thought it would be just fine. Of course the loss of many things run by electricity was a hardship, but not, she realized, nearly as much as it would be in a house without servants.

She did miss television, especially at first. She'd never watched TV much until the last year, but when she was alone in New York, she'd spent many a night with her dinner in front of the screen. Becoming absorbed in a medical show or laughing at a comedy helped her to keep her tension-filled job or her loneliness without her parents at bay. But here, in her new life, they read or played cards in the warm flickering lamplight, looked at kaleidoscopes, family albums, or 3-D pictures of foreign lands through a stereopticon viewer. And always, there was conversation with Constance, whose company continued to make Serena feel at home. Then recently, Trenton had begun to join them after dinner, adding an element of excitement Serena had hardly ever experienced before.

But would that excitement continue? Serena waited anxiously that evening for a sign that their encounter in the afternoon had changed Trenton Longworth's attitude toward her, but he was his usual affable but somewhat distant self, and Serena continued to feel both elation and disappointment. However, elation was the stronger emotion. She was ending her first week in 1908 and she was beginning to feel very comfortable in the era. Trenton Longworth was considerably friendlier than he had been at first and Constance had told Serena that the next day would be even more diverting.

"We do some chores on Saturday," Constance had told her. "But only the most enjoyable ones."

Taking her position as head of the domestic household seriously, Constance entered into many of the chores her staff performed and Serena had enthusiastically done her share during the past week. True to Constance's word, however, their only duty that Saturday was the baking, mostly of Malcolm's blackberry pies.

"Of course, they're for us too," said Constance, with a slight defensiveness in her tone. "It's just that Malcolm enjoys them so much and it's rare to see him smile these days. He used to seem so much more cheerful when he first came to us."

So, conspiring with Frances, they waited until Malcolm had left the house for one of his Dun meetings with the boys, so that the pies would be a surprise.

Frances expertly rolled out the crust, but she let Constance and Serena help her put the pastries together.

"As you shape your crust, imagine you're shaping your future," said Frances, in her infectious brogue. "And as you fill your pie, tell yourself that you're filling it with your hopes and dreams."

Trenton, Serena sighed to herself, as she poured the blackberries into one of the shells. But then she reminded herself she mustn't think such things.

"Hopes and dreams," said Constance, as she crimped the edges of a top crust with a fork. Serena thought that her friend's dreamy but somehow sad expression must echo her own and she wondered what made Constance feel that way.

They had nearly finished straightening the kitchen, with the pies in the oven, filling the house with the aroma of Frances' special blend of spices, when the sound of wood being chopped started outside.

"Oh no!" said Constance, with her hands to her face. "Malcolm is back so soon! He's bound to guess what's cooking from the smell. I don't know why, but I wanted to surprise him tonight."

"We could head him off at the pass," suggested Serena.

Constance looked confused.

"You know," said Serena. "Meet him out there and think up some way to keep him from coming in."

"Ah. Make him run some sort of errand," giggled Constance. "We'll send him over to the Trices to borrow—"

"A dozen sweet potatoes," Frances joined in.

"But he hates those," said Constance, with gleeful eyes.

"That'll make the surprise all the better," said Frances.

"Then when he comes back with the potatoes, we'll send him somewhere else," added Constance, as they all crowded out the back door. "He's so good, the poor thing'll never even complain."

"Oh dear! All our plans were for naught," laughed Frances, coming back through the door.

It wasn't Malcolm in the backyard. It was Trenton. Having returned from his financial meeting next door with Mr. Trice, he had evidently decided to add to the woodpile himself. Swinging the ax with effortless grace, he appeared to enjoy the task. He had removed his coat, which was hanging on a nearby branch, and had rolled his sleeves up, past his elbows. Serena had known that Trenton was well-built, but she was still amazed at the size of his biceps.

"Trenton," she gasped. "You must work out all the time!"

"Work out?" he asked.

"Exercise. Lift weights."

"Well, I do use the weights and the Indian clubs over at the gymnasium occasionally. But I've been chopping wood all my life, so naturally, it's easy for me."

"But your muscles are amazing for a guy with a desk job," Serena enthused.

Too late (when she heard Constance's soft "Ser-reen-na!"), she realized what she was saying. People didn't talk about each other's bodies in 1908, especially not those of the opposite sex.

"I-I'm sorry," she stammered. "I didn't mean to say something shocking. I suppose in the…uh…Wild West, we were a little more casual. Please excuse me."

"Of course," said Trenton. "But that's another thing, along with bird calls and creek-leaping, that you should try to keep to a minimum when you begin teaching."

For all his admonishing words, Serena had a feeling that Trenton was pleased with the compliment. Still, he was actually blushing, something Serena would have thought she would never see, and Constance was biting her lip and staring at Serena with wide amused eyes.

It's a good thing I didn't mention his tight little rear, thought Serena, glancing surreptitiously in that direction. *Not that she'd ever have that much nerve,* Serena realized.

She probably had as much in common with the "proper lady" of 1908 as with the stereotypical bold, young woman the 2000s. But there was no way to explain that to her new friends.

Hoping that her faux pas wouldn't continue to haunt her, Serena prepared for the evening. Saturday nights were always fun too, Constance had promised.

"We often have company," she had said. "Randy McNaught or someone from the college staff. But whether we do or not, we make it a festive evening."

True to Constance's word, a couple of professors and their wives had been invited and the conversation was both topical and witty.

The dinner table was decorated with fresh flowers, even in the finger bowls, and Frances' famous blackberry pie was served à la mode at the end of the meal. No one mentioned Serena's daring comment that afternoon, but there was a lot of spontaneous laughter—"gratuitous giggling," Trenton called it, with a provocative smile, and several amused sidelong glances were sent Serena's way.

When the meal was over, Constance ushered everyone, including any household staff she could find, into the front parlor for a sing-along.

Serena loved to sing and had even done some solos in her school choruses, and she was glad to have Trenton hear her do something at which she knew she was good.

Constance brought out the sheet music for "Down by the Old Mill Stream" (which she called a new song), and the two girls began to sing. Constance was also a soprano, but her range was a little lower than Serena's and their voices blended well. The staff joined in as they could, but Trenton watched from the hall.

"Come on, Trennie. You know this," called Constance from the piano, stopping before the chorus.

Trenton hesitated in the doorway. "I really ought to go and look over the schedules one more time," he offered.

"You've worked on them all week," said Constance. "All summer, in fact. It's Saturday night. Now, come over here!"

"All right," he agreed and came, with a little smile, to stand beside Serena.

"Down by the old millstream," they began again.

Wow, thought Serena. *I'm pretty arrogant, thinking he's going to be impressed with my singing!*

Trenton's baritone voice was as rich and mellow as his speaking voice, soaring easily to high notes and sounding even more enticing on low ones.

"Where I first met you."

But Trenton did appear to be impressed with her high notes too, smiling and nodding his head slightly, and Serena realized that singing with someone, even an old cliché song like this one, could be a sensuous experience.

"With your eyes so blue." Trenton looked significantly into Serena's aqua eyes.

"It was then I knew that you loved me too,"

I've got to stop reading so much into this, Serena told herself, feeling a blush creep up her face.

Was it her imagination or was Trenton blushing too? Serena felt a guilty thrill at the thought of having such power. But just as they finished the song, he looked away and she couldn't tell.

Trenton shook his head slightly. "How about the fair song?" he said quickly to his sister.

"Oh yes. That one's a corker!" said Frances.

Constance drew "Meet Me in St. Louis" from the piano bench.

"We really wanted to attend the fair," Constance said wistfully, when they finished a rousing rendition. "But it was…we were—"

"We were in mourning," Trenton supplied, with a bitter edge to his voice. "Nominally, at least."

There was an awkward silence. Serena knew that the St. Louis World's Fair had taken place in 1904, so that must have been at the time when Anne had died. Trenton was saying that the mourning for his wife was only pretense and, from what Constance had told her, Serena imagined everyone in the room felt the same way.

Just as the silence began to stretch unbearably, Malcolm came through the parlor door with an armload of Trenton's freshly cut logs.

"Malcolm," said Constance, reaching toward him as he deposited the wood in the basket. "I wondered where you were. You must come and sing with us."

"I really shouldna', Mum," said Malcolm, wiping his hands on his leather apron. "There's lots of wood baskets to fill. You know, it sometimes tends to get cool of an evenin', this time of year."

"But it's not cool this evening," protested Constance. "At least sing 'Asleep in the Deep' for us. No one else can even attempt that."

There was a general chorus of approval from the dinner guests and the other servants.

"As you wish," said Malcolm, with a reluctant smile.

Malcolm sang the song by heart, in a strong bass voice that grumbled into intensely low notes with ease and yet still managed to sound rather melodic. Constance watched him in rapt admiration, once or twice forgetting to hit the piano keys.

When he finished the last amazingly deep "deep," there were enthusiastic applause and cheers from everyone. Malcolm laughingly took a bow, but when his gaze met Constance's, his dark brown eyes turned serious.

"I'd better get back to work," he said.

"Oh no, please don't go," said Constance, jumping up and opening the piano bench. "I thought we could sing some Irish songs."

"I-I really need to get the wood," said Malcolm.

Constance followed him to the doorway and, though they spoke softly, Serena could still hear them.

"Why won't you sing with us anymore?" she asked. "I know you used to enjoy it. You even taught Trennie and me some of these songs."

"I'm sorry to disappoint, Mum," said Malcolm, edging away. "But, with the new house and the school, there's always lots of work to be done these days."

"And why do you insist on calling me 'Mum' now? It was 'Connie Girl' when you first came."

"But that's just it, Mum," offered Malcolm sadly. "You were a child when I first came here—you're a lady now. It wouldna' be dignified.

"And I must go," he said, moving away.

Constance stood still for a moment, then turned back to the group with a little shrug and a smile that didn't quite reach her eyes.

"Why don't we sing Irish songs, anyway?" Frances asked, rallyingly.

"Why not?" said Constance. "We don't need old, dignified Malcolm! Frances is as Irish as they come!"

The familiar, lilting, and cheerful melodies soon lightened the mood again and, when they sang "Danny Boy," Serena teased herself that she was close to swooning over Trenton's voice and the quick, soulful looks he sent her from time to time.

All in all, she decided as she prepared for bed, it had been a wonderful weekend and there was still Sunday to look forward to.

Though the college had its chapel, the family and faculty sometimes attended special occasions at the interdenominational church in the valley, and they had been invited to join an event there the next afternoon. A visiting foreign missionary was due to speak about his travels and there would be dinner on the grounds and a general social hour afterwards. It wasn't the kind of entertainment Serena would normally get excited about, but she was anxious to see something of the people and traditions of the surrounding community. Also, it was likely that Randy McNaught, Constance's sometime "caller," who had been in North Carolina on business, would attend, and Serena was curious about him. And most interesting, Trenton would be going with them!

Serena only hoped Estey Wooten wouldn't show up and blow her cover. But Constance, thinking that Serena wanted to ask about her belongings, regretfully said it was unlikely.

Chapter 6

The next afternoon, Serena and Constance met in the columned entrance hall, dressed for the outing. Since the church was expected to be warm and stuffy, due to the crowd, both of them wore light cotton dresses with flower prints—Serena's sprigged with small bluebells and Constance's dappled with pink roses—and they both stopped by the gilt-framed mirror (where Trenton's portrait would hang in 2008, Serena realized), to adjust their romantic but cumbersome flower-laden picture hats. Agreeing with a giggle that they both looked "fetching," they proceeded to the waiting carriage.

Trenton was already waiting for them, looking nothing short of gorgeous in a classic blue suit (it had never occurred to Serena that a historical figure could be so sexy), feeding a lump of sugar to the Longworth's beautiful chestnut mare, Mergatroid.

Constance had told Serena that she and Trenton had been allowed to name all the family's animals since they were children, and Serena knew they always had a mare named Mergatroid and usually one named Mahetable and a stallion named Jehossofat.

With her classic lines and shining coat, the present Mergatroid belied her silly moniker, as she ate happily from Trenton's outstretched hand.

"My, but you ladies look fresh and lovely," said Trenton with an open smile. When he was helping Serena into the carriage, he added. "I've been meaning to comment on that broach of yours. It's very interesting. The three graces, isn't it?"

"I think so," said Serena, fingering the ornament attached to her eyelet collar, but distracted by Trenton's touch lingering at her waist, "I found it at an anti—a-uh…shop in—"

"California?" Trenton finished for her, with a wry smile.

"Y-yes. It was one of the few things I was able to bring with me," she said truthfully.

Even before he guided Mergatroid onto the dirt road, Serena felt that Trenton would be a skillful carriage driver. She knew that he hesitated to buy an automobile because he didn't trust them on the unpaved mountain roads, but Serena had wondered if a horse could maneuver them any better. However, they arrived at the church grounds without incident and even comfortably, in the well-sprung carriage.

The church was the epitome of the old-fashioned house of worship Serena had seen in many movies and TV shows—one large room, built of white clapboards, with a squat-white steeple on the top, surrounded by a few outbuildings, including those with the ubiquitous moon-shaped cutouts on the doors, and a large, well-kept green yard.

Inside, the congregation was already plying cardboard fans against the warmth of the eager, encroaching crowd. Serena found, however, that a place of honor had been saved at the front of the room for the Longworths, and she noted many turned heads and quizzical expressions as she passed down the aisle with them.

The traveling preacher turned out to be a minister-in-training, a kid really, whose parents were foreign missionaries, on the last stop of a summer speaking tour: before his return to college. But he spoke with surprising passion and skill about the exotic climes in which he had grown up, had a speaking and singing voice to almost rival Trenton's, and was handsome enough, behind his round owlish glasses, to elicit audible sighs from several of the women.

Sitting on the rough oak bench between Trenton and Constance, Serena felt as if she'd come home. She didn't even care if the service was overlong. The pews were so packed that there was no way to avoid touching the person next to you. She could feel Trenton's hip and shoulder and leg through her cotton dress, and every once in a while, he looked at her and smiled intimately.

When the service was over, the three of them joined the long line to the potluck buffet, set up on the lawn. The tables groaned with platters of fried chicken, cornbread, potato salad, deviled eggs, all kinds of vegetables and salads, apple cider, and innumerable cakes and pies, including some of Frances', Constance's and Serena's blackberry creations. Serena watched as everyone piled his or her plates up high.

Not a fat-gram counter in the whole crew, she thought, with a laugh.

"Why, Miss Longworth, you're a sight for sore eyes," said a masculine voice behind them. "I got here late and couldn't get up there to you in the church."

"You mean that big red auto of yours couldn't get you here on time?" Constance spoke in a bantering tone to the stocky-built blond, in the expensive-looking brown serge suit.

"I drove straight through from North Carolina," said the young man, blushing to the roots of his slightly receding hairline. "I couldn't leave 'til early this morning, but I didn't want to miss you on this... this occasion, you know."

"My, you must be tired," said Constance, patting his arm consolingly. "But please, let me introduce you to this lady," she added, turning him toward Serena. "Serena, this is Mr. Randolph McNaught. Randy, my very good friend, Serena Cassidy."

"Honored to meet you, ma'am," said Randy, with an appreciative smile and a little bow. "I'm glad to know any friend of Miss Constance's. How long have you known each other, if I may ask?"

"Not as long as we'd like, because she just came here recently from California," said Constance quickly. "She's staying with us for a while, though," she added. "Can you credit it, when she arrived, she actually had to stay with Estey Wooten for a few days!"

"Lord, deliver us, Miss Cassidy!" said Randy. "Don't get me wrong. Estey Wooten's a fine woman. But still, I'm sure you'd rather be with Miss Constance here." He beamed at Constance.

"Of course," said Serena quickly, hoping to get off the subject of Estey Wooten. She had been relieved to find that Estey hadn't attended the gathering that afternoon and wanted to discuss the lady as little as possible. "I can't tell you how grateful I am to the Longworths for taking me in."

"But some of her belongings are still at Estey's house," said Constance. Serena's heart sank. "Malcolm's boys couldn't seem to get a clear answer from Estey. You know how scatterbrained she can be. I tell you Randy," she added, upsetting Serena even more, "Why don't you go around to Estey's when you can and ask for Serena Cassidy's things?"

"Oh no," said Serena. "I wouldn't want to bother Mr. McNaught. I have so few possessions there, it's really not important."

"Nonsense," said Randy. "I live in Belle Vieux. And anything I can do for beautiful ladies like you and Miss Constance is a pleasure for me."

Serena wanted to argue more, but she was afraid it would make her look suspicious, so she subsided into an uncomfortable silence as they began to fill their plates.

Benches and chairs had been set up under a shading oak tree, and Serena, Constance and the two men took their dinners there.

They were joined by the Trice family and other members of the mountain community. Lettie Trice frolicked through the crowd, giving everyone the signs for "hi." Her parents explained that this was a greeting which Miss Cassidy had taught her, and many in the group imitated her, returning the signed greeting, which elicited beaming smiles and giggles from Lettie. Even her brothers copied the movements, though whether in support or derision, Serena wasn't sure. Lettie, however, didn't seem to care.

"You just may be a good teacher, after all, and I may have some apologizing to do," Trenton said quietly, moving closer to her. Serena smiled, feeling a warm glow in her chest.

Conversation was desultory, while everyone ate the rich, delicious food, but someone in the group occasionally managed to ask Serena about her background.

While she tried to think up an appropriate response, Serena would use the pretext of finishing a bite of food for her hesitation. But often, she noticed that Constance would jump in to answer the question. Even Trenton chimed in for her a time or two. Serena thought it was almost as if they knew she had something to hide and were protecting her. While it worried her to imagine what they thought of her situation, she realized it also made her feel very cared for.

Trenton also got up twice to get her a refill of her lemonade and asked if he could bring her more food. Her sense of belonging became even stronger.

Randy had just returned from his second lemonade run for Constance, when one of the most persistent questioners, Mrs. Frye, wife of the general store owner and an obvious community leader, leaned toward Serena again.

"Randy," said Trenton quickly, moving between Serena and Mrs. Frye, to put a hand on Randy's shoulder, "you haven't told us about your trip. I'm sure everyone would like to hear about the newest furniture styles at the North Carolina factories."

This was all the encouragement Randy needed. For the next fifteen minutes, he regaled the group with news of furniture styles and even of machinery innovations he had seen on his business trip. Egged on by questions from Constance and Trenton, he spoke in an ever-more-carrying voice, attracting the attention of picnickers not originally seated under the trees and precluding the possibility of any other conversations or questions.

Released of the necessity to make up personal history, Serena could sit back and observe the group. Away from the rarified atmosphere of the college, the level of sophistication seemed rather low. The Southern mountain accents of this era, before the homogenization caused by modern media, were much more pronounced than they were in the twenty-first century, and the influence of the Scottish, Irish, and Cockney accents, from which most of them were derived was much more noticeable. Some of the men and women wore stiff black suits and dresses, and there were some lovely tucked, white lawns or sprigged cottons like hers and Constance's among them, but many wore simple shirts and trousers or shirtwaist blouses and skirts. Everyone, however, wore hats, most of the women's being lavishly decorated, like the ones Serena and Constance sported. From their rough, red hands and care-worn faces, Serena could tell they were a hard-working lot, but they seemed to be genuinely enjoying themselves at this simple entertainment. Though they appeared to view unexpected strangers with distrust, as well as fascination, they seemed eager for news of the world outside their isolated community, most of them hanging on Randy's every word.

"And I was wondering if you might like one of them for your parlor, Miss Constance," Randy concluded after describing a new style of accent piece that he called a "whatnot" shelf.

Constance, one of the few people not hanging on each of Randy's comments, was gazing across the lawn to where Malcolm was organizing his boys for some sort of activity.

"Of course, I'm sure that would be just the thing," Constance said laughingly, not really trying to hide the fact that her mind had wandered. "I was just noticing that, uh, the boys seem to be preparing a baseball game."

"Ah, baseball," said Randy. "We did enjoy playing that game at the last social, didn't we? What do you say, men?" he rallied the others. "Should we show the boys how the game is played?"

As Constance and Serena strolled with the men toward the baseball site, Serena was glad that no one could read her thoughts. She was hoping Trenton would take off his coat again and felt a little shiver at the idea of watching his body as he swung and caught and ran.

"Constance," said one of the women, catching her sleeve. "Roy's done set up the frame for Charey's quilt."

"Oh, of course," said Constance, turning away from the field with some apparent reluctance. "Serena, we're making a quilt for Thelma's daughter, who's getting married next month. Would you like to help?"

"Sure," said Serena. She was also reluctant to leave the game, but she enjoyed sewing and was anxious to see how a real old-fashioned quilting bee worked.

Thelma's daughter, Charey (short for Charlotte), Constance said was a sunny-aced seventeen-year-old with long honey-brown hair. She was thrilled to be getting married, partly, Serena thought, because it made her the center of attention, and she loved the pastel wedding ring design quilt the ladies were making for her.

"Isaac and I'll sure like snuggling under this of a cold night," she said with a saucy grin, obviously enjoying the shocked expressions her comment caused.

"Charey, you'd best not be talking like that around Isaac," said her mother with a tired laugh. "You'll get enough of that kind a stuff without bringin' it up."

"Oh, Ma, you just can't remember bein' young," said Charey.

"I was younger 'en you when you come along," answered Thelma. "But bein' young like that don't last too long. We was hopin' I wouldn't be so far along with this one at the weddin'," Thelma said in aside to Constance, patting her stomach as she spoke. "But then Roy got hurt. Couldn't help finishin' their cabin for two, three months so they had to put back the weddin'."

"I thought you and Roy were going to try to stop having children," said Constance with mild reproach.

"We was," said Thelma, pulling a sad smile. "But, I prob'ly shouldn't be talkin' about this—you not bein' a married lady—but the way it is with men, and sometimes even with women, you just can't keep the chillin' from comin'."

"How many kids—children—do you have?" asked Serena.

"Fourteen head," said Thelma. "Two of 'em twins."

Serena looked at Thelma as she plied her needle. From what she said, this woman must be in her middle thirties. When she spoke with her daughter and the other women, flashes of Charey's comeliness crossed her face, but in general, Thelma looked much older than her years. Her long wraith-thin visage already showed deeply etched lines; the set of her jaw was tight and grim; the expression in her eyes was one of resignation; her thick brown hair was liberally streaked with gray, and her movements were slow and tired. She had probably had a baby almost every year of her marriage! No wonder Serena Longworth had joined with Margaret Sanger to try to bring birth control to the women of Appalachia!

"Speakin' of you not bein' a married woman," Mrs. Frye's stringent tones cut through Serena's thoughts, as she skewered Constance in her gaze. "Have you and young Mr. McNaught agreed to tie the knot yet?"

"Oh no, Ma'am," said Constance, flushing deeply. "Randy's a fine man, but—"

"But nothin'," answered Lavinia Frye. "He's one of the finest young men in these parts, and you know, with the least bit of encouragement, he'd come right up to the mark."

"But our feelings—" Constance put in desperately.

"Pshaw!" snorted Mrs. Frye. "Feelin's! Feelin's can change, m'dear. What with your brother insistin' that all those professors at your school be married men and you stuck up here in the hills, where're you gonna meet anybody else with the same kind of learnin' you have. You're lettin' your youth slip away, hopin' for some kind of Prince Charmin', and, come to think on it, the McNaughts must be near's rich as princes, anyway!"

"And he looks fine-wrought," offered Charey. "In them tailor-made clothes of hisn."

"And-and he's a fine friend," said Constance defensively. "I know that. I was telling Serena just this morning about his organizing that picnic on the river back when we were in the doldrums about—Anne."

Constance's attempt to change the subject backfired for Serena, as Mrs. Frye's direct gaze centered on her once again. "That reminds me, Miss Cassidy," she said in stentorian tones. "Didn't Mr. Longworth say you come from out in California?"

"Y-yes," said Serena. "I was born there, but my parents are from the south, so after they were—after I lost them, I was anxious to see where their roots were. And I love it here," she went on hurriedly. "The mountains are so beautiful, and—"

"What part of California?" Mrs. Frye cut through Serena's rhetoric. "I have a cousin out there."

"Well, it's a big state-uh-territory," said Serena breathlessly, hoping one of them was correct. "We lived-uh-near San Francisco."

"Well, I'll be," said Mrs. Frye. "My cousin too. Went out there in the seventies by wagon train. But she writes me regular, so I know about a lot stuff out there. Do—"

"That's how my parents traveled too," said Serena, fending off the next question. "They just made it through the Oregon Pass before the snows," she went on, hoping she remembered her old TV dramas correctly. "But of course, I came back on the train. M-most of the way, anyway," she added, when Mrs. Frye gave her a doubtful look.

"How long d'it take you," asked Thelma.

"Oh, several days," said Serena vaguely. "Nearly a week. Of-of course we had stops along the way."

"And you traveled all that way all by yourself?" asked Mrs. Frye in shocked tones.

Serena's eyes darted around the group. Nearly every woman had her eyes glued on her, many of them even held their needles suspended in the air over the colorful squares and curves, and they all seemed to gasp simultaneously, whether in disapproval or in sympathy, Serena couldn't tell. Ladies obviously didn't travel by themselves much in 1908.

"Well, I-I felt I had no choice," mumbled Serena, hating the way her constant stammers must be making her appear. "I had no one left in California after my parents were gone," she said, recalling her genuine emotions after her parent's deaths.

"You poor dear," said a sweet-looking woman named Mrs. McInnes.

"And you do have relatives here?" asked Lavinia Frye, in her no-nonsense voice.

"Well, no," admitted Serena. "But at least, as I said, my roots are here. My parents often spoke—"

At that moment, Mr. Bagby, the young minister passed by the open door of the shed and nodded to the ladies.

"Oh," Serena gasped. "I see Rev. Bagby is free at last. I did want to speak with him on a-a spiritual matter—concerning my parents. I hope you ladies will excuse me?" she asked, rising hastily from her chair.

Far be it from Southern women of the early nineteen-hundreds to interfere with matters of a spiritual nature, Serena had guessed correctly, and most of them excused her from the table with smiles and nods, though Mrs. Frye favored her with a moue of doubt and Constance looked disappointed or concerned or both.

Serena was sorry to leave Constance's company and the beautiful quilt, but she felt she couldn't continue to field Mrs. Frye's questions. Also, she had actually wanted to ask Mr. Bagby about Brazil. She had visited the country on several occasions and wondered what it had been like in 1908.

For his part, Mr. Bagby (who asked her to call him "T. C.") seemed genuinely pleased to be accosted by a young lady, whose questions were of a light nature. The young man spoke animatedly of Rio, Sao Paulo, and the jungle; he described his parents' struggles to establish their churches and schools; he made her shiver with stories of snakes and tarantulas, and he had gray and white photographs of almost everything in an accordion folder he fetched from his buggy. Serena also noticed that Mr. Bagby seemed to react to her as a woman, despite his image as a minister. He was attractive, she thought, and charming, if somewhat opinionated and peculiar. She felt more comfortable with him than she had for most of the afternoon, exchanging a teasing banter along with the travelogue.

The sun was beginning to lay pink lines across the sky when Constance approached them diffidently.

"Con," said Serena, encircling her friend with her arm and pulling her into the group. "I'm glad you came over. Rev. Bagby has been telling me some fascinating stories about Brazil.

"See this odd-shaped peak over the water?" she went on, holding up a grainy, cardboard-backed landscape photo of Rio de Janeiro. "This is Mount Corcovado, which means 'hunchback' in English. The Bagbys and some of Rio's other church leaders are working to get a really huge statue of Christ erected on the top of this mountain. Won't that be impressive?"

"It certainly will," said Constance, her smile a little tighter than usual. "I hope your family is successful in their goal."

"Oh they will be, I'm sure," said Serena, who had flown over the statue several times. "T. C.—Rev. Bagby here is certainly strong-willed enough. If all the members of the committee 're like him—

"I'm sure they'll succeed," Constance put in quickly. "Actually, though, I came to see if you're ready to leave. I believe Trenton wants to go."

"So soon?" asked Serena. "But the ball game is still going on."

"I think he's just a little tired," said Constance. "They have more than enough players, and it'll be too dark for any of them to play soon."

"Sorry I left so suddenly," said Serena, when they had said their goodbyes to Mr., Bagby. "But I did want to, uh, confer with the minister."

"Oh, that's okay," said Constance. "I finished the square you were working on."

"Thanks," said Serena, deciding to be more honest. "The main reason I left, though, was because Mrs. Frye was making me uncomfortable. She's just so—"

"Believe me, I understand," said Constance. "I think she actually means well, but she can pin you down like—like a butterfly in a nature exhibit!"

That set them both to giggling and they were in a lighter mood by the time they reached the carriage. However, Trenton's expression was anything but amused.

"We're all ready to go, then?" he asked with raised eyebrows as he pulled open the door of the carriage.

There were no lingering fingers at her waist as Trenton helped her into the back seat and he hardly uttered a word on the way home.

"How did the baseball game go?" Serena asked tentatively after several minutes,

"Fine," Trenton answered shortly. His long, slender finger looked tight on the reins. "And I trust you had a nice time?"

"Oh yes. Very nice," said Serena. Trenton merely gave her a curt nod and Constance sent her an uncomfortable smile.

Serena shrugged. "Well, I guess it's been a long day," she said, with an involuntary, nervous giggle.

She received exactly the same reactions she had before, so she decided to give up, and the remainder of the journey was accomplished in strained silence.

His face set, Trenton excused himself to complete some work, as soon as they entered the house.

"Do you think I've done something wrong?" Serena asked, as she watched Trenton disappear down the hall.

"No, of course not," said Constance reassuringly. "I'm sure he's just anxious about the first day of school."

He's worried! thought Serena. *He's not going to teach his first class ever, and in an era he doesn't completely understand!*

She also bid Constance goodnight early and went to her room to study River's lesson plans again. But it wasn't actually a matter of learning the material, she realized. It was finding an approach to keep the boys interested and even knowing how to greet them. She and Trenton had never gotten around to having another conference and suddenly she felt completely unprepared.

She went over the material several more times, though she knew it almost by heart, and then spent a restless night, filled with dreams of classrooms, of cynical derisive boys and a disparaging darkly handsome schoolmaster.

The boys were all due to arrive early in the morning, most of them coming into Belle Vieux on the seven-thirty train and then being transported to the school in various buggies and carts, driven by men of the town, under Malcolm's capable direction.

Malcolm had also helped Trenton to organize the dorm assignments and class schedules, Constance said, as well as supervising the renovation of the dormitories to accommodate plumbing.

Serena tried to help Constance with greeting the boys and giving out their schedules and room assignments, but she spent much of her morning fidgeting, stealthily watching Trenton (who seemed to be trying to ignore her as much as he could, without appearing impolite), and feeling like she might throw up.

The students were to have a shortened class schedule; a few moments with each teacher in their assigned rooms after lunch. Serena knew she couldn't eat, so she went to her bedroom to review her first-day remarks for the tenth time that day and then once again checked her appearance in the full-length oval mirror.

She had chosen to wear one of Cousin Violet's more prim morning outfits, a mustard-colored, tucked shirtwaist dress, with a white collar and cuffs at the high neck and long sleeves. It was a conservative look, but not unbecoming.

That's good, she told herself. *I need all the ego-boosting I can get.*

With trepidation in her heart, she walked over to her classroom on the first floor of the liberal arts building. Not even Constance realized how nervous Serena was, because she had convinced everyone she had taught classes before.

Well, she told herself. '*My tutoring students did improve with me and I think I'm even helping Lettie some Anyway, no matter how bad it is, it's only temporary.*'

What was I so afraid of? she asked herself a few minutes later when she faced the group of fresh faces in Basic English Grammar. In their suits and ties, the students somehow looked both younger and also, more mature than their seventeen or eighteen years. Of course, there wasn't a spiked hairdo, an earring, or even particularly cynical expression among them.

But they were kids. When she announced that she was Miss Cassidy, their temporary teacher, a redhead (whom according to his name tag had the unfortunate name of Mortimer Shine) began to applaud, and all the other boys joined in. Serena wondered if she'd be expected to reprimand them for the noise, but decided against it. After all, it was the first day.

"It's only until Mr. Rivers is on his feet," she said, and there was a chorus of "aws."

But when she described the course, their enthusiasm waned, and they presented her with yawns and grimaces.

"It may not be the most exciting subject in the world," she concluded. "But it's very important. In any profession you pursue, you must be able to express yourself effectively and correctly."

This was apparently a good argument, because the boys perked up a little and listened to the remainder of Serena's speech. She finished by calling the roll, making sure to call each of them "Mister," à la *Goodbye, Mister Chips*.

("Yes, everyone does call me 'Mortician'," volunteered Mr. Shine when his name was called.) And the time she had dreaded so much was over.

Of course, there was a full-length class tomorrow, and considering his demeanor since the picnic, Serena doubted she could count on much guidance from Trenton.

Classes weren't quite as uncomfortable as Serena had anticipated, though she never succeeded in engaging her students' enthusiasm for the dry subject matter. While she droned on about punctuation or verb and pronoun agreement, the boys fidgeted with their pencils or gazed out the window, just as she knew she had often done during the same studies. Serena stuck by River's lesson plans exactly. In desperation, she even tried some of the jokes Rivers had included, but they were River's jokes and not her style, and the laughter was no more than polite. Of course, she perceived many admiring glances from the students, but she resolved not to capitalize on them, making sure to keep her smiles distant and her attitude serious.

At least, judging from their homework and test scores, Serena knew the boy's knowledge was improving, despite their boredom.

Her sessions with Lettie were also going well. They were working through the alphabet, in both hand signals and printed letters. Soon, Lettie could associate one symbol with the other, though Serena wondered if she had any idea of their significance. The child seemed to enjoy the classes, however, and Serena found herself forming a genuine attachment to the funny little girl.

Serena did worry that she might be teaching the child some wrong hand motions. She wasn't sure of the symbols for the letters "g, p, and s," and she eventually realized that each time she showed what she hoped was the correct sign for one of these, Serena would give a little shrug. So of course, it wasn't long before Lettie was repeating the hand motions and the shrugs.

Come to think of it, Serena said to herself, at the end of an afternoon lesson. *Didn't Letitia Jenson shrug a bit as she signed some of her letters? Well,* she reassured herself, *'if she really is the same person, at least she appeared to have learned to communicate well, somewhere along the way!*

Serena and Constance continued to enjoy their time together and felt more and more like sisters. Serena even began to feel a family-like bond with the household staff.

The only gray on the horizon was Trenton, but the change in him seemed to make everything else dark for Serena. She told herself that a woman of the twenty-first century wasn't supposed to feel that way and then realized she was no longer in the twenty-first century, at least not for the time being. Serena realized that, whether it was politically correct or not, she had to admit to herself that Trenton's attitudes seemed to color her own.

She had even asked him, a couple of times directly, if she had done something to offend him. Trenton had assured her that everything was fine, but she knew it wasn't true.

Once again, Trenton took most of his meals in his study, pleading his busy workload and when he did join them, he had very little to say. Gone were the light banter and the compliments. He studiously avoided touching Serena when he had to pass her something or hold a door for her. Trenton simply kept his distance from her, both literally and figuratively.

Even the subject of her classes didn't lure him into spending time with her. When Serena tried to broach the subject, Trenton would merely advise her to follow River's lesson plans as nearly as possible. Two or three times, he had ducked his head into the door of her classroom. She had been humiliated that her students were half asleep, but when she mentioned it to Trenton, he said stiffly, though not unkindly, that their drowsiness was probably to be expected, considering the subject matter and the time of day, which was right after lunch.

So Serena continued with the lesson plans as before, hoping her delivery did them justice. But toward the end of the second week of classes, River's lesson plans ran out. Trenton had told her that Rivers would be sending more, but none were delivered.

So on Wednesday afternoon, Serena was faced with a dilemma. There was no ready-made lesson for the next day. Trenton had seemed very busy and had been particularly gruff when she had seen him earlier and she hated to bother him. Couldn't she (she wondered) come up with something on her own and not have to involve Trenton?

She pored over the lessons she had already taught and tried to decide what should be the next logical subject and what part of a grammar course would be the most likely to keep the boys awake.

"Of course!" she suddenly exclaimed to her empty classroom. "Why didn't I think of it before? Dangling phrases!"

Serena had always found the examples of that grammatical error, such as "The man walked by the house wearing the sergeant's uniform," funny, and she was pretty sure the boys would too.

Feeling a lift in her heart for the first time in nearly two weeks, Serena reviewed the rules for dangling phrases and then made up a few examples herself. It was odd to get excited about a grammar lesson, but she thought the boys might actually take an interest in this one. She desperately wanted to contribute to the school and to regain Trenton's approval. And she had come up with this idea on her own!

A new lesson called for a new outfit, decided Serena, standing in front of her closet the next day. For the past two weeks, she had been alternating between the rust-colored dress, a gray one with small maroon "clocks," and black-and-navy skirts with various white blouses. She had been planning to wear the gray again, but the day was sunny and warmer than it had been recently and she felt like a change.

Tentatively, she took out a linen suit she hadn't had on since Constance had passed it on to her. The long-sleeved jacket was a dark rosy-peach in a length that would later be known as "bolero." The slim, wrap-around skirt was a pinstripe fabric in peach, magenta, and tan. It was an unlikely color combination, but somehow it worked and was even surprisingly subtle. Every edge of the jacket and skirt was finished with a neat, pleated ruffle of the solid peach. Serena hesitated. Constance had called this a "morning suit" or a "walking suit." She wished she could ask Constance's advice, but she knew her friend was in a menu conference with Frances and the school cooks. She decided to try it on.

"Well, it certainly looks businesslike." She told herself a few minutes later, "And it's far from low-cut." She laughed, noting how the ruffle at the neck nearly reached her chin. "And it's more becoming than the gray-and-maroon. Why not?"

Among her accessories was a comb with a bow of the peach fabric attached. Serena stuck it at the back of her topknot to complete the outfit and headed for the school.

"I'm going to read you some sentences," she said as the class came to order. "And I want you to see if you can tell me what's wrong with each of them."

As soon as she read the sentence about the house and the sergeant's uniform, Morty Shine who liked to consider himself a wit, shot his hand up.

"The trouble is," he piped, "it doesn't say if the house had won any medals."

This quip and the laughter and groans that followed it were infectious, and soon, all the students were trying to top each other with witty analyses of the sentences. Occasionally, Serena attempted to calm them down and to review the rules of the lesson, but since they seemed to be learning as well as enjoying themselves, she let the boys go and got into the spirit herself. Several times, she found herself leaving the small, raised podium, on which her desk was centered, to walk around the class and then climb back up to write something on the board.

About midway through the lesson, Serena was startled to notice that Trenton had quietly let himself into the room when her back was turned and was sitting in an empty desk. For a while, she felt self-conscious with him watching, but the boys were so enthusiastic that she soon got back into the spirit herself.

Five minutes before the end of class, Trenton left again, but Serena felt sure that he had seen enough to be impressed. She had noticed a very intense expression on his face once or twice. She completed the lesson by assigning the students to make up their own sentences with dangling phrases and show how they could be corrected for Friday's class. Then she dismissed them with a joyous smile.

Today had been her most successful class yet; it had been based on her own ideas, and Trenton had witnessed it. Surely that would convince him that she genuinely cared about the college and that she was doing a good job.

She climbed the steps to the house a few minutes later, whistling and singing "In My Merry Oldsmobile" (which she and Constance and the servants had sung the night before) and opened the door to find both Trenton and Constance in the entry hall.

Trenton must be very anxious to congratulate her, Serena thought, for he was pacing when she walked in. But the blank stare he gave her wasn't what she'd expected.

"I thought the lesson went rather well today—" she began tentatively, before Trenton cut her off.

"What could you have been thinking with that display today?" he asked in the coldest tone she'd ever heard him use.

"Trennie—" said Constance plaintively, but no one really heard her.

"D-display?" stammered Serena, astounded. "I thought you'd be happy with the boys' enthusiasm."

"I've no doubt they were enthusiastic," said Trenton, his voice dripping sarcasm. "However—"

"I realize that the atmosphere was somewhat irreverent," Serena pressed on before she lost her nerve. "But I feel that often people learn more when the lesson is involved with some sort of recreational activity. They've done some studies—"

"That may well be," Trenton interrupted again, his voice still dripping ice water. "Though I think their levity might have been controlled to some extent. However," he continued with renewed emphasis, "that is neither here nor there. The matter at hand is your actions. I won't have a teacher behaving provocatively with the students!"

"Trennie, you know she didn't mean to—" Constance tried again, but Trenton and Serena could only stare in consternation at each other.

"Behaving provocatively?" cried Serena in disbelief. "Provocatively? Maybe I laughed a little too much for your liking, but—"

"Your laughter, though somewhat questionable, is not the issue here, either," Trenton ground out. "The issue is leaving your desk to hover over the students, wearing an outfit that makes you look—like a carny worker!"

"Trenton!" said Constance. "That outfit was Cousin Violet's!"

"Well," said Trenton, taken a little aback, "it certainly was not appropriate for the occasion. But," he added, adamantly, "the most offensive thing, Miss Cassidy, was your displaying your ankles to them!"

"I was showing my ankles?" asked Serena, in surprise.

"Surely you weren't unaware of it," asserted Trenton.

"But I-I was," said Serena sincerely. "I suppose I was just too caught up in the lesson to realize it."

"But, when you're dealing with impressionable young people, you must be aware of everything," said Trenton, in a somewhat milder tone. "No impropriety can be tolerated."

"You think showing one's ankles is an impropriety?" questioned Serena. "I would never do it intentionally, because I know people in this era—area frown on it. But don't you think to call it an impropriety is a bit extreme? It's just an ankle, a-a part of the foot, really."

Trenton said nothing, clenching his jaws tighter.

"Well, I suppose we just looked at things differently in California," ventured Serena.

"Oh no, don't bring up California again," Trenton exploded, inexplicably. "You've used that same excuse too many times already. California, if, that in fact, is actually your place of birth," he added, with surprising venom, "is one of the states of the union, peopled, for the most part, by Easterners, and it can't be that different! There are standards that any properly brought up person would meet. You arrive at our reception under very suspicious circumstances and promptly 'faint' on our lawn. You have no visible means of support, no family backing. You make very unfortunate allusions to others' anatomy—"

"Admit it, you liked that," Constance insisted.

"And then, by some means, you persuade Constance to let you stay," he continued, as if she hadn't said anything. "It was always against my better judgment, but my sister had somehow been convinced that only you could overcome her feeling of isolation. Then you convince her to carry on like a hoyden, shouting through the hills and jumping creeks—"

"I convinced her to do that," said Constance. "And you know very well you've done it recently, yourself."

"And then," he went on, determinedly, "you consort with a poor, young visiting minister."

"Consort?" said Constance. "She was asking him for spiritual guidance about the loss of her parents."

"And-and talking about Brazil," added Serena, gulping.

So that was why Trenton had been acting so peculiar, she realized.

"And the culmination—" Trenton went on "—was your shameful display today. I simply can't have an instructor in my school—even a temporary one—who conducts herself as you do."

"Trenton, I've never known you to behave so abominably," Constance nearly shouted. "You know Serena is our friend and anything she's done was meant with the best intentions."

A muscle in Trenton's jaw twitched. "Perhaps you're still taken in by Miss Cassidy's wiles, Connie," he said stonily. "I, however, am not. If you still wish for her to remain in our household, I can't prevent it, but her association with Longworth College is terminated."

Serena drew herself up like a statue, her anger lending her strength. "I'm sorry that I've done so many things to offend your delicate sensibilities. I certainly didn't intend to," she said, clipping her words with dignity. "But, believe me, I've no wish to be associated with such a pompous a—, with someone as uptight as you are. I won't impose on you any longer. I will m-make other arrangements, as soon as I can." Fighting to hold back the tears, she turned on her heel and started for the stairs.

"Serena, wait—" Constance called after her, but Serena didn't slow her pell-mell flight to the sanctuary of her room. Trenton didn't say anything, she noticed.

Just as she closed her bedroom door and flung herself on the bed, Serena heard the voices below begin to rise. The house was well insulated and she knew that, if she could hear them, Trenton and Constance must have been shouting. She was sorry to cause them to argue, but there was nothing she could do about it. Possibly, some of the household staff could hear her cry, but there was nothing she could do about that either. She felt as if she could never stop.

At first, Serena was consumed by both fury and hurt, but the anger faded fast. (She could never seem to hold on for long to even justified anger, especially with people she really cared about.) She was left feeling humiliated and disappointed that such a promising day had gone so wrong.

When the truly racking sobs had subsided somewhat, Serena got up and took off the offending outfit and put on a cotton robe over her lingerie. She rinsed her face with cold water from the pitcher and basin and sat back down on the bed, trying to remain calm.

But the tears wouldn't stop and rolled unchecked down her cheeks as she stared, unseeing, out the window.

What was she doing in 1908? It had been going on too long to be a dream or an elaborate joke; unless she was completely insane and delusional, she had actually been somehow transported to this different era. But why? Serena had never felt that she completely fitted in the twenty-first century, but at least she knew the rules. Now she was stuck in a time where the accidental display of an ankle could mean you were a fallen woman, where the words you used (not even curse words, just slang) could make you seem questionable, and where ideas of ladylike behavior were tight and restrictive. (Serena had even heard Frances admonishing one of the local girls for trilling a merry tune a couple of days ago. "Ladies don't whistle," she had said.)

And in the twenty-first century, she had known people. True, she hadn't felt genuinely close to anyone since her parents' deaths, but there were people in the world to whom she could have appealed in times of crisis. In 1908, conversely, she was without funds, a home, marketable skills, verifiable background, and just about everything else that would make it possible for her to take care of herself. She had no one to turn to or depend on except Trenton and Constance.

And what cruel twist of fate had brought her to Trenton and Constance?

In Constance, she had found the best friend she'd ever had, except for her parents. But, as Serena had learned today, her many faux pas could also make Constance's life uncomfortable. And what if Serena had to leave, which she felt was probably unavoidable? Serena knew the pain of separation would be almost equal to what she'd felt for her mother, and she hated to bring that kind of hurt to Constance, who seemed curiously vulnerable already.

And then there was Trenton. Why had she been sent to fall in love—yes, in love, she sadly realized—with a man whose opinions of her were so ambivalent? Serena knew that Trenton had some tender feelings toward her, but she doubted that what he felt was love. She knew also that he fought those feelings as hard as he could. She was sure that he distrusted her and disapproved of her and that today, she had made him furious. She doubted there was anything she could do to explain her "failings." And even if she could find a way to overcome his present anger (and her own wounded pride) and could convince him to accept his attachment to her, what good would it really do, when she knew he would meet the other Serena very soon, anyway?

Then it hit her with force, the thought that had (of course) occurred to her before, but which she had managed to push down and keep from full consciousness until now. What if she were the other Serena? What if there were only one? What if she were Serena Longworth, merely repeating the odd events of a fractured life over and over again?

Serena's recall was almost photographic when it came to important conversations, and, once again, she went over the peculiar reactions she'd elicited at the 2008 party.

Martha Whitter had said Serena would probably look very much like Serena Longworth, when she was older, and had asked if Serena was a relative. Also, Serena thought she had said something about Mrs. Longworth's ability to predict events before they occurred.

Then Martha's mother, Letitia Jenson (Lettie?) had insisted on calling Serena "Miz Reenie" and had gotten very upset when Martha told her she was mistaken.

Also, Senator Marshall had behaved very strangely. As soon as Serena had given her name, the senator had stared at her with bug eyes and had taken Serena's hands in both of hers, in a gesture that was effusive, even for a politician. She'd also gasped something like "It's real!" or "It's really true!" and had insisted Serena talk with her later.

If this amazing theory of time travel were correct, Senator Marshall, that sophisticated older woman, was Serena's granddaughter!

A new memory occurred to Serena. Hadn't the senator said. "Grand," right before she had been called to the podium? Serena had assumed she had intended to say "Grand to meet you," or "Grand party," but could she have started to say "Grandmother?"

No! It was impossible! But if time travel were a reality, why couldn't this be too?

If she actually was Serena Longworth, Serena thought, were all those things she had done for her parents at the school just a result of selfishness on her part? Was she just doing them to make sure she, herself, would have a good life? It certainly put the old lady's altruism in a different light.

Also, how can I marry Trenton, she asked herself, *delicious as the thought may be? He acts like he practically hates me right now and I don't see how I can ever get him to completely trust me, when there's so much of my past I have to hide.*

Besides, there's all that stuff Grace Pierson said Serena Longworth did in her life! Work with Margaret Sanger to help bring birth control up here! Start some kind of business with Constance! Bring the arts to Appalachia! Help start the college for women! Be a mother to two outstanding people! Be a grandmother to a senator! she shouted in her head, the stress of the argument and these new realizations robbing her of her usual optimism and energy.

I'm not some damn superwoman! How am I supposed to do all that?

No matter what—even if it changed the future—she couldn't be Serena Longworth, she decided. She really should leave, she thought, maybe tonight after everyone was asleep. But what would she do? Simply trudge down the hill in the blue-and-cream 2008 party dress, which was the only thing she truly owned? And how would she support herself after that?

She also wondered what would happen if she went and stood in the closet that had been a bathroom in 2008. She had found out that the closet was in Connie's room, so she'd have to sneak in when Constance was occupied somewhere else. But was there a way to get back to the future? She hadn't liked 2008 all that much, but at least it made sense to her.

At some point during her internal ranting, she didn't remember when, Serena had gotten up from her bed and was pacing back and forth between her dresser and the window, until she was interrupted by a light tap.

It was no surprise to hear Constance's voice. "Serena," she called tentatively, "may I talk to you for a minute?"

Serena went immediately to the door and found her friend looking anxious.

"I'm so sorry, Rena," Constance said as they hugged each other.

"No," said Serena sadly. "You have nothing to apologize for. I'm the one who made the indecent display, but I swear to you, Constance, I didn't mean to."

"Oh, I know that," said Constance, with an emphatic flip of her hand. "Trennie is blowing the whole incident completely out of proportion. He's behaving like a self-righteous prig and I told him so too!"

"Self-righteous prig," said Serena with a wry smile. "Perhaps that was the expression I was searching for."

"Well, it certainly fits today," her friend answered. "And what makes it really silly is the way he acted when the same thing happened to me last year. Randy was trying to teach me the Castle Walk and Trennie told me later that I showed my ankles several times, one time even part of my calf. What made it even worse was that Randy's parents were there too. But they didn't seem upset, I'm not even sure they noticed, and all Trennie did was tease me about it afterwards and call me 'Careless Connie.' You can be sure I reminded him of that. And he admitted that his attitude had been completely different."

"Well," said Serena, wrinkling her brow. "Maybe he reacted so strongly because the school was involved. Or maybe it's just that he-he doesn't like me very much!"

"Oh, that's ridiculous!" snapped Constance with a deprecating smile. "It's just the opposite, I'm sure, and I think you know it too. The real reason he got so upset is…No, I promised to let him talk to you about that. But there is one thing I can tell you," she added, lowering her voice.

Serena cocked her head expectantly.

"Remember when I told you that I thought that Anne had other men?" Constance was almost whispering now. "Well, that wasn't completely true. I know there were others, even here at the school. She caused one of the professors to lose his job and probably his marriage, and there was even one of the students—one of the younger boys too—with whom Trennie had to forcibly intervene. And we suspected others. One reason Anne was so mean to Malcolm was that, no matter how much she flirted, he seemed immune to her charms. What was even worse was that she didn't care anything about these men. She was just using them for amusement and to prove she was still attractive. She laughed behind their backs and didn't care what she did to their lives and she threw it all in Trennie's face."

"How awful," said Serena. "And they say only the good die young," she added with a bitter laugh. "No wonder poor Trenton has a hard time trusting anyone!"

"True," said Constance. "He always gave everyone the benefit of the doubt before that and he was never—. There I go again, starting into something that's better for him to discuss with you. He's gone for a walk to mull it all over now, but I'm sure he'll come to see you soon, to apologize and—"

"Oh, Con, he doesn't have to come. I mean—if he has to mull it over so much, it must be because he feels he'll have to compromise in order to apologize. I've been thinking," Serena continued, "that maybe I should just go. Trenton's never felt especially comfortable with me here, and if I can't help with the school. I can't really pay my way, so—"

"No, Reenie," cried Constance. "You can't go! It's my house too, you know. It's so isolated up here. I'd miss you so much. I've tried to make friends with the village women and with the professors' wives, but I've never felt I had much in common with any of them. But you felt like family from the start."

"Somehow we'll keep in touch," Serena assured her friend. "But of course I'll miss you and-and Trenton too, but if my being here makes him uncomfortable and unhappy." She shrugged hopelessly.

"It's not that at all," Constance said determinedly. "And Trennie knows it too. He just needs to sort out some of his feelings. Please just promise me you won't do anything rash 'til you talk to him?"

"Okay," Serena agreed. "If you think it'll help."

"Definitely," said Constance, squeezing Serena's arm. "You'll see. Everything will come out right. Oh, I almost forgot," she said retrieving a covered china cup from a little table in the hall. "Frances sent you some special blend of peppermint and chamomile tea. It's very soothing. And" she added, with a mischievous smile, "she wanted me to tell you something her mother always used to say. She said, 'A pot never boils over unless there's a fire underneath.'"

The tea was delicious, but whether or not it was soothing, Serena wasn't sure. She continued to pace as she contemplated Frances's message and the nerve-racking notion that Trenton was going to come talk to her.

Remembering the way he had behaved earlier, it was hard to believe Trenton would come to see her at all, despite Constance's assurances. And if he did come, Serena couldn't imagine what he would have to say. According to Constance, everything was okay, but Serena wondered.

Well, she certainly couldn't receive him in her corset and wrapper, she decided, what with the way he'd reacted to an ankle. She quickly pulled on the flowered housedress, rearranged her hair and even sneaked her evening purse from the bottom back of her wardrobe and powdered her nose. But it was still red and so were her eyes.

"Oh well, I guess it's the best I can do," she said aloud to her image. Then she replaced the purse deep in her wardrobe and resumed her pacing.

Once, when she moved close to the window, Serena thought she heard a masculine yell echoing from far away, toward Butler's Peak, but surely that was her imagination.

If he's going to come, I wish he'd hurry up and get it over with, she told herself, close to an hour later, but when the knock sounded at the door, she wished he'd waited a little longer.

"Miss—Ser-Serena-uh-Miss Cassidy—"

He sounded as ambivalent and nervous as she was, Serena thought, trying to swallow past the lump in her throat as she turned the knob.

Serena had never seen Trenton looking even slightly unkempt before. Whether chopping wood, boiling with indignation, or playing baseball in dress clothes, he had always appeared "together," but not when she opened the door. His shirt collar looked damp; his tie was tightened unevenly, and his thick black hair looked like he had run his fingers through it many times. But he still looked marvelous, she reluctantly admitted to herself, and his eyes bore a look of contrition.

"Serena, I owe you an apology," he said quickly, as if trying to get it over with, as soon as she opened the door.

"Yes," she answered facing him with a shy smile. "But I'm sure I owe you one too. I know how important your school is to you and that Victorianism is still rampant in these days," she continued, in her nervousness not realizing what she was implying. "I should have been more careful."

"Perhaps," conceded Trenton. "But you were enthusiastic about your lesson and that should have impressed me more than anything else.

"I have to admit—as Connie was quick to point out to me—I was judging you by an-another standard, which was very unfair of me. I really don't believe you're—"

"I didn't do it on purpose, if that's what you mean," said Serena, knowing he was thinking of Anne. "And I'm very sorry if you think it'll reflect badly on the school."

"Don't give it another moment's thought." Trenton reached out to jostle her shoulder reassuringly, if somewhat awkwardly. "I was definitely overreacting. It's just that the boys are so impressionable and you're so—"

He moved very close to her, studying her face. His expression was almost grim, but his eyes, she realized, were burning into hers. A muscle in his jaw twitched. He moved his hand from her shoulder to her chin, but then dropped it to his side and straightened quickly.

"Well, you must know you're a very attractive young woman," he said with an overbright smile. "And the boys are at the age where they get…uh…crushes easily. So in the future," he finished bracingly, "please, just try to be extra careful around the students."

"In the future?" Serena repeated. "You mean I can continue with the classes?"

"Oh, of course," Trenton gave a dismissive wave of his hand. "That is, if you will."

Serena nodded.

"Thank you," he said softly. "As I mentioned, I realize I overreacted and it's good of you to continue to help us out, under the circumstances. I suppose I should tell you what Constance and I were discussing about this situation," he continued, with reluctant resolve. "She says I've behaved the way I have recently because of jealousy. And as much as I hate to admit to being controlled by an emotion of which I don't approve, I'm afraid she may be right."

Serena felt a flush of pleasure run through her. She had never approved of jealousy either, believing that it implied that people were each other's property. Yet it thrilled Serena to know that Trenton was jealous. She knew that she was taking a chance of appearing too bold, especially in light of the afternoon's discussions, but she simply had to let him know.

"I don't generally like jealousy, either," she said softly. "But I don't seem to mind it—since it's you."

For a moment, the same burning lit up Trenton's eyes, then he shrugged resignedly and gave her a sad smile. "I might as well tell you the rest," he said. "I believe Con has shared with you something of the life I lived with my late wife, Anne?" he asked.

Serena nodded and risked reaching out to give his hand a squeeze.

"Con made me see that the main reason for my distrust and jealousy of you was because of the way Anne behaved, and I know that's not at fair to you. Just because you too are a…beautiful woman, does not necessarily mean that you're conniving and selfish and duplicitous," he ground the words out past clinched teeth, then shrugged the anger away. "Sorry…and I'll do my best not to judge you by that standard. But," he continued with a sigh, "as you can see, my marriage has left me bitter and suspicious, and I'm afraid, not fit for any other relationship. So I've realized it's better for me not to give anyone—or myself—any false hopes."

"But surely," Serena asserted. "Over time—"

"Maybe," agreed Trenton. "I'd like to think so, but I'm not at all sure." He squared his shoulders. "The boys seemed to really enjoy and learn from the lesson today, so you might want to continue with that for tomorrow and, maybe for the next day, we'll receive more lesson plans from Rivers."

"I…uh…gave them the assignment of making up their own sentences with dangling phrases," said Serena, adjusting with effort, to the abrupt change in subject. "And then to show how they can be corrected."

"Very good," said Trenton stiffly. But then he added, with a sincere smile. "I think you're doing a fine job with the boys, Serena. There're a few things you need to be careful about, but overall, I think you have a real flair for teaching. And I want you to know it's appreciated."

Serena could only manage a smile, feeling oddly choked up by his speech.

"Well," said Trenton. "I'll leave you alone now. I'm sure you've seen enough of me for today."

Before she could protest, Trenton had moved quickly down the hall, but as Serena watched his elegant back, she broke into a dazzling grin.

She was Serena Longworth!

Somehow or other, she would help Trenton overcome his hesitance, she'd marry him, and they'd be together for almost forty years and have outstanding children and grandchildren. She'd do all those things Grace Pierson had talked about by taking one day at a time. And in 2008, they would be talking about her life and her accomplishments! She could settle in, knowing she wouldn't suddenly be zapped back, and enjoy this elegant era, in this beautiful house, with these wonderful people. The world would slowly change in ways she would be expecting. And someday, she'd see her beloved parents again, introduce them to each other and help them to establish their future! What more could she want?

But somewhere in the back of her mind, some doubt still niggled.

Despite his apologies, Serena sensed that Trenton still felt some distrust for her, specifically. It probably wasn't surprising, she realized, with the huge gap in her experience, caused by the time travel. Yet what could she do? She would just have to teach Trenton to trust her, she concluded, by always being completely honest and straightforward about everything except her past.

But there was something else, she realized, playing at the edge of her consciousness, something she couldn't recall. She thought it might be an anecdote about Trenton she had read a long time ago. It was a small thing, she felt, yet it had left a distressing impression with her.

Chapter 7

Yesterdays/Deal

The next day, Serena returned to the classroom, decorously dressed in the gray-and-maroon shirtwaist dress. The boys had all done their assignment, most of them correctly, and they were almost as enthusiastic as they had been the day before.

At the end of her class, Trenton met Serena in the hallway to announce that he'd received a wire from Rivers. The reason no more lesson plans had arrived, Trenton related, was that Rivers' doctor had deemed him fit to travel, so he should be arriving within a day or two. Serena received the news with mixed emotions, realizing she would miss the students more than she had expected.

Since Rivers still hadn't sent lesson plans, Serena decided to show how dangling phrases might be avoided, by the use of sentence diagrams. She tried to make the potentially dull exercises seem like puzzles to be solved and managed to keep the interest of about half of the class.

On the second diagram day, during which more of her students had begun to nod off, Rivers and his wife arrived.

Frank Rivers was a pleasant young man with very short whiteblond hair and an athletic build, who lifted himself with no trouble on his wooden crutches.

"Isn't it ridiculous? I was in sports all during school and then hurt myself on a train platform," he said.

Trenton, Rivers, and Serena had a conference to acquaint Mr. Rivers with the material that had been covered and also with the students' work. Rivers seemed impressed with the progress Serena had made, including that in her improvised lessons. He announced himself ready to take over the class the next day, but said it was good to know so capable a substitute was available, should he ever need one again.

When Rivers had gone, Trenton detained Serena for a moment. First, he assured her that she would still have lots to do, helping Constance with household and entertaining decisions and reminded her how much her companionship meant to Constance. "And to me too," he added emphatically. Then he told her again how much he appreciated her help and reiterated what a good job she had done.

"We don't have to worry about Rivers' class anymore," he said. "He's very good at holding a class's attention. But some of our other professors can, frankly, be stultifying at times. I'm sure even I," he said, with a wry smile, "can use some help sometimes, though I try to make my classes interesting. I'm definitely a believer in innovation in the educational process. Learning shouldn't seem like punishment.

"One thing I realized, when I stopped being angry the other day, is that you're very good at finding ways to make education seem like a game and, therefore, to make the students pay a lot more attention."

Serena thought about the sea of drowsy faces that had often confronted her and decided that Trenton was being very generous.

"I wonder if I might bring some of our—mine and the other professors—problem subjects to you for ideas on how to teach them more entertainingly?"

"Of course," answered Serena, feeling a lump rise in her throat. "If you really think I could help."

"Definitely," said Trenton. "But…uh…maybe it would be better if we didn't let them know I was consulting you. It's not that I want to take credit for your ideas, it's just that some of the men might not like for their lessons to be discussed with a woman. I guess they tend to be—"

"Chauvinists?" supplied Serena.

Trenton knitted his brow.

"You're not familiar with the term?" asked Serena.

"Well, yes?" he said. "Chauvinism is extreme loyalty to one's own country to the exclusion of all others. But I don't understand how that applies—"

"Well, in—" she hesitated to use the 'California' excuse again, "in…recent times, I've heard it used to mean a person who irrationally favors his own gender over the other."

"Or her own gender?"

"I suppose so, though I've really only heard the term 'male chauvinist,' referring to men who're threatened if a woman shows ambition or intelligence and who just want women to cook and clean and be se—to look good for men."

"Oh," said Trenton. "Yes, I suppose we do have some of them at the school. I…uh…hope I'm not one of them?"

"Occasionally, a bit," said Serena with a smile. "But I think you can probably learn not to be."

"Hmm," he answered, quirking his brows. "Then, in that case, I hope you'll point out to me when I'm showing those tendencies. And I do hope you'll give me your suggestions for our classes. I was truly impressed with your handling of the class."

"Except when I showed my ankles," Serena ventured, stopping in the doorway.

"Well, yes," said Trenton with a grin. "But I suppose, if I were a true male chauvinist, I'd say that had certain compensations too."

He caught on quickly, Serena decided with a chuckle, this future husband of hers. He could also be generous when he took a mind to do so. She doubted that Trenton actually needed much help in teaching techniques. He had probably asked for her assistance because he knew that she needed to feel that she was making a contribution to the household. And she thought, he had stressed how much her companionship meant to Constance for the same reason.

Trenton had not been physically close to her at all, keeping the desk between them for most of the conversation. Yet more than at any other time, Serena felt that he was extending his friendship and that they had been closer in spirit than ever before.

Chapter 8

Yesterdays/Deal

Life in 1908 continued to improve for Serena during the first few months of the school term. As the leaves turned their beautiful fall colors and transformed the Blue Ridge Mountains and foothills, Trenton and Serena's friendship continued to deepen.

At mealtime, she and Trenton and Constance made the painted dome in the dining room ring with their laughter, as Serena was included more and more in the freewheeling, often goofy humor the brother and sister shared. As Serena became more accustomed to the idioms and current events of her new time, she felt more comfortable adding her own puns and jokes to the silly mix, and she found she was enjoying herself more than she had since her parent's deaths.

Trenton continued to keep his physical distance, touching Serena only incidentally, as he pushed in her chair or helped her from the carriage, but he didn't seem to have the same qualms about drawing closer to her emotionally, treating her more and more, as Constance always had, like a sister. Since her physical attraction to Trenton hadn't diminished (it had, in fact, gotten stronger) and as Serena sensed that Trenton felt the same way about her, this "sibling" relationship was sometimes frustrating. Still, she decided, the best romances were based on strong friendship and emotional trust.

Serena was treated so much as a sister, in fact, that when Malcolm acquired for the household an Irish setter puppy, Constance and Trenton insisted that Serena name him. Serena, determined that the name should be as silly as the Longworths' horses', reached back in her memory and christened the dog "Cahudalin," after a Carolina

Native American her mother had once met. The Longworths were so thrilled with the name that they declared Serena an official member of the family, and Constance even drew up a highly embellished "adoption document," which she and Trenton both signed. Since she knew it was meant as a joke, Serena fought hard and managed to hold back the tears.

Oblivious his ridiculous moniker, Cahudalin frolicked on the lawn between the houses with the Trices more sedately named collie, Lady, while Serena and Lettie watched from the side porch and finished the lessons in the alphabet. Serena became even more convinced that the child was very intelligent because she learned with phenomenal speed, even with an untrained teacher like Serena. But Lettie also took in misinformation like a sieve, mimicking Serena's every unconscious gesture and expression with equal accuracy.

It wasn't long before Lettie could sign all twenty-six letters in correct order, but Serena was a bit concerned about what she'd taught the child. Every time she signed the letters G, P, and S (the ones that Serena was unsure of), Lettie continued to give an exaggerated shrug. Serena tried to correct the habit, but no matter how many times she demonstrated the letters with her shoulders determinedly stiff and still, Lettie, who obviously enjoyed motion for its own sake, repeated them with the vaudeville-style shrug.

However, when Serena voiced her doubts, Lettie's mother reassured her. "At least she's learning something and she's trying to communicate, which is more than I can say—for sure—she's ever done before. I'm positive it won't take long for her to learn new ways to do just three letters, if need be," she continued. "And I think she'll stop that shrug pretty soon, if no one repeats it to her."

But Serena wasn't sure. Even though Letitia Jenson had seemed able to communicate well (despite the fact that no one believed her about "Miz Reena"), Serena wondered if Lettie had gotten the best education available. She determined to try to find out about other sources of education for hearing-challenged children. She had briefly studied the teaching of the deaf during the early 1900s, but she was having a hard time remembering all the details. One thing was for sure—she couldn't go on the Internet for the information, the way she might have in 2008.

Serena was glad that Mrs. Trice had agreed to learn the signing alphabet and had said that she taught what she learned to her husband at night. Lettie seemed happy about it too, laughing uproariously as her mother went through the signs.

When she thought they had the alphabet down pat, Serena decided to introduce the concept of spelling, starting with proper names. She showed the little girl the signs for "Lettie," "Miss Rena," "Mama," and "Papa," pointing to each person before and after she signed.

In a remarkably short time, Lettie was spelling the names and pointing to the correct person, though whether or not she understood what she was doing, Serena didn't know.

On the day when Serena announced that she would be teaching Lettie how to spell their names, the child's brothers, Mathew and Nathan, said they wanted to learn the signs too. When they were all three correctly signing, "Mat" and "Nate" and pointing to the right person, Serena taught the boys to spell "Lettie" and they even agreed to start practicing the complete alphabet.

One thing her lessons with Lettie had accomplished—and if it was the only thing they'd accomplished, it would still make it worth her time, Serena decided—was that the little girl's brothers treated her much better. The fact that Lettie was learning her own language seemed to make them respect her more. They had agreed with Serena that Lettie wasn't really a "dumbbell" and that it was unfair to call her one, and often at the end of the lessons, the boys came to escort her to play with them, jumping with the dogs into the newly raked piles of crisp autumn leaves or covering each other with mounds of gold, brown, and scarlet.

Just as Constance had promised, Saturday night continued to be sociable night, with professors and their wives and visiting dignitaries often joining in the festivities. Randy McNaught was a frequent guest, with his parents accompanying him on one occasion.

Conversation at these dinners often turned to education and Serena was quick to put in her bid for a fine arts program at the college and for women to be admitted. After all, not only were these issues dear to her heart, but also Grace Pierson had said she had been instrumental in bringing them to Longworth College. So she figured she might as well start.

Trenton was quick to agree that he'd like a fine arts program, but said the school didn't yet have the resources to build the studios and hire the talent that such a program would require. Serena was satisfied when he told her he'd work toward such programs in the future.

"And you can be sure we can use your background in art, when we do start the program," he assured her. "At least in an advisory capacity," he added, a teasing light in his steel-colored eyes.

About the idea of a women's branch of the school, Trenton was less positive, however.

"It would require more dormitories, more security, more involved medical services, to say nothing of a completely different curriculum," he told her.

Serena postponed her questions concerning his other objections to zero in on the most important. "Why a different curriculum?" she asked.

"Well," said Trenton slowly, "if we had a fine arts department, I'm sure that would be of use to the ladies, but otherwise—that is," he glanced at her, with an uncertain look on his face. "Wouldn't we need to offer home economics, deportment, and the like?"

Serena bit her lip 'til she found a way to phrase her response diplomatically. "I'm, uh, sure there are women who would find those courses helpful," she said patiently. "But there are quite a few schools, already, which offer that sort of an education. What I'm thinking about is more general education which women might use in their careers."

"Well, there are nursing schools and teachers' colleges for those women," said Karsten, of the math department, with his slight Norwegian accent.

"Yes, I know that," said Serena. "And I realize no one college can offer every course of study a woman might want, just as it can't offer everything for men, but why can't the women just take the same courses that the men do?"

"Do you really think many women will have any use for subjects such as advanced mathematics and science and political studies?" asked Trenton.

"Yes," said Serena emphatically. "Especially as the years go on. I think you'll be surprised how the need for such courses for women increases."

"And if I doubt you, you'll probably say I'm a chauvinist, right?" asked Trenton, flashing his perfect teeth in a grin.

"I might," said Serena, chuckling in return.

The Rivers and the Karstens knitted their brows questioningly and Randy gave them a suspicious squint, but Trenton and Serena didn't bother to explain, enjoying their private moment.

"I can't understand why you lovely ladies don't just relax and let us men take care of you, like we want to," said Randy, making a well in his mashed potatoes and ladling in copious amounts of gravy.

Taking into consideration the attitude of the time and Randy's sincere, uncondescending expression, once again Serena schooled her own expression and searched for a moderate response. "But Mr. McNaught, surely you must realize there are women who have no husbands or families, who have no choice but to fend for themselves in this world," she said, deciding not to mention, at the moment, the women who wanted their independence. "And having a better education could only help them to find adequate employment?"

"That's right," interjected Constance, appearing in command, in her ruched lavender dress, despite the fact that she was so tiny she was almost hidden behind the tea service. "There are women who really have no choice. Many immigrant women are in that position, aren't they, Malcolm?"

Serena saw Malcolm, who was holding the gravy boat for her, give a slight tremor. "Y-Yes, Mum," he said. "Many immigrant women come here because they are without family or they must leave their families behind, hoping to send them funds or to bring them over later, and they often are without the skills they need in this country. Especially those who are not lucky enough to find a household such as yours," he added solemnly, his gaze encompassing both Trenton and Constance.

"It pains me to think of any lady who doesn't get the support and care she deserves," said Randy, staring with devotion at Constance. "And please," he directed to Malcolm, "contact me, if you know of any women in such circumstance, so that my family and I can help them."

Malcolm thanked him, with a dignified nod, before retreating to the kitchen, and all the other guests smiled at Randy, obviously relieved that the discussion had been brought to so diplomatic a conclusion. Later, however, Trenton pulled Serena aside, to tell her that he would give her ideas serious consideration. Serena felt a warm glow spread over her. Trenton might not let himself love her yet, but at least he respected her and her point of view.

When the meal was over, Constance gathered everyone, including several of the servants, around the piano for the weekly sing. Always cooperative, Randy sang in a thin but enthusiastic tenor, his eyes never leaving Constance, as she played and sang and requested solos from everyone.

Though Constance always cajoled him, Malcolm rarely joined the Saturday songfest, except to deliver his amazing "Asleep in the Deep," and Serena began to realize he didn't even do that one on nights when Randy was there. In fact, he made himself so scarce on those occasions that Serena wondered if he disliked the wealthy young man.

But if Malcolm wouldn't sing, there were certainly enough willing amateur entertainers. To Serena, accustomed to 2008s people, who were evidently afraid they would look uncool if they joined a sing-along, it was remarkable how quick these people were to risk looking foolish by performing duets or solos. But, without TV, singing was one of the major sources of entertainment, and, she realized, these participants didn't have as many polished performances with which to compare themselves.

Most important was that everyone seemed to have fun. Frances regaled them with Irish songs; Karsten and his wife sang a Norwegian piece (a capella, since Constance couldn't play it); Mrs. Karsten, who was classically trained, entranced them with her rich contralto in several solos; Randy and Frank Rivers gave them a raucous rendition of "Take Me Out to The Ball Game"; and Constance had everyone in stitches with a little piece called "Daddy Wouldn't Buy Me a Bow-Wow," sung in baby talk.

With everyone else being so cooperative, Trenton and Serena could hardly demur when Constance asked them to sing the last chorus of "When You Were Sweet Sixteen" as a duet.

As always, Serena thrilled to the physical feeling of singing with Trenton and performing a duet, especially one this unabashedly sentimental and romantic, was such an intimate experience it felt like they shouldn't be doing it in public.

But their audience was also enthralled. When the chorus began with the very evocative line, "I Love You Like I Never Loved Before", there were audible sighs, and then, at the end, when Constance directed Serena to sing the first "When you were sweet", and then for Trenton to sing "When you were sweet", and them for sing together "When we were sweet sixteen", everyone applauded; several of the women actually had tears in their eyes, and everywhere there were comments about how beautifully their voices blended and that they seemed born to sing together.

Trenton (whom Serena felt sure had experienced some of the same sensations she had) gave a comic bow and said he was so glad they'd enjoyed the effort. But, he continued with a thinner smile, that would have to be his swan song for the night. Pleading "unfinished work," he retreated to his office.

Serena watched him go, wondering if he'd ever let himself physically react to her, without feeling guilty about it.

As the days grew cooler and Lettie's lessons were moved indoors, Serena began to look forward to the fall and winter holidays. She'd always adored these special days, which came in such quick succession, but she hadn't felt like celebrating them since she'd lost her parents. Now she had a new family. Of course, the Longworths would never take the place of her parents, but being with them filled up places in her soul, which she had thought would never again be filled.

Serena found that adults rarely dressed up for Halloween in 1908, but the students had no such qualms. Mostly dressed in sheets or inside out, mismatched outfits, they raced around the courtyard and even bobbed for apples in the huge washbasins Malcolm had set up. But Morty Shine and a group of his friends dressed as women, in clothes borrowed from their sisters, packed just for the occasion. At the end of the evening, they insisted on serenading Constance and Serena, who had earlier accompanied the students' festivities with ghostly notes and shrieks through megaphones. Decked out in ruffles and long skirts, with bows perched precariously in their short hair and singing, "My Wild Irish Rose," with simpering gestures and fluttering eyelashes, the boys presented a ludicrous picture that rivaled the most outlandish drag queens on the 2008 talk shows. Yet no one made any snide comments about their "orientation;" they all just laughed and appeared to have a marvelous time.

In November, William Howard Taft was elected president by the men of the United States, following "the cowboy," Teddy Roosevelt. Taft was one of those presidents who had never left much of an impression with Serena, from history classes. But now, she studied his pictures and credentials in the paper and wondered if the nearly three-hundred-pound jurist, qualified though he might be, would have had any chance of being elected, in the body-conscious twenty-first century. In contrast, the new first lady was willowy and stylish. Serena remembered, from tours of Washington with her parents, that it was Frances Taft to whom the king of Japan had given the beautiful cherry blossom trees, which lined the Potomac River and had given rise to Washington's annual spring festival, which she had attended several times with her parents.

On the Saturday night after the election, Serena dressed with particular care, her heart racing. Constance had accepted an invitation to a dinner party honoring visiting relatives at the McNaught's and, therefore, hadn't invited guests to dine at the Longworths. So Trenton and Serena found themselves alone for the evening.

Just before leaving her room, Serena pinched her cheeks and bit her lips, which had become a new habit. It was the 1908 substitute for makeup (bringing a rosy hue to the face), and she wanted to look especially glowing tonight. Actually, though, she doubted that she would need any artificial enhancements. In just a few moments, she would be facing Trenton, alone, over a candlelit table. It was bound to be a momentous occasion.

But the conversation over dinner wasn't momentous. It was light and cheerful and slightly stilted. Over Chicken Kiev, asparagus, and white wine, Trenton and Serena spoke of some of the human interest stories that they had read in the recently delivered newspapers, of the new president's campaign promises, of the Trice children's games, and of the puppy Cahudalin's latest exploits. Once or twice, their eyes held for a little too long, reflecting the candle glow and each other, but then, they looked away and returned to their current topic.

When the last of the dishes were taken away, they smiled self-consciously at each other and retired to the back parlor, where Malcolm deposited the coffee tray.

"Some new viewer pictures were delivered today," said Trenton, pointing, with a slightly shaky hand, to the small table where the stereopticon and its picture cards were kept.

"One set is views of Paris, and the other is one of those comic picture series Con is so fond of."

Settling herself in one of the Chippendale chairs, Serena untied the first pack and put the top card in the viewer's wire holder and looked through the eyepiece. The two nearly identical pictures on the card merged to form a 3-D image of a man in a driving cap, duster, and goggles, polishing a large, expensive-looking automobile.

Serena passed the viewer to Trenton, who had pulled his chair tantalizingly close to hers, and selected the next card.

In the next scene, a pretty girl was shown, driving a donkey cart. Both the girl and the donkey had on flowered hats. Serena was sure she knew what was coming. With a wry grin, she handed the contraption to Trenton, brushing his hand with hers, in the process. His eyes glinted silver.

Other scenes followed a predictable route, showing pedestrians shaking their fists at the auto driver and birds perching (à la Disney) on the girl, her cart, and donkey.

Serena studiously avoided brushing Trenton's fingers again, but, with the fourth card, his fingers grazed hers.

The next picture showed the automobile, with a ridiculous amount of smoke billowing from under the hood and around the wheels, and the man angrily waving a huge wrench in the air.

"I've been expecting this," said Serena.

"E-expecting it?" asked Trenton, oddly. "Oh, you're talking about the pictures."

"Uh, yes," said Serena, wondering what he had thought she meant. "See," she said, leaning closer, to show him the scene. "Wouldn't you say it's predictable?"

"Typical, and probably accurate." Trenton nodded, with a mischievous grin. He and Serena often argued about the practicality of the automobile. But as he spoke, Serena noticed he moved his chair a little closer.

She'd certainly go along with this trend, thought Serena, sliding her own chair nearer to his.

"His rescuer." She shrugged, as she handed him the card that showed the girl in the donkey cart stopping beside the car, while the man looked underneath it. "How trite!"

"Oh, I don't know," Trenton smiled directly into her eyes. "Any man worth his salt would be happy to be helped by a pretty girl."

Serena could feel the happy blushes spread over her face while she looked at the last card. As she knew it would be, the auto was tied to the cart and being pulled by the donkey, while the man and woman looked at each other soulfully.

"True love!" she intoned.

"Yes, I think maybe it could be," said Trenton, reaching for her, rather than the stereopticon.

The viewer clattered to the rug, as his lips grazed hers.

Kissing Trenton was all that Serena had known it would be. Even this light touch sent heady vibrations throughout her body. Reveling in the sensations, Serena shifted slightly and put her hand on his shoulder. The kiss began to deepen, and she heard his breath—or was it hers—begin to quicken.

Suddenly, there was a light tap on the parlor door, and the knob began to turn, as Trenton and Serena jumped apart like guilty children.

"Frances insisted that I bring you some of these scones to try," said Malcolm apologetically, as he entered the room with a platter. "Mrs. Karsten gave her the recipe."

"T-that was nice of her," said Serena, as she bent to pick up the viewer. The T-frame that held the picture was slightly askew, and she tried to tighten the screw with her fingernail.

"Yes indeed, it was. Please thank her for us," Trenton added, with false heartiness. He was already standing beside the tray. "May I pour you a cup of coffee, Miss Cassidy?"

"I suppose so," said Serena, distractedly, as Malcolm left the room. Trenton hadn't called her Miss Cassidy in weeks.

Trenton handed her a delicate cup with a scone perched on the flowered saucer.

"I'd better go," he said, picking up his own cup.

"Don't you want to see the last picture?" Serena asked, as if that were the important thing. "And the views of Paris?"

"I can see them later," he said with finality. "You must know, Serena, it's just too tempting to stay right now. I didn't intend to do anything like-like kiss you, and yet I did. And if Malcolm hadn't come in—"

Serena decided it was time for her to also be straightforward. "Trenton," she said, looking into his eyes. "Don't you know me well enough now to realize that I wouldn't have kissed you back, if I didn't think there was genuine feeling between us?"

"But that's just it, Serena. As we've become better friends, I've been even more determined not to lead you on or to take advantage of the yearnings that I believe we both have. Don't you remember the conversation we had about my late wife and my inability to become involved again?"

"I was hoping," Serena interjected softly, "that you would eventually see that you could once again learn to-to care and to trust—"

Trenton's eyes flickered oddly at the word "trust."

"Trenton," Serena said with determination. "Is there something else bothering you?"

Trenton looked at her for a long moment. "I think we all must sometimes do things to protect ourselves," he said enigmatically.

"But—"

"We can discuss it another time," he finished, moving toward the door. "Right now, though, I'm going to go. Constance should be home soon, to keep you company."

Serena stared at the closing door. It appeared that Trenton might distrust her specifically, not just as he would any attractive unknown woman. And who could blame him, with all her faltering and half-truths? But what choice did she have?

But, no matter what, she told herself. *I have to find a way to win his confidence. especially if I really am going to be Serena Longworth.*

By the middle of November, Frances and the household and school staffs were already beginning their preparations for Thanksgiving, since the holiday was jointly celebrated with the family eating with the students in their dining hall.

Thanksgiving hadn't changed much in the hundred years between 1908 and 2008, Serena was happy to discover.

Malcolm had arranged with a local farmer for the turkeys to be delivered, ready to dress and cook on the day before the holiday, but it still took careful planning between Constance, Frances, and Neva, the attractive young widow from the community, who served as the school's main cook, to schedule their baking even with the usually ample ovens provided by the house and school kitchens.

The preparation of the less-perishable items had begun in advance. At the beginning of the week before the big event, nutmeg was ground, walnuts and pecans were shelled, and corn was husked. Serena helped with these simple tasks and found that she rather enjoyed them, though she wouldn't want to be responsible for the preparation of the many meals every day, as Frances and Neva were.

The great day dawned bright and cool, just as Thanksgiving should. After special chapel services, Serena and Constance had repaired to the dining hall, to put the final touches on the table decorations, when they were interrupted by Randy McNaught, bearing a huge bouquet of yellow roses.

He'd come, he said, to ask Constance one more time to change her mind and come to Thanksgiving dinner at his home in Belle Vieux.

Constance laughed and thanked Randy for the flowers and for driving so far just to speak with her, but she explained, as she had several times before, that Thanksgiving was a time when one should be with family. Then she placated Randy with an invitation to dinner on the following Friday.

"Though we'll probably have to settle for some kind of leftover turkey stew," and he left, hiding his disappointment manfully behind wishes to both her and Serena for a happy day.

When Randy's big red auto could be heard gunning out of the yard, Constance split up the bouquet of yellow roses and added them to the various table decorations of polished fruit, autumn leaves, and gilded, paper-mache cornucopias. With this chore completed, Serena and Constance checked final details with Frances, Neva, and their assistants in the school kitchen and finally went to change into the elegant fall-colored dresses they'd picked for the sumptuous feast.

As the Thanksgiving prayers were offered up that afternoon, Serena silently gave her own thanks for the unusual twist that fate had brought her and for her new friends, Frances and Malcolm and dear, dear Constance and especially Trenton, whose resonant voice was filling her, at that moment, with a somewhat unreverent thrill.

Suddenly, the Christmas season was upon them. Serena had been amused—sometimes to the point of annoyance—in the twenty-first century with the way the sales-conscious merchants had moved the Christmas season earlier each year, 'til it had almost overlapped with Halloween. But she found the situation almost the same in 1908, though for different reasons.

In 1908, the season was started early because almost everything used during the holidays—from food and baked goods, to special party clothes, to decorations, to presents—had to be made by the members of the household.

Since the school would be closed during Christmas, Frances and the staff didn't have too much planning to do for the Christmas dinner. However, the Longworths hosted three separate parties each year: one for the students on their last day before vacation, one for the staff, and a much more elegant one for the Longworth College's board, contributors, faculty, and other interested dignitaries and all of these had to be arranged from soup to nuts.

In addition, there were events to which the Longworths were invited, many of them covered dish socials for which to prepare.

But by far the most involved seasonal activity for the kitchen staff was the baking. Nearly every Yuletide treat Serena had ever heard of was annually turned out in Frances' kitchen, including a traditional plum pudding, which Serena was not sure she'd be able to appreciate.

Many of the Christmas decorations had to be made also. Constance explained that, since the students left in the middle of December, very little decorating of the school was done, except for wreaths on the doors of each building.

"Of course, they can decorate their dorm rooms themselves," said Constance, "just as the professors and their wives can, in their suites. But we have enough to do, what with this house, without worrying about the school."

Constance also told Serena about the glass ornaments and candleholders for the Christmas tree, most of which were bought on trips to Richmond or New York, and that she and Trenton also hung old beloved toys and trinkets on it. But since all the other decorations they used were perishable, they had to be made fresh each year. So they worked many evenings on popcorn and cranberry chains and ornaments carved from dried apples, and they helped Frances make chains and ornaments of rock candy crystals, some of which were dyed with beet and other vegetable juices.

With so many edible decorations, Serena wondered why these old-fashioned trees didn't have the additional "ornaments" of bugs or mice, but she was relieved not to see any. She did know, however, that the trees of 1908 often caused fires, due to the use of real candles. Trenton had told her that, though they did have candles with tiny clip-on holders for the tree, they were seldom lit and that the surrounding branches were always dampened beforehand.

Even without lights, Serena thought the tree would be spectacular and eagerly helped to trim it. Since she didn't have any old toys to contribute, she had decided to make paper snowflakes and origami birds and to tie her pin with the three graces on a branch.

But the most time-consuming projects for the season were the gifts. Constance and Trenton had bought some presents on a visit to Richmond last spring and there were some things available from catalogs, trips to Belle Vieux or even Fry's General Store, but much of Christmas giving was handmade in 1908.

Serena and Constance were making clothes for Lettie's dolls and embroidered hand towels for the professors' families and the Trices, as well as embroidering handkerchiefs for the servants and some of the women of the community. They enjoyed sitting on the side porch and working together, when the weather permitted. Malcolm, who was whittling spinning tops and other wooden toys with peculiar mountain names like Jim Crackey and whatever for his Dun members and the Trice boys, would sometimes join them, sitting on the steps and, at Constance's urging, telling them of Christmas in Ireland. Constance always said she was happiest when creating, and she did seem to glow with Christmas spirit more at these times than at any other.

Occasionally, Trenton even joined them, to help Malcolm, but he wasn't as adept a whittler as Malcolm, who had carved the beautiful chess set in the Longworth's parlor and the manger scene they would be putting out soon.

Constance told Serena that Trenton usually managed to order all his gifts or buy them on trips, so he had nothing of his own to make.

Soon, Trenton decided he could contribute more by entertaining everyone else, so when he had time, he read Dickens' *A Christmas Carol* (already considered a classic) or a newly published story called *Byrd's Christmas Carol.*

In her room at night, Serena worked on her gifts for the family. She was hemming and initialing a dozen linen handkerchiefs for Trenton and painting a miniature of Cahudalin, in a mosaic tile frame fashioned from bits of glass and pottery stealthily gleaned from the trash dump behind Frye's General Store, for his office desk. It didn't seem like enough to give the man she loved, even if no one knew how she felt, but she hadn't found anything which inspired her in the few shops she had access to; her money was very limited, and it was too late to order anything. Also, there were so few things that were deemed proper gifts between unrelated people of opposite sexes.

She was more pleased with her inventions for Constance, though they still seemed hardly adequate, considering all her friend had done for her. With leftover bits of ribbon and beads from Constance's sewing room, she was making a set of pastel silk flowers, some of which she was attaching to hair combs and the rest to an old, jewel stick pin she'd found in the bottom of her vanity drawer. Her second gift for Constance was also made from leftovers—remnants of clothes and projects she and Constance had worked on together. She was making a crazy quilt wall hanging for the sewing room.

Serena enjoyed all the handwork, baking, and carol singing and she loved the readings by Trenton. The weather was cold and crisp, as the season should be, in fact, everything seemed to be the way the season should be. But, in the midst of all the fun, Serena had several concerns.

Ever since the night they had dined alone, Serena had worried about Trenton's odd comments about people's "protecting" themselves. She had tried to engage him in conversation about it several times, but he had always, politely put her off, the most recent times suggesting that they might talk after the holidays. But he had never told her that her suspicions were unfounded and, though she racked her brain almost constantly, Serena could think of nothing she could say to make him trust her more.

Another thing that bothered Serena also pleased her. The Trices had decided to try to get Lettie into a legitimate school for the deaf, as soon as possible.

"She's made remarkable progress," Serena told them. "But she needs to be trained by people who really know what they're doing. And I think it would do her good to be around children like herself."

"We'd miss her," said Mrs. Trice, with conviction. "But I guess it'd be best for her."

Serena realized that she would miss Lettie, also, to say nothing of the income the teaching provided, but she knew she had gone about as far as she could with the child.

At Serena's urging, the Trices had written to several schools in the area, and the Gallaudet School, in Washington, DC, had agreed to an examination and interview. However, they said it would have to be in the middle of December, when school was out of session.

So, in the midst of their own holiday activities, the Trices packed up themselves and Lettie and took a carriage, ferry and train trip to the nation's capital, leaving their two active boys in the care of the Longworths.

"If we didn't have Malcolm at times like this, I don't know what we'd do," said Constance, as she watched him keep Nate and Mat entertained by "letting" them help him with chores.

When the Trices returned, they had both good and bad news.

"They said she was intelligent and they were very impressed with how much she's been able to learn in such a short time especially from [if you'll pardon the expression] an amateur, but as you warned us, most of them thought she shouldn't be learning sign language at all," said Mrs. Trice of the Gallaudet committee.

"Still, they told us, just as you said they would, that Lettie was too young to be in the school," added Mr. Trice. "Mrs. Trice and I told them about how you said that they were beginning to find that the younger the deaf child's training begins the better," he went on.

"They asked where you got your information," said Mrs. Trice, huffily. "Since they're supposedly the experts and say they keep up with all the news and research from other places. I told them that anyone who could make the kind of changes you have made in my little girl was expert enough for me! And we told them we're going to continue having you work with her, whether they thought it was a good idea or not."

"They reluctantly agreed," offered Mr. Trice. "Well, actually, there's no use in arguing with Mrs. Trice when her mind's made up. But they did show us some methods you can add to your lessons, which they said can help facilitate lip-reading later."

"And they agreed to see her again next year and possibly let her enter then," said Mrs. Trice, with a proud smile, "Even though she'll still be younger than the school usually admits children."

"Not that it will be easy, as far as Lettie's concerned," said Mr. Trice, biting his cheek.

"That's true," Mrs. Trice reluctantly agreed. "I thought Lettie would enjoy the trip, but everything seemed to irritate or scare her."

"She's always hated to have doctors' examinations, and when they put the tuning forks by her ears, she gets very annoyed," said Mr. Trice. "And when they tried to test her intelligence, she didn't want to sit still and she didn't like it when they wouldn't let her use sign language. She even yelled a couple of times. At least they have no doubt she'll be physically able to speak.

"All the motor cars and trolleys in Washington scared her," he added. "And she didn't like having to stay in the hotel, instead of roaming the hills."

"And she was afraid when the train first started," admitted Mrs. Trice. "Though, after a while, she calmed down and enjoyed watching the scenery fly by. But then, she wouldn't stay in her seat—just like on the ferry and everywhere else, and she wanted to sign to everyone, which the people didn't understand. But at least she wasn't scared anymore."

"Except," said Mr. Trice, "when we went from car to car. She was petrified of the vibrating floor, over the connections, you know?"

"We had to pull her-practically carry—her over those," said Mrs. Trice.

"Forcibly," her husband added, emphatically.

"And she's been pouting ever since," said the child's mother.

"Well, perhaps she is a little young to go off on her own," said Serena. "But maybe during this year, we can change her mind about some of those things," she added, thinking of her behavioral psychology classes. "We can show her pictures of trains, autos, and ferries and…uh…doctors and classrooms and teach her to sign the names and maybe give her special treats when she learns them. That should give her pleasant associations with them."

"You always have such good ideas," said Mrs. Trice.

But it was several days before Serena was able to effectively work with Lettie again because the child was unusually irritable and withdrawn. However, she recovered in time to play a lovely, if over-animated angel in the community church's annual Christmas pageant. Though the boys had played shepherds or wise men before, it was Lettie's first time to be asked, and the Trices attributed this to Serena's lessons. They were very anxious for Lettie to make a good impression, but no one seemed to mind her signing and other antics, which weren't so different from those of the other giggling children. It wasn't a very sophisticated production. In fact, after the slick Christmas pageants she had seen on TV, Serena found the performance refreshingly amateurish, with its bathrobe and dishtowel costumes, wobbling, pasteboard scenery and live animals, some of which added their own embellishments to the proceedings.

By far, Serena's biggest concern, however, was the two receptions which were scheduled for the next to last Friday before Christmas. The party for the students would take place in the afternoon and the one for the dignitaries and friends of the college would be held that night, and Estey Wooten was expected to attend both of them.

"She brings some of her best girls from the boarding house to socialize with the boys at the party, like she did with you," reported Constance. "Then she stays around all afternoon, ostensibly so she and the girls can help with the preparations for the evening event, but all she really does is try to get Trennie alone and then they all stay for the evening. She contributes a lot to the school, so we can't really deny her the privilege, but sometimes she just gets in the way."

It wasn't just her getting in the way that was a problem, Serena thought. This woman could be a major problem to her, exposing her to the Longworths in front of everyone.

Serena visualized over and over Estey Wooten's declaring, "No, I didn't bring this woman up here. She never stayed in my house. In fact, I've never seen her before in my life!" loudly and dramatically. Serena could just imagine Trenton's eyes turning a harsh iron gray, as he stared accusingly at her. He'd never learn to trust her, after that!

Once again, Serena tried to think of some way to justify her arrival there, but she could think of nothing plausible. She considered playing sick the day of the party, but she knew that, if she were sick enough to miss such important events, the Longworths would insist on calling the doctor. Again, she thought about sneaking off in the night or going to stand in Constance's closet to try to be zapped back to 2008, but she had no idea that it would work, and she didn't want to leave Trenton and Constance, if there was any way to avoid it.

So Serena helped to make the cookies and the canapés and the star-shaped sandwiches, to mix up jugs of punch, to decorate the parlors and the dining room, and she got a gown for the evening. And she did it all with growing trepidation. December 11th could be the day of her downfall.

As they set out the refreshments for the students' party, Serena told herself she should savor these moments, which might be the last peaceful ones she ever knew in this household.

While she and Constance and Frances spread the snowy tablecloths, put the star and ivy centerpieces on the tables and set out the refreshments, Trenton and Malcolm moved the furniture and put more garland around the doorways. Trenton was in his shirtsleeves and Serena stole surreptitious glances at him, as his muscles rippled under the fine material. Everyone else appeared to be in a good mood, and Serena tried to give the same impression. It wasn't so hard, in this atmosphere. As they all exchanged jokes and hummed bits of Christmas carols, Serena smiled in spite of her fears, especially when Trenton caught her eye with looks that seemed more than friendly. If only things could stay like this!

The day unfolded quickly. The professors and their wives began arriving at about 1:45 p.m. When the boys descended on them at

2:00 p.m., Estey Wooten and her boarders still hadn't appeared, and Serena crossed her fingers that they had decided to stay away. But within ten minutes, she heard a very loud car rattling and backfiring its way into the yard, and she somehow knew her wish had been denied.

"That'll be Estey," said Constance. "She never keeps that auto in good repair."

Serena hurried over to Morty Shine. "Good," she said. "The other guests have arrived. Now you boys can begin your skits."

Morty accommodatingly took up her cue and, as soon as Estey Wooten and the six young women she had in tow were introduced to the group at large, he sprang up and announced the first skit.

As was traditional, each class presented a short playlet pertaining to Christmas or school or both. Of course, the boys tried to make their sallies amusing, and Serena actually found herself enjoying the entertainment, but she was particularly happy that they took up time and put off the confrontation between her and Estey Wooten.

As the presentations went on, Serena ducked behind a column on the other side of the room and observed Estey Wooten.

Serena knew that Mrs. Wooten had been married twice to much older, wealthy men and had also been widowed twice. With the bequests of her last husband, she had bought her lucrative boarding house, but now seemed to be looking for husband number three and had evidently settled on Trenton. She used her donations to gain access to a group with whom she had little in common, and Trenton, though appreciative of her contributions, did not enjoy having to dance attendance.

The woman was about Trenton's age and tending toward what the Edwardians called "pleasingly plump," however she was more attractive than Serena had expected. Serena was beginning to be able to assess the clothes of the period, and she was sure that Estey's dress was expensive, but it wasn't especially becoming.

The fact that it was too dressy for an afternoon party could be excused by the fact that Estey would be attending the evening festivities, with no chance to change. However, the outfit had too many ruffles and too much jet beading for Serena's taste and the iridescent purple taffeta did nothing for Mrs. Wooten's strawberry-blond coloring. Black feathers waved in her intricate hairdo and heavy jet jewelry decorated her fingers, wrists, and earlobes. Still, she was lithe and exuded surprising vibrancy and her face still retained most of its small-featured prettiness. Estey affected graceful motions and postures, especially when Trenton was close by, a situation she seemed determined to continue.

For just a moment, Estey's eyes strayed from her quarry and came to rest, with a frown, on Serena. Serena quickly shifted her glance to the decorations behind the couple, and then she moved over to congratulate Morty Shine, on his comic performance as Father Christmas. Estey, apparently deciding that Serena was no threat, went back to posing and batting her eyelashes for Trenton.

But Serena knew she couldn't continue to be so lucky.

Amazingly enough, though, the student's party passed without incident, taken up with the boys' hijinks, Estey's boarders' flirtation with them (and vice versa) and Estey Wooten's more outrageous attempts to dally with Trenton.

When the crowd dispersed, Serena moved as far away from Estey Wooten as she could, but it wasn't far enough to miss Estey's announcement to Constance in a loud loquacious voice. "I'll be along shortly to help you, Constance dear," she trilled. "But first, this dear man," Estey gestured theatrically toward a very stiff-looking Trenton, whom she was actually anchoring to her by holding his sleeve, "has agreed to advise me on how my next contribution to this hallowed institution might best be allocated."

Over his shoulder, Trenton gave Serena and Constance a comical grimace as Estey tugged him away.

Serena watched the man she loved—if her assumption were correct, her future husband—being ushered away by an attractive woman who obviously had designs other than financial discussions. Serena was not a jealous person, and she knew Trenton didn't really relish going with Estey Wooten, but she might have tried to intervene, if she hadn't needed to stay away from the woman.

As it was, Serena doubted that Estey's designs would give her much respite from her worries. No self-respecting woman in 1908 could feel comfortable letting other women do housework, without offering to lend a hand. Though the kitchen would probably be overrun with extra helpers as it was, Serena was sure Estey Wooten would feel obligated to join in shortly.

As all the other women filed into the kitchen, Frances began to give the directions on what they might do to help and Serena decided to put a plan she had devised earlier into motion. "I'll get out the other dishes," she told the housekeeper.

Maneuvering her way through the kitchen, crowded with females of every description, Serena found the cabinet in which the best serving dishes were kept and began to set them out on the counter. Making sure that no one was watching her, she began to squeeze and tap her forehead in much the same way Edwardian ladies brought color to their cheeks. Then, before she lost her nerve, she brought the heel of her hand down on the counter in front of her with a loud thwack, and, at the same time, moved forward to the edge of the open cabinet door and lurched quickly back, as if bouncing away from an impact. As Constance and several others looked around, Serena grabbed her forehead, giving it an extra squeeze for good measure, and staggered slightly.

Frances and Constance rushed to her side, helped her into a chair, and insisted on looking at the "injury."

"Well, at least the skin's not broken, said Constance. "But it looks like a welt is already forming."

Serena sighed in relief, especially when Frances called for a cold compress and told Serena not to take it away. The cool, damp cloth felt good against her nervous brow, besides hiding the absence of a wound.

"How do you feel?" asked Frances.

"A little dizzy, maybe kind of nauseated," said Serena.

As Serena hoped they would, Constance and Frances insisted on helping her upstairs.

As they passed the brilliant stained glass windows on the landing, Serena made a feeble protest about leaving during the party preparations.

"Don't be silly," said Frances comfortably. "There are so many women in that kitchen, we could prepare for a dozen parties! Though I could wish it had been one of those girls Estey Wooten brought who had injured herself. It takes longer to tell them where things are and what to do than to do it yourself!"

"That's not very charitable," laughed Constance.

Later, as the shadows on her walls began to shift toward evening, Serena lay on her bed, covered with her pastel afghan and ballasted by every pillow in the house.

Frances and Constance had had a mild disagreement about how to treat a head injury, so as a result, both her head and her feet had been propped up, and there was another stack of pillows under her arm, so that she could comfortably hold the ice against her head.

The cold compresses had been replaced by a canvas bag, full of ice someone had probably had to chip from the icehouse. Serena was drinking her second cup of peppermint and chamomile tea and had also endured a dose of crushed, strained willow bark, to ward off a headache. If Serena remembered correctly, willow bark was the basis for aspirin, which would be invented in the next year or so. It couldn't be too soon for her, considering how bitter the bark concoction was.

At least once a half hour, someone came to check on her, so Serena rubbed her forehead red as she heard footsteps in the hall and then smiled weakly and said she thought she was feeling a little better, when her visitor arrived. Whoever came always told her not to be silly, when she made tepid protests about trying to get downstairs to help with the preparations.

"We just want to make sure you're well enough to come to the party," said Constance.

Trenton even came a couple of times, though he didn't venture into the room. He knocked on the door and, his wonderful voice, full of chagrin, expressed his concern for her from the other side of the wooden barrier. The second time, he also said he hoped she could attend the party later, and Serena said she would try her best.

Serena felt guilty about fooling her friends and about causing them concern—she even felt bad that someone had had to interrupt the preparations to brew her tea and chip extra ice, when she actually felt fine physically, but she knew that she was putting on this show for self-preservation. Nearly her whole existence depended on this deception, but she knew she couldn't use this ploy for long.

If she missed tonight's party, Serena knew the Longworths would definitely send for the doctor, who was expected to be in attendance at the party, to examine her.

Besides, self-preservation or not, she didn't think she could bring herself to miss the entire Christmas party.

Serena gazed at the dress she planned to wear, pressed and ready, hanging on the wardrobe door. It had been one of the few of Violet's dresses that she hadn't particularly liked at first. A translucent gold tissue, it had been trimmed in a heavy gold and maroon braid. But the trim was just tacked on and easily removed and, underneath, the dress was simple, beautifully constructed and wonderfully becoming. Serena had trimmed the neckline and sleeves with a delicate tracing of gold-colored beads, in a flower and vine design and she had some gilded flowers for her hair. Though she liked all of Violet's clothes, this dress (which she had redesigned herself) felt more like her own than any garment she'd had since she'd been there, and she wanted to wear it for Trenton.

So when the sun began to get low in the winter sky, Serena got up and began to prepare for the evening, with a mixture of excitement and trepidation in her heart. Reaching to the very bottom and back of her wardrobe, she pulled out the little beaded handbag, at which she had rarely even dared to look since her first day in 1908.

Next, after making sure no one was in the hall, on the way to check on her, Serena applied a dot of pink lipstick to her forehead, where the bump was supposed to be. She thought it was a pity she had no lavender eye shadow to add just the hint of a bruise, but she decided (rejecting the other cosmetics she had brought with her) that the lipstick would have to do. After a moment's consideration, she applied a thin coat of mascara to her eyes. It was a special occasion, she justified, as she carefully separated her lashes and blotted the residue. And Estey Wooten sure didn't stay away from the "paint pots!"

Just as she finished redressing her hair, making sure to leave a few curls free around her face for a more festive look, as well as to conceal her "lump," Constance burst into the room.

"Serena!" she reproved. "You should have rung for someone when you were ready to get up!"

"I'm feeling a lot better," protested Serena. *Except for this feeling of impending doom!* she thought.

"But we want you to feel well for the whole party," said Constance. "And look, your head is still red!" she added, reaching toward Serena.

"It…it's getting better," said Serena, deflecting Constance's fingers from the makeup. "But it still hurts a little to the touch."

"Sorry," said Constance with real concern. "But, at least, let me put your flowers in for you, so you won't have to turn your head all sorts of ways."

Serena gladly sat still while her friend attached the gilded flowers to the back of her hair. Then, she added delicate, gold filigree earrings and bracelets and surveyed the final results with pleasure. Even with the extraneous, new coloring on her forehead, she thought she looked the best she'd ever looked in 1908. This would be such a wonderful evening, if only Estey Wooten weren't there!

But as soon as she and Constance descended the stairs, Estey Wooten approached them. "So this is the invalid everyone was so concerned about," she said, looking significantly at Trenton, who was smiling at Serena over Estey's shoulder.

"But of course, you must recognize Miss Cassidy," said Constance firmly. "Miss Cassidy was one of your boarders. You brought her up here on your last visit and left without her. In fact, I believe you still have some of her belongings."

Estey Wooten glanced at Serena with a vacant look in her eyes.

Serena had decided that her only defense—though a lame one—would be to say she had been mistaken about knowing Mrs. Wooten and that there had been another woman with whom she had boarded and who had brought her to the last party. She was just about to say that, when Estey Wooten spoke.

"Of course," she said, still looking blank. "But you must remember, my dear, that I stressed that since my auto was so crowded, we must all meet there at the appointed time, in order to leave together. After all, you're all grown young ladies now and I can't be responsible for looking after you at every minute. And as far as your belongings go, as I told Mr. McNaught when he asked after them, you're welcome to come to look in my storage area, but I can't keep unclaimed things forever. Eventually, I must…uh…donate them to charity, you know."

With that, Estey Wooten excused herself to load up her plate at the buffet. Serena was still staring at her with wonder, when she felt a nudge at her elbow.

"She doesn't know you from Jack's hat rack, you know," the woman beside her said, in a carrying aggressive voice.

Serena's heart sank. Trenton and Constance were still standing close by and were bound to have heard. She turned to face one of Estey's boarders, a girl from New York City, whom Serena had already decided fit many of the stereotypes for which the city was known.

"Why? What do you mean?" Serena said softly, hoping Miss New York would follow suit and lower her voice.

"Don't you know we're all interchangeable to Miss Wooten?" asked the girl. "One of my friends had lived in the house for a week, and, when she came in from work one day, Estey tried to rent her a room, like she'd never seen her before!"

"I suppose you're right," said Serena with relief. "She did look pretty vague."

"You said it!" said Miss New York. "And, you know, the only reason she offers to bring us up here is so she can charge us that 'excursion fee.' And, of course," she continued conspiratorially, her voice finally lowering, "bringing us to meet the students gives her more excuses to come and see Mr. Longworth there. Not that I blame her," she added, with a comical quirk of her cheek. "He's a real looker, if you like the studious type."

Yes, thought Serena. If that was what Trenton represented, she definitely liked the studious type.

It had all been so amazingly easy, thought Serena dazedly, as she moved through the lavishly decorated rooms and festively dressed people, as she was introduced to notables and Longworth family friends and received everyone's concern and good wishes.

She couldn't believe the situation with Estey Wooten had been resolved. It was the encounter Serena had been dreading since her arrival in 1908. But instead of causing any kind of trauma, the confrontation had been almost anticlimactic!

Everything was dovetailing so well that she once again felt a little guilty.

At Constance's insistence, the doctor gave Serena's forehead a cursory glance, asked her a couple of questions and stated that she seemed to be recovering as she should be.

But the most perfect event of the evening was that Trenton momentarily escaped the company of the visiting dignitaries and the grasp of Estey Wooten and came to stand by her side. "You look very beautiful tonight," he said, with a dark resonance in his voice. "Very beautiful!"

"So do you!" she answered, not caring that men in 1908 were not called 'beautiful,' or that 1908 women rarely commented on men's looks. Trenton didn't seem to care either.

"Dear, Mr. Longworth," came a pretentious, raspy voice, that was becoming all too familiar. "If I may be so bold as to interrupt your tête-à-tête," here, she flashed Serena a distressingly malicious smile, "but I believe our presence is requested on the porch, and I thought perhaps you would be so good as to escort me."

"Oh, are the boys ready for the caroling?" asked Trenton. "Of course, I'd be happy to escort you, Mrs. Wooten. Come on," he said to Serena. "Let's get our coats. You'll be sure to enjoy this!"

"Didn't dear Constance tell me that the reason you didn't leave with my group—and, by the way," she gave a dramatic pause and looked at Serena with narrowed eyes, "when was that again, Miss… uh…was that you were sick? And then today, weren't you feeling poorly again? Dear, I don't want to be a killjoy, but I would think the prudent person who suffered from a weak constitution would stay inside on a cold night."

Serena was, once again, quaking. Would Estey expose her after all? But Trenton seemed unimpressed with her performance.

"As I believe you already recalled," he said, his tone pleasant, but firmer than any Serena had ever heard him use with Estey Wooten, "it was last fall when your group left Miss Cassidy here. She had retired for a moment, due to a food allergy. Today, she had a bump on her head, and the doctor has given her a clean bill of health. In any case, I don't believe either condition would be worsened by her going out on the porch for a few moments on a crisp night. Naturally, I would expect her to bundle up. As I would wish of all you lovely ladies," he continued, seeming suddenly to remember himself and giving her a gracious smile. "So if you'll help me locate your wraps, I'll collect my sister, and we can all go out together."

"O-of course," said Estey, apparently somewhat cowed by this lengthy speech. "Collect your sweet sister." She brightened. "We'll tend to our own coats, won't we, Miss…uh," she went on, motioning imperiously toward one of the Longworths' staff. But, when Trenton had gone, Estey's expression became much less friendly. However, she didn't seem to be able to think of anything threatening to say.

They all crowded out on the side porch to hear the students, who had spent the afternoon packing for home and celebrating the holiday, regale them with Christmas carols from the yard below. Even Estey Wooten seemed placated, as Trenton brought all three of "his ladies" hot toddies and made sure they were all bundled up, especially—because, at Serena's and Constance's urging and surreptitious elbow jabs, he made his addresses to Estey especially flowery. However, when the crowd on the porch joined in the singing and there were several comments about how Trenton and Serena's voices blended so beautifully, Estey started to frown again.

Standing under the stars, on the cool crisp night, snug in Cousin Violet's elegant black velvet coat, with its fur-trimmed hood and matching muff (which no one had called "politically incorrect") and singing the old familiar carols with her new loved ones, Serena felt she was experiencing the true spirit of Christmas. Yet still, Estey

Wooten was sending her dirty looks and, when Constance raved on what a "magical" evening it was, her comment once again tweaked that unpleasant trace of a memory that continued to play just on the other side of Serena's consciousness.

Chapter 9

On the day after the very eventful Christmas party, the students and many of the professors and their wives left for the season. As usual, Malcolm organized the departures, in various conveyances, piloted by the men of the community.

For a couple of hours, the courtyard was filled with noise and bustle, to be replaced suddenly by the kind of silence Longworth College hadn't known for the past three months.

"Well," said Malcolm, rubbing his hands together. "That'll be that. And Saint Finnian be praised, it all went off without a hitch!"

"Now it's time for us to celebrate," agreed Frances.

The staff's Christmas party took place every year, in their dining room, and all the help had the remainder of the day off, to celebrate.

Frances, who had already laid out sandwich makings and other cold cuts for the household's dinner, began to do the same for the staff, adding fancy Christmas pastries and other traditional delicacies, while Malcolm and some of the other men rolled in kegs of strong dark beer.

Also, as part of the tradition, the Longworths went down for a few minutes, at the beginning of the party. This year, naturally, they took Serena with them.

It was a very relaxed and cheerful event, with lots of eating and drinking and laughing. One of the men who worked on the school grounds had brought his "fiddle" and regaled them with not only Christmas music, but also mountain music and rousing Irish tunes.

Even Malcolm forgot his usual butlery dignity to join Frances in an Irish jig and then to swing Neva into a Virginia reel.

"Shall we, Ma'am?" asked Trenton, with mock formality, offering Serena his arm, as other couples joined in.

Even as she attempted to pick up the unfamiliar movements and tried to dodge chairs and tables in an area too crowded for the laughing, jostling group, Serena felt a tingle each time she linked arms with Trenton or caught his hand. She was just getting used to the steps, when the reel ended and the fiddler launched into a faster, more complicated one. Disappointed it was over so soon, Serena started to move away, but Trenton, with a wide, boyish grin, held her firm.

Neva, however, backed away from Malcolm, clutching her chest. "That's enough for a while, Malcolm," she said, fanning her becomingly flushed cheeks. "You may never seem to feel the advance of the years, but I'm afraid I do!" She sat down in a nearby chair.

Malcolm gave a comical frown.

"I know the steps," said Constance, holding out her hands.

"That, I believe you do!" said Malcolm. "You taught it to me, when you were a wee girl."

"In exchange for the jig you taught us!" said Constance, with glowing eyes.

They all swept into the complicated reel. Serena was glad to see she wasn't the only one having trouble among the giggling group. In fact, only Malcolm and Constance danced with happy assurance.

But when the fiddler segued into a lively waltz, Malcolm interrupted him.

"Sure, that's a pretty tune," he said affably, "but why don't we have some more Christmas music? If I'm not mistaken, we haven't even heard 'Jingle Bells' yet."

Everyone sang the already-familiar ditty, but when the chorus was over, Constance nudged Trenton and Serena. "We should go now and let these people enjoy themselves," she said soberly.

Though surprised to leave so soon, Trenton and Serena agreed.

"Have a good time," said Trenton, good-naturedly. "Our only request, as you know, is that we'll have at least a skeleton crew who feel up to working tomorrow."

"Sure, we may all look a bit like skeletons," Malcolm laughed.

Trenton took Constance's arm, as they mounted the stairs. "We still have those holiday stereopticon pictures to look at," he said, in a rallying tone.

"And Frances laid out a little feast for us," added Serena, for some reason feeling that she should add a cheerful note. "We'll have our own party!"

The next week passed quietly but quickly. With no students and the remaining teachers planning for their own celebrations in their individual quarters, the Longworth household was free to complete their own preparations.

Serena spent more time than usual in her room, finishing up her gifts, but everyone else seemed to also be busy with secrets.

As she completed the white-on-white silk stitching on Trenton's dressiest handkerchiefs and embroidered Constance's and her initials, "Best Friends" and birds, butterflies, and flowers to complete the crazy quilt, Serena thought, with continued wonder, about her experiences in the last three months. Strange as it all was, she felt she had arrived where she belonged. Yet she was essentially living a lie. Gradually, a radical and rather frightening, thought and then a conviction, formed in her mind. There was something she had to do, she concluded, she just had to decide how to do it.

But as the conviction grew, so did a doubt of another kind. If only she could bring into the foreground that memory that was playing at the edge of her consciousness, though Serena had a feeling that remembering it would not make her happy.

On Christmas Eve, Constance and Serena set out together to deliver baskets to the neediest families in the area. Instead of the carriage, Murgatroid, with red and green ribbons and jingle bells braided into her chestnut mane, was harnessed to a wagon, to accommodate the many baskets and pails they carried.

As Constance drove the wagon, Serena read off the list of the many stops they needed to make.

"I hope we get back before the weather changes too much," said Constance, looking up at the milky sky.

Even those in the grimmest of circumstances seemed happy today, and all were thrilled with the pretty baskets, filled with food, household necessities and even a few trinkets. At many of the houses, Constance also handed out one of the specially decorated pails of milk.

"For the cats," she'd say.

"Bless you," said Thelma Privette, rubbing her rounding stomach. "We sure need all the help we can get these days!"

"What's with the cats?" asked Serena, as they were riding away.

"Oh, it's an old Appalachian superstition," said Constance. "It's supposed to be bad luck if your cat cries on Christmas day."

It's lucky we don't have any cats, then, thought Serena. *I sure need all the good luck I can get tomorrow too!*

That evening, the Trices hosted a festive dinner party for the remaining faculty and their wives, the Longworths and Serena. The food and the drink and conversation were very convivial, and as they were leaving and wishing each other happy holidays, in both spoken words and signs, the first puffy flakes of snow began to fall.

To finish the evening, Trenton read the Christmas story in St. Luke to them, and then they hung their stockings and lit sparklers over the fireplace, as Trenton and Constance had done every year since their childhood.

After they'd all added their brightly wrapped packages to the bottom of the tree, Constance gave a rather stagy yawn. "I think I'll turn in now. You two don't mind turning out the lamps without me, do you?" She kissed each of them on the cheek and received kisses in response. "Merry Christmas," she called, as she mounted the stairs.

It didn't really take two to put out the lights, but neither Trenton nor Serena pointed that out. They moved slowly together from light to light, taking turns working the gas knobs. It vaguely reminded Serena of a scene from a movie she'd seen, but she didn't bother to mention that either.

"This has been the best holiday season in years," said Trenton, as they entered the back parlor.

"For me too," said Serena, significantly. "The best one I've had since my parents."

"All of us have seemed to find new family feelings," said Trenton. He stopped, reaching the hook up to the Tiffany lamp, its colors playing across his face as he looked at her. "If only—"

"If only?" she asked softly.

He shook his head, as if to clear it. "It's okay. We have a big day ahead. We'd better be heading to our beds, like good little boys and girls," he concluded with a rueful smile.

As they headed toward the parlor doorway, Serena couldn't help staring at one of Constance's many bunches of mistletoe, its waxy leaves glowing dully in the dim light from the hall. She saw Trenton's eyes, flashing white-gold in the darkness, follow hers to the kissing bough.

When he had kissed her before, they had been interrupted by Malcolm. This time, Malcolm, and everyone else, had retired for the night.

But when they stopped under the mistletoe, Trenton gave her a chaste kiss on the cheek, just as he'd given Constance. "Merry Christmas, dear," he said, a little sadly.

"See you in the morning."

Serena shrugged as she followed her elusive love up the garlanded staircase. She was sure Trenton had wanted to give her a real kiss, and yet he had avoided it.

Obviously, he still didn't completely trust her. And how would he feel, if she carried out her nerve-racking plans for tomorrow evening?

A blanket of dazzling white greeted Serena outside her window, when she woke the next morning. *Christmas, 1908,* she thought. *Amazing!*

The Longworths appeared to love her handiwork and were amazed that she'd spent so much time working on their gifts.

"You seemed so concerned with finding ready-made gifts," explained Trenton.

Coming from a world where everyone had to have the latest video games and brand-name shirts, Serena supposed she had made her insecurity about her homemade presents more apparent than she'd realized.

"What could possibly be better than these?" asked Constance, indicating Serena's offerings.

"Yours!" Serena answered confidently.

Constance's main gift to Serena was an outfit that she had "saved" from the rejects of Cousin Violet's wardrobe. A dark lavender velvet skirt, which Serena had loved, had been judged too skimpy across the hips (due to Serena's shorter measurement from waist to hips) and had no extra material in the seams. Constance had added insets of dark wine-red braid, ending at about the knee, with yellow-gold tassels, between the narrow tops of the six gores. Then, she had embroidered a beautiful white lawn blouse, which Violet had sent only as a work blouse, because of an indelible scattering of stains. Constance had added a pattern of cross-stitched pansies, in the colors of the skirt, over the stains. It was an unusual, but striking combination, of which even Trenton seemed to approve.

"You mean it doesn't look like a carny girl's?" asked Constance with gentle sarcasm.

Trenton screwed his face into a comical frown. "Haven't I done enough penance for that yet? I'm sorry! But don't give me such a hard time. It's Christmas! Don't you like your gifts?" he added.

"Oh sure. They're great," Constance conceded.

"They're wonderful," said Serena.

Just as Constance had told her, Trenton had ordered his gifts or bought them locally, rather than making them, but Serena thought they were, indeed, wonderful.

Constance and Serena had received identical Kodak "Brownie" cameras, which were "all the rage," and Trenton had given both recently published novels—Constance's was *The House of Mirth* by Edith Wharton and Serena's Baroness Orczy's *The Scarlet Pimpernel*, an old classic in 2008, which Serena had always thought she would enjoy reading, but had never gotten around to. Serena was glad to know that books were as important a part of Christmas to the Longworths as they had been in the Cassidy household, and she had insisted on going in with Constance on O. Henry's *The Four Million* for Trenton.

The only real difference in Trenton's gifts to her and to his sister was in the jewelry. And Serena realized, that was only due to availability. Trenton had bought Constance a complete set of pearl and marquisette pieces which she had admired on a summer trip they had made to Charlottesville. Serena received intricately carved tortoise-shell combs and two bracelets of blown glass beads in delicate colors.

"They're the best things I could find locally, even in Belle Vieux," he said.

"But they're wonderful!" Serena enthused. Even more wonderful, she thought, was the fact that Trenton had gone to so much trouble to pick gifts for her and that he had obviously done it soon after her arrival. Even in 2008, sometimes you had to allow three to four weeks for delivery. Heaven only knew how long it would have taken in her new era!

So even when she'd thought Trenton didn't want her there, he'd obviously been treating her like a member of the family. Even if he had only done so then for Constance's sake, Serena thought, it was very generous.

Serena took a deep breath. Her place seemed nearly secure. Would that change tonight?

That Christmas afternoon was a time of childish delights. All three of the Trice children had received bicycles that morning—shiny red, blue, and green models with the brakes by the pedals, but the blanket of sparkling white on the ground made the gifts temporarily useless and they stood, resplendent, on the side porch still adorned with big red bows while the children chased by the jubilant Lady and Cahudalin, sledded down the embankment in their front yard and made snow angels on the ground. The Longworth's household joined them to try a few slides, to make a comical snowman, to make snow angels, and even to challenge the kids to a snowball fight. A perfect white Christmas, thought Serena, worthy of Frank Capra. If only her plans for the evening didn't keep her from feeling as lighthearted as everyone else seemed to be.

After another sumptuous holiday dinner, Serena ushered Trenton and Constance into the cozy back parlor. The coffee tray included a bottle of brandy, as she had requested; a fire blazed cheerfully in the hearth, and she was dressed in a festive and becoming green corded-velvet dress, which she hoped would give her extra confidence.

When they had all helped themselves to coffee and brandy, Serena stood before her friends and took her evening bag from behind the sofa pillow, where she had secreted it earlier.

"I have one more Christmas gift for you," she said quickly, before she lost her nerve. "The truth."

Neither Trenton nor Constance looked surprised, Serena noticed.

"First, I have some things to show you," she said, and, with shaking hands, spread the contents of the little purse she had been so careful to hide, on the table before them.

Trenton knitted his brow, as he looked at the money and driver's license and credit cards. Constance tapped the plastic makeup containers with her fingernail.

"What's the meaning of all this?" asked Trenton.

"They show you where I really came from," said Serena with an almost comically pleading grimace. *Please, don't think I'm stark raving crazy!* she silently begged. "Just before I met you at your tenth anniversary party and passed out at your feet from the shock, I was attending a party here for the hundred and tenth anniversary of your school…in 2008."

"What?" exclaimed Trenton and Constance together.

"I was born in 1984," said Serena with deliberation. "I grew up in the nineteen eighties and nineties and, then, in the twenty-first century, until August of 2008, when I came to this house for a celebration of this school, which both my parents attended, and then, somehow, I came back through time to 1908 and met you."

"So you're seriously telling us you can jump back and forth in time, like some character from H. G. Wells," said Trenton, in whose library Serena had already noticed a copy of the recently published soon-to-be classic, *The Time Machine*. Serena realized Trenton was making a conscious effort to keep his tone pleasant and light, as if this whole scene were some sort of joke she'd prepared for their entertainment.

"Well, no, I didn't travel by time machine, if that's what you mean," said Serena. "At least I don't think there was one. And I don't know how to go back, not that I want to," she hastened to add. "I don't know how or why it happened," she continued. "I really did have an allergic reaction to crab, like I told you, and I was taken up to the second floor, to a powder room, off a room the museum staff used as an office. But when I came out a few minutes later, I found myself in a closet, attached to a bedroom, which I later found out was Constance's."

"Good heavens!" said Constance, clutching her arms across her chest and giving a little shudder.

"Oh please," said Serena, "don't let that upset you. I tried to go back into the powder room, and it was a completely solid closet wall, like nothing else had ever been there. And anyway, it's nothing sinister. Coming back has turned out to be a wonderful thing for me [though it freaked me out, at first]. I always thought that I would love this era, and it turned out I was right."

"So is it a common practice for people to travel in time from the twenty-first century?" asked Trenton, still sounding as if he thought it was all a joke.

"No," said Serena. "At least, not that I know of. Of course, I'm sure there must be anachronisms, people who don't feel they fit in, in every time, so maybe it has happened before, but I've certainly never heard of it. I honestly don't know how it happened to me, but I'm glad it did. I had felt so lost and alone since my parents died, and now I-I don't, anymore."

"So your parents really did pass away?" asked Trenton quietly.

"Yes. I'm sorry to say, that's true," answered Serena. "I tried to tell the truth as much as possible. Mostly, what I avoided was the fact that I've lived all over the world—my father was in the diplomatic service—because I was afraid transportation might come up."

"So you didn't really go to school in California?" asked Trenton deliberately.

"No,' said Serena. "I've spent very little time in California. I just picked it, because it was so far away, that I figured..." She stopped, the light dawning. "You knew that, didn't you? Did you check up on me?"

"Well, I attempted to contact the school, Berkley Seminary for Women, wasn't it?" asked Trenton with a rather sheepish look. "I... uh...felt that since you were becoming involved with our school, and my sister...and myself..."

"That you should know something about me," Serena finished for him. "That's understandable. After all, I arrived here out of the blue, more literally than you even realized. But what did you find out, when you tried to contact the school?"

"That it doesn't exist," answered Trenton, "and schools with similar names I wrote had never heard of you."

"So that's why you were so angry that day you watched my class," concluded Serena. "And yet, you didn't expose me, and you even allowed me to continue teaching the boys until Rivers arrived." How generous, thought Serena, once again.

"Well," said Trenton, still looking sheepish, "against my better judgment, I decided you must have had a good reason for your deception and would tell us the truth when the time was right. Though I never expected anything as fantastic as this. But," he added, "your belongings here," he indicated the contents of the purse, in front of him, "are pretty convincing."

"They are convincing," said Constance, who had been quietly contemplating Serena and her 2008 cache for several minutes, "but there are some other things which persuade me too."

"Like what?" asked Serena.

"Some of the words and phrases you use," answered Constance.

"You mean 'cursing'?" asked Serena with trepidation. "I try not to do it, especially back here, but it's done so much in the twenty-first century, it almost gets to seem like second nature, and I—"

"It's not really the, uh, cursing," said Constance, giving Serena a mischievous smile. "You usually manage to stop yourself in the middle of those words, anyway. It's words and phrases you use in unusual ways. Let's see, you…uh…"

"For instance," interjected Trenton, "you must change the word 'era' to 'area' ten times a day!"

"I was hoping you didn't notice that," said Serena, shrugging comically.

"That's true," said Constance. "You do say that a lot. But that's not it either. It's—for one thing—the way you put the word 'like' in the middle of a sentence, where it has no meaning. I've never heard anyone else do that."

"I guess that was one of those holdovers from the hippie era," said Serena. "That was a rather strange trend that took place in the 1960s," she added, at their blank stares. "Before my time—or after it. I'll have to tell you what I know about it sometime. I guess that couldn't hurt."

"What do you mean?" asked Trenton.

"Well, you know, like they always say in the movies," said Serena, "we have to make sure that nothing I tell you will change the course of history."

"But wouldn't your coming back to this time automatically change things?" asked Trenton.

Serena couldn't tell whether he was just testing her or beginning to be convinced.

"Well…," began Serena. *I think maybe I was—will be—your wife?* "Well, I believe there was a 'Serena' mentioned on the house tour, so maybe I was already here in a past before…now… Oh, it's too confusing!" she finished in frustration. "And I know you must think I'm just nuts or a con woman."

"Whatever that means," said Trenton with a resigned smile.

"You mean, our school is still here a hundred years from now?" Constance asked, in awe.

"Oh yes, and very well thought of," answered Serena. *And you and I start a business together and Trenton is a US senator!* she thought, but didn't say. What she told them might change things in some way, and besides, she hoped to avoid other, more painful subjects, like life spans.

As her friends continued to sift through her meager belongings from 2008, Serena spent the next couple of hours telling them about her life and as much as she thought she could about the twenty-first century. From their general attitude and the questions they asked, Serena felt that Trenton and (especially) Constance were beginning to take her amazing story for fact.

Finally, when Serena was nearly hoarse from the monologue, when she decided that her friends had taken in all that they could in one sitting and when they had put a considerable dent in the brandy, the inhabitants of the parlor began to wind their way toward bed.

"It's all so awe-inspiring," said Constance sincerely, hugging Serena. "I'm just glad you've finally decided you could tell us!"

"It is remarkable," interjected Trenton, still with a wry note in his voice. "I suppose we should all sleep on it and talk about it more tomorrow.

"You go on, Con. Serena and I'll get the lights again tonight, won't we?" he added with a little smile.

"Oh, of course," said Serena, her heart fluttering in her chest. The mistletoe was still waiting over the parlor doorway.

As they went from fixture to fixture, Serena and Trenton made desultory conversation, neither mentioning the mistletoe or her revelations of the evening.

But, when he had extinguished the back parlor light, Trenton pulled Serena gently toward the mistletoe, and she followed, her heart beating even faster.

It wasn't a chaste kiss on the cheek tonight, and, though his lips met hers for only a few seconds, Serena felt the difference in Trenton's touch. There was a sense of trust and even surrender she had never felt with him before.

"You believe me, don't you?" she asked, still breathless, as they began to move toward the stairs, his arm around her shoulders.

"About the time travel?" asked Trenton with a lift of his brow. He bit the side of his cheek, considering. "You know, there's a place in the mountains close to here, where they find perfect, cross-shaped stones. Many of them. No one knows how they're formed—they seem to appear out of nowhere."

"The fairy stones?" asked Serena. "Yes, I've heard of them. In fact, my parents gave me one once. But how are they connected with my experience?"

"Well," said Trenton, pausing by the statue of Artimus on the landing, "some people think that fairies make the stones, others think that they're made by God. But either belief seems to bolster peoples' morale. They have them attached to jewelry, wear them on their wrists or necks and sincerely believe the stones bring them luck…"

"Are you trying to say you think I'm sincere, but delusional?" asked Serena, with fire in her eye.

"No," Trenton said, hastily. "I'm saying I think you're sincere, but not delusional. I think something happened to you. I think you really believe that you traveled in time, but I do wonder if there's not some other explanation. Still," he added, touching her shoulder reassuringly. "You do present a pretty convincing argument, with all your stories and all the dates and the plastic," he said the word with the emphasis of a novice, "from your purse. I just don't know what to think, but if I promise to keep an open mind, will you forgive me for not being sure of your story?"

"Of course," said Serena. "Believe me, if it hadn't happened to me, I'd probably have trouble with it too."

"I'm glad you understand," said Trenton, standing very close to her. "It's important to me. Merry Christmas, Serena dear," he whispered.

This time his kiss was only on the cheek, but Serena was so elated that it was hours before she was able to sleep. Two kisses in the same evening, and evidently no regrets on Trenton's part. Certainly not on hers!

Chapter 10

The next day, the day after Christmas, was a very leisurely one in the Longworth household. No one had to rush back to work, as was often the case in the twenty-first century, and neither did anyone feel impelled to hurry out to return Christmas gifts or to fight deluged parking lots, hectic crowds, and endless lines to take advantage of gift money or after-Christmas sales. In fact, many of these dubious holiday treats weren't even available in 1908, at least not in the foothills of Virginia.

Serena found that the holiday didn't end in the Longworth household as soon as the last present was torn open.

Since school didn't begin again for a couple of weeks, everyone in the household was able to relax a bit, after the holiday preparations and parties and to take time to enjoy their Christmas gifts. Trenton and Serena and Constance tried on and modeled their new finery and dreamed up exotic places where they might wear it. Armed with hot tea and the remains of the Christmas pastry, they settled down in the back parlor, to delve into their novels, and even to read passages aloud to each other.

In the evening, there were more songfests, and then Trenton continued to read to everyone. Having finished *A Christmas Carol*, he enthralled them with his interpretation of *Byrd's Christmas Carol*, a touching family tale, which often had all the women in tears and even left the men a little damp-eyed.

But not all the household's activities took place inside. The beautiful snow, unmarred by the onslaughts of traffic, provided a sparkling background for innumerable pictures. Serena and Constance aimed their new Brownie cameras at each other, Trenton, Malcolm and Frances, the Trice children, Lady and Cahudalin and the various snow people, which now dotted the side lawn, and then they started all over again.

Three days after Christmas, they all went on a sleigh ride. Even on her visits to other countries, Serena had never had a chance to ride in a sleigh, and she had always wanted to. She wasn't disappointed.

Snuggled under thick down coverlets, with Trenton's arm linked through hers, Serena enjoyed the rush of crisp cold air. Mehetable's tail and mane were still braided with Christmas ribbons, and she and the sleigh were decked with bells, which filled the air with their cheerful jingles.

"Every time I saw this in a movie," Serena trilled happily. "I longed to do it. And it's every bit as great as I thought it would be!" And now that she'd told the truth, Serena thought, she didn't have to pretend sleigh rides were old hat to her.

On the first Saturday after Christmas, Malcolm declared the small lake across from the church sufficiently frozen for traversing and organized a skating party. The entire Longworth and Trice households and many other surrounding families joined in the fun.

Ice skating was another cold weather pastime Serena had never tried, and since she's never been very good at roller skating, she was a bit leery of it, especially when she realized how thin the blades actually were.

"Don't think about the blades," said Trenton, kneeling in front of her, as he tied the skates onto her shoes, sending delicious vibrations up her legs and to other parts of her body. "It's all a question of balance."

Trenton, a natural athlete, hadn't been able to resist showing off a little, leaving Serena and Constance, to perform graceful swirls and perfect figure eights, as soon as his own skates were in place.

Soon, however, he returned to escort Serena and his sister onto the ice.

"I've never been very good at this, either," said Constance, struggling to keep her feet under her. "And I've had lots of opportunities to learn."

"Just hold on tight to me," said Trenton, with an intimate smile.

They took a few awkward turns around the lake, with Trenton continuing to encourage them. But when both Serena and Constance fell at the same time, pulling Trenton down to sandwich them in an inelegant heap on the hard ice, even he decided they should stop for a while.

"We can try again later," he assured the girls, ushering them off the ice.

But Constance spent the rest of the afternoon at the far end of the lake, helping Malcolm organize his boys into an impromptu hockey game with tree branches for mallets and a pine cone puck.

And Serena was completely content to sit with Trenton, on a bench close to one of the campfires Malcolm had built, with Trenton's gloved hand in hers, and Trenton didn't seem to want to go anywhere either. As the skaters before them swirled, shuffled, or clambered down on the ice in their long full coats and skirts, top hats, muffs, and capes, in a scene straight out of an old-fashioned Christmas card, Serena quietly told Trenton about ice rinks in shopping malls, Zamboni machines, sequined, gossamer skating miniskirts and international Olympic telecasts.

Trenton listened to her stories with rapt attention, rarely letting his eyes leave her face to observe the scene before them. He asked an occasional question, often smiled, raised his eyebrows in surprise, or shook his head sadly. Once or twice, he even laughed and squeezed her hand, but at no time did he show any distrust of Serena or any doubt that what she was telling him was fact.

One of the best things about that holiday week was the fact that Constance and even Trenton had evidently come to believe that what she had told them about her time travel was true.

Every evening, since Christmas, when Trenton had finished his reading and the servants had retired to their quarters, Trenton and Constance had eagerly questioned Serena about the future. Serena had decided not to tell them about specific events, for fear it might somehow change history, but she did relate everything she could about the twenty-first century's lifestyles and about future inventions.

Trenton and Constance were fascinated with Serena's stories and with continuing to look at the contents of her purse, and they never seemed to tire of trying to figure out how Serena's time travel occurred. They examined every inch of Constance's closet, closed themselves in it, to see if anything would happen, but they could find nothing unusual. Because she told them she had bought the broach of the three graces from a local antique store, they wondered if it could have any connection with the time warp, but they could find nothing significant about it either. Serena had been trying to solve the mystery of her presence in 1908 for the last four and a half months, but now that she had allies to join the search, the solution seemed no closer than before.

"Well, we'll just have to say that you're here because we needed you, to teach us to…uh…care again," said Trenton.

"Just as I needed both of you," Serena answered.

On New Year's Eve, the snow still covered the ground in deep drifts and the roads to Belle Vieux, primitive at best, were impassible, making it impossible for Serena and the Longworths to attend the McNaught's annual New Year's gala. So they decided to have their own little party at home in the front parlor.

"It's just as well," said Constance. "Randy would probably propose to me again, and I'd just have to refuse him again."

"Oh, you mean he's proposed before?" asked Serena, who thought Constance had shared all her secrets.

"The last three years in a row. On New Year's Eve, with his family and everyone probably within hearing distance," Constance answered. "I hate to hurt him. He's such a dear soul, but…"

On the lawn outside, the gaslights shed amber shadows on the snowdrifts, but inside, there was warmth and song and laughter. Everyone had dressed in their best clothes and spent the evening playing charades and telling riotous stories.

When the grandfather clock in the hall and the enameled Ormolu clock on the mantle struck midnight, Trenton, Serena, and Constance and the household staff lifted their champagne glasses.

As the chorus of, "It's 1909!" echoed from one to the other, Trenton whispered softly, "And 2009?" Then he kissed his sister on the cheek and, in front of her and the staff, kissed Serena full on the lips.

Serena felt a glow of pleasure. She had a new family and a new love, and even something as remarkable as time travel seemed to be within the realm of their acceptance. She felt a sense of belonging she'd never thought she'd have again.

Trenton, devastating in his velvet-collared evening jacket, didn't even hesitate to kiss her before others. True, it was a chaste kiss, as a public kiss should be, but in some ways, it said more about his feelings toward her than the more heated kisses they continued to exchange alone under the mistletoe each night. Serena had to admit that even the private kisses were more proper than she'd like, only hinting at the passion she dreamed of, but she supposed that was what could be expected for an "unpromised" couple in 1908–1909.

The important thing, she told herself, as they all joined hands to sing "Auld Lang Syne," was that she had found love and was sure she was loved in return. She had found comfort and contentment. She looked forward to the future with shining eyes.

But outside, the wind howled eerily, milky clouds roiled over the sky, and Serena's world, capricious as the wind, was poised to jolt on its axis once again and leave her scrambling to hold on to its curve.

Chapter 11

Yesterdays/Deal

"Mr. Trenton! Miz Serena! Miz Constance! Mr. Malcolm!"

The clamor of names echoed sharply through the afternoon chill, accompanied by insistent bangs on the front door and nearby windows.

"Hald yer harses!" said Malcolm, as he opened the door for the Trice boys.

"But you don't understand," said Nate emphatically.

"Dumbelin—I mean, Lettie's gone," chimed Mat, at the same time.

"Gone where?" asked Trenton as he, Constance, and Serena gained the doorway, their arms wrapped with garland and other Christmas decorations they'd been removing from the front parlor.

"Run off!" said Nate.

"We searched the whole house, ten times over," said Mat, "and she's nowhere to be seen! Ma's getting scared 'cause it's getting cold and—"

"Of course," said Trenton, giving a worried glance toward the milky skies. "Have you searched our grounds?"

But the search of the Longworths' house and outbuildings also proved fruitless, and soon, Malcolm and the boys went out to organize the neighbors for a thorough search of the entire area.

"It's all my fault," Mrs. Trice said tearfully. "I got the boxes for the Christmas decorations out of the hall closet and I never even thought about the fact that I'd also taken out the suitcases and left them in the hall. Lettie took one look at those Gladstones and bolted out the door, and by the time I could get down from the ladder and could follow, she'd just vanished! If only I'd thought...," she mourned. "I guess she thought we were going to drag her on the train again."

"Don't worry," said Serena, patting her hand. "We'll find her. It's lucky the school is still closed and all the buildings are locked up. At least we don't have to worry about searching all those classrooms and dormitories."

"That's true," said Mrs. Trice, with a sniff. "But we have to find her soon. Look at the sky! I know it's going to snow again and she'll be out in the cold by herself, and—"

"No, no, dear," said Constance, hugging her. "Just look at all the people arriving. And Malcolm is going to organize us all. Why, we'll find little Lettie in no time!"

Indeed, it appeared that everyone from the surrounding area had been rallied.

Men, women, and children, in their sturdiest clothes, were converging on the Trice lawn, carrying an assortment of ropes, ladders, and other hardware implements, as well as whistles, bells, bullhorns, and even some musical instruments!

The remarkable Malcolm had made up a map of the surroundings and began to assign groups of two or three to each area. To expedite the search, it was best they split up, but they still needed to be able to communicate with each other and Serena soon learned (in the age before walkie-talkies and cell phones) that purpose was served by the musical instruments and other noisemakers.

"We'll take the far side of Butler's Peak," Trenton volunteered quickly, as Malcolm began to pencil names on the diagram. "I grew up climbing that peak and Serena can communicate with Lettie, if we find her."

Despite herself, Serena felt her heart skip a beat. Her main concern was Lettie, she assured herself, but she couldn't help giving some thought to being alone with Trenton, amid such beautiful, romantic scenery. But, as penance for her straying thoughts, Serena made sure to spend extra time comforting Mr. and Mrs. Trice and assuring them that Lettie would soon be found.

When all the areas had been assigned, Malcolm began to go over the numerical code for the noisemakers—one ring or whistle, etc. at fifteen-minute intervals, to check in; two, if help was needed and so forth. When this instruction was completed, he had each group make their sound, so he would know which was which, and found that several of the bells sounded too much alike to be distinguished from a distance.

"Why don't some of us use animal sounds," suggested Constance. "They echo very well through the hills." She proceeded to crow like a rooster and to suggest additional beasts and fowl, which other groups might imitate.

When Constance turned to Trenton, who had given up his Chinese gong to the Fryes, he held up his hand. "I have our call, already," he told his sister. Hollowing his cheeks and flattening his tongue, he gave an unmistakable Tarzan yell. Everyone from Johnny Weissmuller to Carol Burnett had done the Tarzan yell in the years since 1909, but Serena doubted that Trenton had heard it at any time, other than on the fall afternoon when she and Constance had climbed Butler's Peak. Yet he executed it perfectly, making several of his neighbors chuckle, despite the serious situation, at the idea of the dignified educator making such a spectacle of himself.

"Vera well," said Malcolm, with a wry smile. "Mr. Longworth's call will be...what'ere that is."

Serena took a quick moment to show all the searchers a few signaled words and signs that might lessen Lettie's fear, if she were found by a near stranger. Then the group split up and headed toward their assigned areas.

"Even if they don't get the signs right," Serena told Trenton, "the fact that they're trying to communicate might reassure her."

"Or amuse her," answered Trenton, handing her a walking stick.

Going up the far side of Butler's Peak was a much harder climb than the way she and Constance had taken in the fall. Even without the snow, it was a strain, Trenton said. And of course, there was snow. Even the magnificent views couldn't keep it from being a chore. Rocks were slippery and jagged and the trail all but disappeared at times.

"It makes it so much harder to hunt for Lettie," said Trenton, "because she can't hear us call."

"But if she's still hiding, that might be to our advantage," said Serena, fighting for footing in the icy brush.

Lettie Trice was a very stubborn and resourceful little girl, they knew and if she didn't want to be found, she could make their search very difficult.

With that in mind, they began to investigate every clump of trees and bushes and even gently probed areas of thick underbrush with their walking sticks, but to no avail.

"We'd better move higher," said Trenton, giving her back a rallying pat.

"It's so upsetting, thinking of Lettie lost and frightened out here," said Serena.

"Oh, I can assure you," Trenton answered, "she knows her way around. The only thing that really bothers me is the weather. I'm afraid we may get a storm."

As if in answer, the wind began to gust and a few white flakes drifted down from the doughy sky.

With renewed vigor, Serena and Trenton searched every nook and cranny at that level and Serena even lifted her hands high and signed Lettie's name, in case she might see it from afar. But the only response was the whistle of the wind, which was becoming more biting by the moment.

"No matter how tough she acts," said Serena, "she's really so small, and she—"

"Wait!" said Trenton, lifting his hand to his mouth.

Serena heard it too, a rustling nearby. Hopefully, she scanned the scene, but no movement disturbed the view. Then—from the corner of her eye—she saw something stir. And again. Breathing a little prayer, she turned as unobtrusively as possible and caught the erratic movement of a clump of bushes, several yards away.

"You go around to the other side, in case she still feels like running," whispered Serena, though she knew the child couldn't hear them.

With as much stealth as possible, they approached the clump of bushes from different directions. Gingerly, with his stick, Trenton brushed the vegetation aside. Unconsciously holding their breaths, Trenton and Serena leaned around the brush…and startled a family of brown and white rabbits.

"I hate to drive them from their beds on such a cold day," said Serena, watching the animals' white cottontails disappear into the drifts of snow.

"Don't worry," said Trenton, squeezing her arm and looking into her eyes in an oddly intimate way. "They'll find shelter. As will we all," he added, almost under his breath.

"But that's what worries me most," said Serena. "I'm afraid Lettie won't be able to find adequate shelter tonight."

"Oh, I wouldn't worry too much," said Trenton. "She's usually quite resourceful. But I don't need to convince you, of all people, of her intelligence."

"No," said Serena, beginning to climb again, "but intelligence doesn't always win against the elements, particularly with a child."

"We'll find her," said Trenton, heading toward a clump of small birch trees, their bleached bark made even whiter by patches of snow. "Or someone else will."

"I wish I had your confidence," said Serena, striking out on her own. Trenton's offhand attitude seemed odd to her, and she felt the need to get away for a few moments, before she started an argument. Trenton was usually so concerned about the children in the community, especially the Trices.

They were nearing the top of the peak and the wind whipped ruthlessly through their inadequate clothing. Snow obscured every surface, a beautiful but treacherous landscape, and flurries of it continued to fall. Even as it began to grow darker, the sky retained the blanched look of a snow sky and the clouds continued to threaten.

Could the child have climbed this high in the time she'd been gone?

"Lettie?" Serena called ineffectually, as she approached a large rock. Was there a shadow on the other side?

Weighted by the thick-soled shoes she had borrowed from Frances and by her long skirts, Serena began to edge her way to the other side of the rocks.

Like the moon in the night sky as you drive toward it, the shadow seemed to move farther back as she approached.

Pulling back the heavy sleeves of her tweed work coat, Serena grabbed off her gloves and reached around the rock to sign Lettie's name and her own with shaking hands.

The shadow didn't waver. Serena let go of the rock and tried again, just as a gust of wind wrapped her cumbersome skirts around her legs.

With a cry, Serena felt herself slipping backward. Reaching for anything, she found herself clinging to nothing more substantial than a small snow-covered scrub bush, which felt dangerously close to pulling out of the ground.

This was no time to hold on to any hard feelings, Serena quickly decided and lifted her voice. Before she got out the second syllable of "Trenton," delivered in a panic-stricken voice, he was above her.

"I'm here," he said in his reassuring voice, wrapping his strong arms around her shoulders.

"Do…you th-think you can lift me from there?" she quavered.

"Of course, I can," he answered. "If it's necessary."

"If it's necessary?" gasped Serena.

"Well, naturally, I'm here if you need me," said Trenton, "and I won't let you go. But…" Serena staring, in amazement, up at him through the bush, could have sworn that he was fighting a grin. "I believe, if you'll just try to put your feet down, you'll find that you can stand—on a slant, of course—and I can help you walk up."

"Walk?"

Serena, who had been clinging for her life to the girth of the bush, had only managed to kick up some showers of ice with her flailing feet. Now, with Trenton holding onto her, she moved her hands farther out on the branches and found that she was able to put her feet through the snow and touch solid ground and that the slant was not nearly as steep as she'd imagined.

"Now let go of the bush," Trenton urged.

Reluctantly, Serena relinquished her hold and realized that she could stand up, with Trenton helping her.

"You needn't look so amused!" she railed, as she came up beside him. "I thought I might fall to my—"

"Never!" said Trenton. "Butler's Peak is not that steep anywhere! Don't you know I'd never have brought you here, if there were any real danger?"

"What do you mean?" asked Serena, incredulously. "We came up here to find Lettie and to make sure that she didn't meet withwith any kind of danger."

"Well, of course," he answered rather sheepishly. "But I wouldn't have brought a woman into real danger. You may call it…chauvinism, but this isn't 2008 and that's the way it is. I wouldn't risk the life of a woman, especially one I…especially you! Besides," he continued, "Lettie usually…" With that, he shrugged and then held out his hand to gesture in the direction of a far-away sound, as if he'd been expecting it.

Serena heard it too, through the gusts of wind and snow, three distinct "rooster" crows from the throat of a boy, probably Nathan Trice. She remembered that the crow had been the sound picked by Nathan, who had been assigned to thoroughly research the grounds around the Longworth's house with one of the Campbell boys. Three repetitions of the call meant that the team had found Lettie and that she was okay. Joyously, Serena turned back to Trenton, whose own smile was a little too knowing.

"As I was saying," he went on, "she usually stays close to home, when she runs away."

"Usually?" asked Serena. "You mean she runs away often?"

"Well, yes," said Trenton reluctantly. "At least two or three times a year. Though, of course, not recently."

"Why didn't you tell me she did it a lot?" asked Serena, wrinkling her brow. "I wouldn't have worried as much."

"Well…I didn't want to raise false hopes," offered Trenton. "Anyway, as I was saying, she would never run far—just wanted to make a point, I think. I always believed it was just her way of expressing her feelings. But now, she probably doesn't need it so much," he went on, in a placating tone, "since you're teaching her to communicate in other ways."

"And she's always been found close to home?" Serena persisted. "So why'd you bring me way up here?"

"Just to be sure," said Trenton. "Besides…Well, you know, it was important to check all possibilities, what with the storm coming up."

As if on cue, the wind set up a ferocious howling, sending a barrage of icy flakes in their faces.

"Visibility is getting really bad," said Trenton, with an odd little quirk to his cheek. "I think we'd better stay up here tonight." Before Serena could even react, he had given the call that told Malcolm that they were all right but had shelter for the night.

"Up here?" asked Serena, belatedly, scanning the dismal, twilit scene.

"At the McNaught's hunting shed?" said Trenton, pointing to thatched roof, which Serena hadn't noticed before, dimly visible through the trees.

"It's always open for just such eventualities."

"Oh, a shed. Well…," said Serena, following him dazedly through the snow.

The "shed" turned out to be a sturdily constructed tidy log cabin with two bedrooms and a rustic but cozy living room. There were logs laid for a fire, beef jerky, and canned fruits in the pantry and even covers on the beds.

Serena shook her head. For months, she had been wishing to be alone with Trenton. Ever since their kiss under the mistletoe, she had wished he would be more ardent. Yet now that the chance had come, she couldn't seem to help feeling manipulated.

"I think McNaught might have a bottle or two of brandy here somewhere," called Trenton, evidently unaware of her feelings. "Eureka!" he cried in a moment, holding up a bottle and two glasses. "Why don't you come over here by the fire and have some of this? You're bound to still be chilled, as well as having had a real scare."

"But I thought you found my scare amusing," said Serena, joining Trenton on the dark plaid couch and facing him with a challenge in her eyes.

"Is...something wrong?" asked Trenton.

"I guess I...uh...well, it all seems so canned," Serena answered, accepting the sturdy brown glass which Trenton supplied with a delicate brush to her fingers.

"So...what?" he frowned at the unfamiliar phrase and moved closer to her, as if intent on the answer.

"Well...you know," said Serena. "A man and woman who're... attracted to each other go off on a supposedly dangerous mission of mercy—which turns out to be basically a wild goose chase—and then suddenly they find themselves stranded by the elements and have to spend the night in a 'shed,' which turns out to be a cozy little well-supplied lair." She took a gulp of the brandy.

"I...thought you wanted...," said Trenton, his face showing real concern.

Serena took another big sip of the warming liquid. This was the man she loved.

Why was she intent on upsetting him? She reached across to brush his forehead, as if to wipe the lines of distress away. His hair sprang crisply against her fingers, yet it felt incredibly soft.

"I'm sorry," she said. "I guess it's nerves. Or maybe I've just seen too much TV. It's just that it seems like the plot of every soap opera or miniseries..."

"And dime novel and penny dreadful and temperance drama and even stereoptican viewer slide," said Trenton. "You don't have to have watched your television to know a cliché when you see one. But the reason clichés develop is that they're based on truths," he continued, moving closer to her. "And..." He went on, taking her empty glass and putting it with his on the table by the sofa, "the truth of this particular cliché is that men and women..." He began to draw little circles on her shoulders with his thumbs, "who care for each other..." He moved aside her heavy collar and began to caress her neck, "want to be together...." He began to kiss her neck. "And sometimes, take advantage of an opportunity to do so. Don't you agree?" he murmured, his kisses now following the path his tender fingers had found.

"I suppose...," Serena began, her lashes fluttering involuntarily. "Oh, of course, I do!" she agreed, giving in to the delicious sensations he was causing.

"I'm so glad," Trenton murmured, capturing her lips.

This kiss was a world away from any kiss they'd shared before. Serena felt herself falling into an endless well of pleasure and desire. She answered Trenton's caresses restlessly, hungry for more. Yet at the same time, she felt comforted, as if she had come home at last.

"Because I've imagined this since the first moment I saw you," Trenton continued, drawing her even closer into his arms.

"From the first?" asked Serena, stroking the tantalizing traces of silver at his temples. "But you acted as if you disapproved of me, and"—she pouted prettily—"you made me miserable because you stayed as far away from me as you could."

"Because I was...afraid of you," he admitted with a wry grin. "Because I didn't know what a wonderful person you actually were and because you were too alluring and so absolutely beautiful and because I sensed this..." He brought his mouth down in an even more devastating kiss.

Serena lost all will to protest, and immersed herself completely in thrilling vibrations.

When Trenton once again pulled back her collar to sear his lips down her neck, Serena could have sworn that they were actually burning her skin. He moved away from her slightly, but only so he could look into her eyes and pull back her neckline even more.

"It's okay," she said, when he hesitated over the buttons. To make her point, she undid the first one herself, and he quickly followed suit with the others. But when he took off the heavy outer jacket, there were still several layers of warm clothing, to say nothing of the chemise and corset cover and the unwieldy corset itself. Serena had never had much experience with seduction and all that she had known had been at a time when only a couple of buttons or zippers, a bit of soft elastic and the plastic hook on a lacey front-closing bra had stood between her and nudity.

All the complicated layers with their myriad of hooks and buttons and lacings suddenly struck Serena as being an insurmountable obstacle, but somehow those layers seemed to melt away, as if by magic. With each layer he removed, Trenton left a trail of kisses, until he slowly began to unhook her corset.

"Oh god, Serena, you're so beautiful!" he breathed, devouring her creamy skin with his eyes. Serena moaned softly, her breasts aching for his touch.

For one more excruciating moment, Trenton made himself hold off, tantalizing Serena. And then with a deep groan, he brought his mouth down on her rosy nipples.

Serena sighed in ecstasy. Being this close to Trenton and hearing his passionate sighs in return was all that she could ever ask for. Soon, however, she began to notice a serious inequity. She was naked to the waist, while Trenton had on every heavy layer he had donned that day, except his overcoat. Serena decided it was time to rectify that situation. She was pleased to discover that men's clothes weren't very different from those of the twenty-first century, and, in very short order, Trenton's top was as bare as hers.

Even the time watching Trenton chop wood hadn't prepared Serena for the sight of his beautifully bare chest. With a breath of awe, she ran her palms over his smooth rippling muscles and let her fingers play through the springy black hair in the center.

Now it was Trenton's turn to gasp at her touch.

"No," he groaned.

Serena drew back, surprised.

"No," he repeated, gripping her arms. "I want you against me."

Serena happily complied and was literally breathless with elation. Nothing else mattered but this moment, this feeling.

When Trenton lifted her into his arms, it felt completely natural. With no apparent effort, he carried her into the bedroom and laid her tenderly on the voluminous feather mattress.

Serena would have pulled him down beside her, but Trenton forestalled her. As she watched, spellbound, he reached for his belt buckle. She knew she shouldn't watch him so boldly, surely a 1909 woman wouldn't, but she couldn't help herself. Trenton was magnificent. Even the throbbing evidence of his desire didn't bring an appropriate maidenly blush.

"Young women have certainly changed in a hundred years," said Trenton, with mock disapproval, but he couldn't keep the grin from breaking onto his face.

Serena's courage didn't extend to taking off her own clothes, however. While watching Trenton, she had worked off her shoes, wool stockings and garters. But she hadn't divested herself of her bloomers. The gathered "drawers," with ruffles at the knee, were not Serena's idea of seductive wear, she would have rather had on lacey bikinis but she still felt too shy to remove them.

But as soon as Trenton lay beside her, his body plastered against her, all reticence fled.

Together, Serena and Trenton got rid of the voluminous bloomers and then felt the wonder of completely bare skin against bare skin.

"Oh god, Serena, my angel! Nothing will ever be the same!" Trenton gasped. "I've never wanted anything as much as I've wanted you against me like this!" But wonderful though the contact was, he soon pulled away to torture her with whispering kisses on her neck and shoulders and breasts. His body was hard against her softness and she had never felt so feminine before.

Trenton's kisses became more demanding and Serena matched him kiss for kiss.

"This is why you came back," he whispered. "This is where you belong."

Serena knew it was true. She knew that her whole life had been a preparation for this moment. Even as she moaned her ecstasy and echoed Trenton's almost agonized cries of need, a part of her felt calm and at peace. This was right.

When they both reached a fervent fever pitch and he plunged deep within her, Serena whispered, "This is where you belong!"

"Yes," cried Trenton. "Forever!"

Serena clutched at his back, drawing him closer still, feeling as if she encompassed the whole world in her grasp.

As the dawn began to break, Serena opened her eyes to gaze at her beloved's sleeping face, so near to hers. She was surprised she had even stirred so soon; after all, she and Trenton had only given in to happy exhaustion an hour or two before. But her lack of sleep did not weigh on her now, as she remembered the evening just past.

Trenton was all she ever could have hoped for as a lover—tender yet passionate, considerate yet demanding, controlled at the same time he was uncontrolled. Still, Serena, who thought of herself as inexperienced, had surprised him once or twice.

When her kisses had trailed down below his waist, ever lower and lower, she thought she heard a gasp that held more than ecstasy.

This must not be something he's used to, she told herself. Even as she felt him writhe against her and heard his profound groans of pleasure, Serena was afraid she had shocked Trenton too much. But his beautiful smile, as he held her later, reassured her that everything was all right.

"It's remarkable." Trenton shook his head, when they were propped up against pillows later. "You truly seem to revel in the... uh...union of man and woman. I really didn't realize that women..."

"Of course, we do," cried Serena. "It's wonderful, if you're with someone you truly care about." She snuggled against Trenton's chest until a thought occurred to her. "But you must have known other women who liked sex," she blurted. "Surely Anne—uh..."

"I suppose Con told you some things," Trenton concluded.

Serena gulped guiltily, for possibly breaking Constance's trust, but Trenton didn't seem upset.

"It's true. Anne did have other men, but I don't believe she actually enjoyed the sex. I think it was just her way of using and controlling men."

"It was just a power trip for her," Serena supplied.

"Yes," Trenton laughed. "That seems like a good term for it. Anyway, she didn't seem very fond of the actual act, and she certainly didn't appear to associate it with love...at least, not with me."

"In that case," said Serena, tenderly brushing his cheek with her fingertips, "whatever else Anne was, she must have been at least a little crazy and completely lacking in taste!"

"Thank you, sweetheart, for the vote of confidence," Trenton drawled playfully, pushing her over onto the mattress once again.

Serena shivered happily. It had been a wonderful night, beyond all her imaginings. Time and again, she and Trenton, sated and spent moments before, had reached for each other again. When they had finally fallen asleep, it had been in each other's arms. Sleep began to overtake her again, but not, she was determined, before she drank in the vision of Trenton in the half-light of the coming dawn, stirring softly in his sleep and moving even further into her heart.

Chapter 12

The next time Serena awoke, the sun was blazing through the crack in the brown sackcloth curtains, and she thought she could smell coffee brewing. Pulling the drapes aside, she drank in one of the most beautiful mornings she had ever seen. The snow formed a smooth, untrammeled blanket across the landscape. Every branch of each tree and bush sparkled with a frosty coating. Crystals glittered like jewels, almost hurting her eyes with their brilliance. The picture was one of complete purity and joy. Remembering the night before and viewing the natural beauty before her, Serena felt as if the morning's sunshine were filling her soul. The happiness bubbled over as she pulled on a few garments and tried to make some order out of her hair.

Of course, it may not stay in order very long, she smiled to herself hopefully, as she headed for the kitchen.

Trenton, who was brewing the coffee, was turned away from her when Serena came into the room. For a moment, she reveled in the straight slim back, the broad shoulders, the slender hips—her Trenton! Then, before he had time to feel her eyes on him, she sneaked up behind him and caught him around the waist. With a happy bark of laughter, Trenton grabbed her hands and pulled her closer. Then, keeping both of her hands in one of his, he turned around to tickle her. As they scuffled and giggled like kids, Serena realized that, even with his sister, she had never seen Trenton seem quite so happy and childlike.

Breathless and giddy, they faced each other, gazing sunnily into each other's eyes. Slowly, the depth of the look changed, 'til it became one of profound longing, and they were clinging to each other, their lips seeking each other's, as if they had not just spent an entire night satisfying each other's every desire.

Finally, Trenton pulled away and smiled ruefully into her eyes. "I'm afraid we'd better stop," he said," before we…uh…"

"End up back in bed?" Serena asked with a wicked little smile.

"Yes," said Trenton, raising his brows. "Exactly. And we do need to start making our way back down pretty soon. It cleared up outside and we really shouldn't keep people wondering too long. Besides," he added, "my bunkhouse coffee's getting cold."

"That's true," laughed Serena. "Even on this rare and wonderful day, some laws of nature still apply."

"I guess so," smiled Trenton, handing Serena a coffee cup and making sure to touch her fingers with his. "But you're right, it is a very rare and wonderful day—very nearly magical, in fact."

Serena's coffee cup jerked slightly on the way to her mouth, spilling a few drops.

"Is something wrong?" asked Trenton, with quick concern.

"Oh… uh… no," said Serena, blinking and showing him a wide smile. "The coffee cup was just a little hotter than I expected." She blew on the dark liquid for emphasis and took a tentative swallow. "But it tastes delicious," she added.

It was true. Serena wasn't normally a coffee drinker, generally asking for tea instead, but today, the sweet pungent brew tasted wonderful. Even the beef jerky and preserved peaches they rustled together were delicious. The storm was over, it was a beautiful day, and she was sitting across the breakfast table from her gorgeous beaming lover. Everything was as it should be, she assured herself.

"In about a week, we'll announce our engagement, have Malcolm try to get the notice to the Belle Vieux Courier through his boys, and maybe soon we can have a little party to celebrate—maybe on Valentine's Day."

Serena's lips parted in surprise. "En-gagement?" she asked softly.

"Oh god," said Trenton. "How stupid of me." He immediately dropped his spoon and took Serena's hand in both of his. "I haven't even officially asked you yet!" He looked straight into her eyes, a tender smile playing about his lips. "Serena, I love you very much. You mean more to me than anything else in my life. Will you please do me the glorious honor of becoming my wife?"

"Of course," said Serena. "Someday. Someday soon. But to announce it in a week? Don't we need time to adjust to our new relationship first—before changing it again?"

"Someday?" Trenton exclaimed. "But, darling, we've just spent the night alone in a cabin! We've essentially declared ourselves to the world. Why should we wait, when we both feel…?"

"Oh, I see," said Serena, hating herself for saying it, but being unable to stop herself. "It's all because we spent the night here and everyone knows it!"

"No, of course not!" said Trenton, his eyes dark with hurt. "You know I'd never marry just to please the neighborhood! But as long as we want to anyway… That is," he added in a moment. "I thought that was what we both wanted."

Serena looked at the man she loved. More than anything, she wanted to throw herself in his arms, accept his proposal, and live happily ever after. But she felt she couldn't agree to marry a man who felt honor bound to uphold her reputation. Also, something else was worrying her, though, if pressed, she couldn't have said exactly what it was.

"Of course, it's what I want," she answered, touching his arm across the table. "But…." She swallowed with difficulty. "But I just think we should…wait a while. Can't we just enjoy being together for a few weeks?"

"Just…?" asked Trenton in exasperation. "Serena," he began again, with a noticeable effort to be calm. "I know you say that many people indulge in what you call 'casual sex' in 2008, but you've told us you didn't agree with that. You said that you didn't feel you should be involved in that way unless you had serious feelings for someone. Is it wrong to think that last night was important to you? I love you and you did say you loved me—last night, anyway."

"Of course, I love you, more than anything in the world," Serena tried to assure him, coming around the table toward him. "All I want is to someday be your wife. I just thought we could savor the romance for a little while, before we start worrying about the wedding."

"But why would our being engaged keep us from savoring the romance?" asked Trenton, furrowing his brow. "Sweetheart, we're not in the twenty-first century. I'm just thinking about how this will affect you in the community. And the school…"

"The school and your precious reputation!" Serena cried. "I should have known that was all you were thinking of!"

"And I should have known you didn't really care about the school as you claimed to," answered Trenton sadly. "And maybe not even about me. Is it just a game for you too? Are you really just like…"

"Just like Anne, you were going to say, weren't you? Anne, who you called manipulative, selfish, and deceitful, among other choice things! Well, thanks a lot! I'm really glad I've gotten to know you so intimately. So let me give you my conclusions on your character, Trenton Longworth. You're a self-righteous prig!"

Trenton rose stiffly from the table. "Well, if that's your assessment of me, I don't suppose you'll be too surprised if I'm concerned that we've been up here too long. I believe it's time that you and I clean our romantic hideaway"—he sneered—"and try to make our way down the hill. I'm sure even you would agree that we should no longer impose on the McNaughts' unknowing hospitality."

Serena only nodded, the pain too choking for her to speak.

Getting dressed to go out was an even more embarrassing experience than getting undressed had been.

Though they had been joyously naked together the night before, Trenton and Serena were no longer comfortable with so much intimacy. Serena tried to don the underwear she had left off earlier, underneath her coat, thrown cape-like over her shoulders for privacy, and Trenton even turned his back to her when he unfastened his fly to tuck in his shirt.

The corset was, once again, Serena's worst problem. She wished she hadn't worn the wretched contraption on this physically active trek. She had considered leaving it off, but had decided to wear it for warmth, and now, again, she had to contend with it. She had to put it on, Serena decided. She surely couldn't leave it, as guilty evidence, in the McNaught's cabin, or chuck it in a bush on the way down, or arrive at the Longworths' with it tucked under her arm. The decision made, Serena put the offending garment, with its ties very loosely strung, over her head and somehow got it under the coat. Then she had the lacings to deal with. Adjusting the ribbons by herself was usually an interminable process (even without a coat over it) and Serena generally ended up asking Constance or one of the maids for help. But with no woman to help, she squeezed and tugged, trying to look over her shoulder, with the coat hanging down in her way and nearly choking her with its weight.

Finally, in frustration, Serena tore the coat off, but her nervous fingers still fumbled over the job. She didn't know Trenton was watching her 'til he made an exasperated sound in the back of his throat and charged over to her.

"We don't have all day," he growled prosaically. He gave the strings a couple of tugs and tied them in a tight knot at the bottom. The corset still wasn't adjusted evenly and she'd probably have to cut the string because of the knot, but Serena knew that at least the thing wouldn't fall off. So deciding that would have to do, she quickly donned the rest of her clothes.

Once dressed, Serena rushed to make up the bed and then went in to clean up the kitchen. She insisted on going by the stoop to wash the dishes at the pump, though Trenton angrily complained that the cold water would badly chap her hands. "I won't have you complaining that I've mistreated you," he muttered savagely, chafing her fingers ruthlessly.

"I'm fine," Serena ground through clenched teeth.

"Good," answered Trenton, in the same vain. "Then we can finish straightening up here, so we can get out!"

It was with a heavy heart that Serena preceded Trenton through the door of the cabin a few moments later. This place had been the site of the happiest moments of her life, but now it was all spoiled. She wished she could get the joy back, wished she could reach out to Trenton, but somehow, she couldn't.

Trenton pulled the door closed with a slam that echoed through the hilltops, and they began to work their way down.

The trip down was considerably faster than the one to the top the day before. It wasn't necessary to stop and search behind every tree and rock and the wind and snow were not assailing them as they had the day before. Fear and dread about Lettie were not weighing Serena down, but new feelings hounded her just as painfully. She stole furtive glances at Trenton, but he remained tight-lipped and distant. Knowing the situation was at least half her fault and that it was probably within her power to correct things did not make Serena feel better; it racked her with indecision and guilt.

Everything around her seemed to make Serena feel uncomfortable. The dazzle of the sun on the snow, which had looked so beautiful to her through the window that morning, reverberated painfully into her eyes. The ill-adjusted corset joggled and sagged under her breast at the same time it bit painfully into her buttocks. The downward momentum, coupled with the slippery snow made the descent very treacherous, and several times, Serena felt herself falling. And when Trenton reached out to help her, his expression grim, Serena felt even guiltier.

Finally, the roofs of the school came into view. Serena sighed and darted her eyes toward Trenton. He caught her look and returned it sadly, but then he squared his shoulders and turned directly toward her.

"Serena," he said quietly. "This is foolish. I love you and I truly believe you love me. Please, let's not argue. Please, sweetheart, say you'll marry me."

Serena sighed sadly. "Oh, Trenton, of course, I love you, more than I could ever say, and it makes me miserable to fight with you. But I can't say I'll marry you yet. Please, can't we just agree to wait a while?" she begged.

Trenton shook his head in confusion. "I'm sorry we can't seem to understand each other," he mourned. He shrugged resignedly. "I suppose we might as well be on our way." He turned from Serena once again and began to move quickly toward the Longworths' grounds.

Serena watched him, unable to fight off the feelings of desolation. She wished she could call after him. She wished she could tell him that she'd forget her apprehensions and marry him right away.

But she couldn't. She had to be sure that there wasn't any obligation in his offer and that he wasn't asking just to save her reputation or the school's. Besides, there was something else on Serena's mind, which she couldn't deny.

When Trenton had called the night before "magical," he had triggered the impressions that had been skittering around at the back of Serena's mind for the past month, and as they had slogged down the hill, the total memory had burst on her full-blown.

When she was thirteen years old and of a very romantic frame of mind, Serena had discovered a miniature book on a visit with her parents to a used bookstore. It was an anthology on love, featuring quotations from famous people, and Serena had been so enthralled with it that her parents had to nearly drag her away from the shop. It was only when they'd returned to the hotel that Serena learned that her mother had sneaked back and bought the little volume for her.

Ecstatic, Serena had spent the evening holed up with her book, reading the tantalizing quotations, some of which she shared with her parents.

Then she had come across the quote from Trenton Longworth.

"My Tabby," he'd said. "Is not only the love of my life, she's the most important part of my existence. Our meeting was magical and absolutely awe-inspiring. Just the fact that we were able to find each other makes me happy every day. She made me believe in life again and nearly all I've accomplished, I owe to our remarkable union."

Serena had rushed into her parents' bedroom, shaking the book in front of her, with tears already starting in her eyes. She couldn't believe that her parent's dear friend and benefactor, the icon for whom she was named had been betrayed. Serena had imagined an idyllic love between her namesake and Trenton Longworth, and suddenly it appeared that he had actually given his heart to another. And to a woman with a ridiculous name like Tabby! Even her parents had seemed incensed at first, but they had tried to soothe Serena and perhaps themselves, with adult logic.

"Tabby's probably just short for Tabitha. Trenton Longworth was a widower when he met Serena," they'd said. "Maybe his first wife was named Tabitha."

"Or maybe Tabitha was Serena Longworth's middle name. I don't think she ever told us her full name."

Their arguments eventually eased Serena's adolescent angst and she finally forgot about Trenton's eloquent, if treacherous statement, until it burst full force and word for word on her as she followed him down the snowy hill. Now, however, she knew the arguments didn't hold. Trenton's first wife had been Anne, and Serena's middle name was Elise, not Tabitha. So unless she wasn't to be Serena Longworth after all, she concluded, Trenton would betray her after she became his wife. Someday, he would meet a woman named Tabitha, to whom he would give his true devotion.

Chapter 13

Yesterdays/Deal

Serena looked out the parlor window at the remains of the snow. Gray slush patched the lawn and shrubs between the Longworth and Trice homes and a sickly sun liquefied the remaining mounds at the same time that it sent its rays toward Serena's weakened eyes.

It was only to be expected that her eyes would be weak, she decided. *Crying every day'll do that for you*, she thought, with a bitter laugh.

It was true. In the week since she and Trenton had returned from Butler's Peak, Serena had succumbed to tears at least once each day. She had tried to tell herself that she could go back to life as it had been before that night and just be grateful for the unique experiences of her life. Traveling in time should have been enough for anyone, she decided. But the pep talks weren't working very well.

Serena had met many wonderful people in this new time; people to whom she was closer than to anyone she'd ever known, except her parents. Yet without that one person, she had to admit she couldn't fully enjoy the other relationships.

And naturally, Trenton was keeping his distance, going back, once again, to being polite and cold, just like the scene before her.

Serena nodded at the melting forlorn-looking snowman in the yard. She could definitely see Trenton's point of view, she whispered toward the chilly sculpture.

Trenton, after all, was a man of 1909, and no matter how much she had told him about the values and mores of the twenty-first century, he couldn't be expected to take all of those ideas as his own.

He couldn't understand how Serena could have made love to him without being ready to marry him, and the fact that she had, made him think of Anne, who had played at love to get what she wanted and used sex as a weapon.

Trenton was an honorable man, from an era in which honor was highly prized. He would never have taken her to the cabin, where he knew they would make love, unless he already knew he loved her enough to marry her. He hadn't just proposed because she was "compromised."

Serena had loved him too and wanted to live her life with him. She didn't know why she had reacted the way she had when Trenton had taken for granted that they would marry. She decided she would have been willing to run to him and overcome his defenses and say she'd become his bride anytime he wanted her to, if it weren't for…

Tabitha.

She had asked Constance about her.

"Does Trenton know a woman named…uh…Tabitha?"

"Tabitha? No, not that I know of."

"Has he ever known anyone named that? Like an old girlfriend or something? Maybe in college?" she added hopefully.

"I don't think so. Why?"

"Nothing. I…uh…just thought I heard about someone by that name. Never mind."

"Tabitha," Constance mulled over the word. "It's a rather old-fashioned name, isn't it?"

"It's a witch's name," Serena had answered, with more force than she'd meant to.

Constance had looked at her strangely.

Not that it was unusual for Serena to receive strange looks these days. Ever since she and Trenton had returned from the cabin, the atmosphere around her had seemed strained. Neighbors, some of the household staff, even people she considered friends had given her odd, expectant looks, and, when whatever they were looking for—probably a marriage announcement—had not been forthcoming, many had turned away from her.

On the morning after their return, Serena had heard whispering and giggling on the landing when she was coming around the corner, but when they saw Serena start down the stairs, the whisperers immediately clammed up and commenced with very ostentatious dusting.

When she and Constance had managed to make it through the snow, down to Frye's General Store, Mrs. Frye was characteristically outspoken.

"So when can we be expecting an announcement, Miss Cassidy?" she called archly across the store.

"I don't know what you mean," Serena answered, knowing that a deep blush was spreading to the roots of her hair.

Mrs. Frye gave a snort of laughter. "Well, from what I've heard, tootsie," she said with her hands on her hips, "if you don't know what I mean, it's time you were finding out."

"Don't pay any attention to her," consoled Constance, as they were leaving. "You know how she is. You can't expect someone like her to understand... Not that I do completely."

"Con, I wish I could tell you everything," Serena answered sadly. "I wish I could...make Trenton understand too, but I—"

"Serena," Constance cut in decisively, "I don't know exactly what happened up there on the peak, but I do know that, no matter how he's acting now, Trenton really loves you, Serena, more than he ever thought about loving Anne, even at first. And I know you care about him too."

"Of course, I do," said Serena. "I wish I could explain it to both of you, but right now, I just can't. But believe me, if I could think of any way to avoid hurting Trenton—and myself—I'd jump at it!"

"I know," said Constance. "But don't worry. You'll find an answer."

Serena wished she could be that confident. But no matter how hard she tried, she couldn't resolve her feelings about the "Tabitha" quote. It seemed silly to damn Trenton now for something he would evidently do, or at least feel, in the future, but she couldn't give herself completely, being sure that someday that gift would be bested.

So she would continue to have to face the hurt in Trenton's eyes and offer no explanation. What could she say? "You did something in the future, and I can't forgive you?" Even if he could actually accept her time travel, how could he possibly accept that?

And since she couldn't tell him the truth, there was nothing to say to anyone. She had begun to avoid Trenton as much as possible, just as he avoided her.

"I simply must accept the fact that that night was just a diversion for you," Trenton had told her, after they had been back for a couple of days. "I'm afraid you were just 'playing games,' as you say."

"No," Serena protested, so relieved that he was finally speaking to her. "It's not like that at all. But I just can't think of any way to explain it to you. Please, try to trust me, until I can come up with a solution."

Trenton had shrugged resignedly. "I will try, Serena, but please don't expect me to act as if nothing has happened." With that, he'd retreated again to his study, where he'd been almost constantly since their return.

That was where he was right now, she knew, hiding out in his study, so he wouldn't have to face her. But at least he didn't appear too furious and contemptuous like he was for the first day or two. It seemed he had decided they couldn't live on a battlefield. So he no longer seemed to be in a rage. Not that sad and hurt and withdrawn were much better.

Serena looked back at the pitiful snowman and laughed bitterly. He was the only man of any kind she had any chance of being close to these days. And he wouldn't be any colder than Trenton, or even Malcolm or even—for that matter—the college boys, who, on their return after the holidays had apparently sensed the tension in the Longworth household and were steering clear of her too. Even Morty Shine hadn't come up with any jokes for her.

She wondered if the students had heard rumors. She was sure the neighbors and household staff were all speculating and gossiping about her and about poor Mr. Trenton too.

Of the household staff, only Frances and Malcolm managed to keep the smirks off their faces when addressing her, and even they gave her perplexed glances and kept their distance when possible.

Serena kept her distance too, not knowing how to improve their opinions of her.

Even the Trices had changed toward her. At first, they had all rejoiced together that Lettie had been found so quickly, her having evidently doubled back to the Longworths' smokehouse after it had been checked initially. But then, the atmosphere had changed. They assured her they still wanted her to continue the lessons with Lettie, who appeared no worse for wear due to her adventure on New Years' Day, but there were subtle differences in Serena's visits. Mr. Trice, always a busy man, whom she had seldom seen before, was simply never there during her visits. The differences in Mrs. Trice were even harder to point her finger on. Before "the incident," as Serena bitterly dubbed it to herself, she and Alice Trice seemed on the way to being real friends, confiding secrets or sharing jokes on almost every visit. Now they seemed to be merely acquaintances again, polite, even cordial, but in no way intimate. But at least the Trices still wanted her for lessons. She had to have something to keep her mind occupied.

"And I thought I was a stranger in a strange land before!" she told the snowman, who, just like many others, studiously ignored her.

The only thing to do, Serena had decided, was to simply ignore the changes she encountered and, as much as possible, to go on with her life as usual.

At least Trenton continued to be civil, even as he continued to stay away. Serena supposed she would have to be content with that until she could find some way to resolve the "Tabitha" situation. But it was one of the hardest things she had ever done. She continued to completely adore Trenton, and it was wrenching not to even be able to explain herself to him. She missed his touch and his care. Her arms ached to hold him, to pull him to her, to comfort and love.

Love. Her heart ached; her whole body ached for him in ways she wished she could forget. Night after night, she lay looking at the beautiful, crocheted canopy and remembering that night in the cabin. And from his bleary looks and the embarrassed way he avoided her eyes on some mornings, Serena thought Trenton was remembering it too.

But longing was just another thing she'd have to learn to live with, Serena knew, in the long days that stretched ahead.

Trying her best to stick to that decision, Serena threw herself into as many activities as she could. She helped Constance organize the housecleaning after the decorations were taken down and even polished all the mirrors herself. She'd always been fascinated by mirrors and loved to shine their surfaces, but now it wasn't easy to face her own reflection. And if there was anyone who didn't need to go "through the looking glass," Serena knew she was the one.

Spurred by their Christmas projects, Constance and Serena decided to work together on more needlework and began to design the patterns for table and breakfront runners, featuring grapes in various shades of wines, purples, golds, and greens. As usual, the girls worked wonderfully together and were bubbling with ideas about future projects.

It amazed Serena that she could enjoy anything so much while the pain about Trenton still hovered in the back of her mind. Still, the creativity was one of her greatest respites. Serena remembered Grace Pierson's mentioning that she and Constance were to start an embroidery pattern business, and she imagined this was the beginning of it. But how could she go along with this part of her future with Trenton's sister, when she couldn't accept the part that involved the man himself?

When she wasn't involved with "womanly pursuits," Serena threw herself, with renewed zeal, into teaching. Since Trenton was no longer consulting her on the college programs, her only outlet for this newfound enthusiasm was her lessons with Lettie.

They had come to a point where Serena felt she should do more than just teach the child to spell and identify objects. She began to try to convey concepts or emotions. But visually representing something like "love," especially with her own feelings so mixed up at the moment, seemed beyond Serena. After spellings and demonstrations, it appeared that Lettie thought that l-o-v-e stood for "hug," which was one of the main ways Serena had chosen to explain the word. Realizing that she hadn't taught Lettie any simple verbs, and that the child seemed able to pick up these meanings more easily, Serena decided to pursue this simpler course of study for the time being and deal with the lessons on emotions later.

So somehow, life went on. At times, Serena thought the time would never pass, but pass it did. More than a month went by with Serena facing virtual isolation and Trenton sad and withdrawn.

Serena wished desperately that they could establish at least a friendship once again and often she felt that he wished the same thing, but they couldn't seem to dispel the awkwardness between them.

And, as the end of the school year neared, another problem began to plague Serena. How would she contribute to the household without her duties around the college? Though she no longer taught there, she performed myriad small duties and errands around the campus, and these would soon end for the summer. Serena knew that the Longworths would never allow her to do something like putting on a uniform and plying a dust mop in the back parlor, but especially with the present uneasy atmosphere, the meager amount she still earned from the Trices seemed an insufficient offering.

Finally, she arrived at a solution she thought should have been obvious all along.

One March afternoon, Serena approached Trenton in his office, her heart beating double time.

"I've…been wondering how I might…uh…earn my keep, what with the students leaving soon."

"That's not necessary," Trenton snapped. "You are…my sister's dear friend and, as such, a member of the household for as long as… you both wish it. Also, you give us what you earn from the Trices."

"That's just not enough," Serena insisted. "But I think I may have solved the problem. As you know, I used to do advertising," she hurried on, when Trenton seemed about to interrupt her. "So I've been working on some ads and ideas that might make the school a little better known."

"You must know—uh—Serena, that we at Longworth College don't wish to engage in the sort of…er…'hype' you say is prevalent in the twenty-first century." Trenton was definitely in what Serena thought of as his "stuffshirt mode," but since she realized he acted that way mostly when he was nervous or hurt, Serena tried to ignore it.

"If you'll just look at what I've come up with..." Serena placed an ad layout with copy and a short press release on the desk in front of him. "This ad is what we called 'camera ready' in 2008. I don't know if it conforms to the specs of these days, but I can find out..."

"Besides the fact that I'm not sure what you're talking about," Trenton began stiffly. "I just don't think that... Well...uh...this is actually quite good, subdued and yet rather compelling."

"Yes, that's what I was trying for," said Serena. "I'm aware that you don't want some jumped-up jive and Day-Glo campaign." She couldn't resist sticking in some twenty-first century lingo, just to nettle him, though it probably wasn't the best strategy. "But, if you keep it low-key, I don't see why you couldn't run ads with scholarly publications without losing your dignity. And the article is about when the Adams boy won the science award. If we sent out this sort of publicity occasionally, it would—"

"Yes," Trenton interrupted. "It might do... If we needed it," he added. "Our enrollment is up to our dorm capacity now, so—"

"I've thought of that," said Serena quickly. "You could double up the freshmen in bunk beds for a year or two 'til a new dorm could be built."

"Possibly," said Trenton.

"And then, with the extra revenue, you could begin to work on the girls' facilities."

"Let's not get ahead of ourselves," said Trenton, trying to hide a little smile. "But, uh, I'll consider your ideas and, uh, thank you for your concern about the school."

"Oh, I'll always be concerned for...the school and for...everyone here," said Serena.

They stared at each other across the empty space.

"Trenton," Serena began, "I wish..."

For just a moment, Trenton lifted a hand tentatively toward her and Serena thought he might bridge the gap between them. Then, his hand moved into a gesture of frustration and his mouth twisted into a callous line.

"Yes, well, so do I," he sighed bitterly. Then, he turned his back on her and drew a book from the case.

Serena assumed the interview was over. It wasn't all she had wished it would be, but she had to admit that Trenton had been generous, under the circumstances. Possibly, the meeting might have helped to allay some of the strain between them. All she could do, she decided, was hope.

When the weather began to turn and a hint of new buds showed on the trees, Serena felt her mood lightening a little.

Serena had always loved winter and was sorry to see the season end without a conclusion to her problems. Despite the past winter's negative connotations, Serena enjoyed the snow and there was very little here to turn the white to the familiar dingy gray of city snow in 2008. Still, there was something about the coming of spring that somehow made her feel more optimistic about Trenton. Maybe her memory wasn't as dependable as it usually was. Maybe she'd misinterpreted what Trenton had said about this Tabitha.

As the last patches of snow disappeared and her blood began to warm, Serena decided that it was possible that she could find a way to deal with the "Tabby" question, even if her memory had been correct.

CHAPTER 14

On a golden afternoon in early April, Serena tossed aside her embroidery with a restless motion. Constance was away with Randy on a day trip to the Natural Bridge and the handiwork just didn't seem as inspiring without her.

"Spring has sprung—or just about," murmured Serena, responding to that indefinable stir in the atmosphere that heralds a new season. "Change is in the air. High time for a change too," she added decisively as she opened the sewing room door.

The windows all over the house were thrown open to the touch of warmth in the air, and Serena caught the sounds of birds chirping and children playing from outside, but inside, it was unusually quiet.

The night before had been another largely sleepless one. Serena considered a nap, but rejected it. Today she felt a heavy-lidded languor, rather than the unpleasant exhaustion those nights often left her with.

Descending the staircase, Serena ran her hand along the cool walnut rail, savoring its smooth curves.

Then, just as she reached the vivid colors of the Tiffany windows on the landing, Serena spotted Trenton coming through the front door. She sighed, ready for him to turn away from her and dart back to his office. But instead he looked up with a tentative smile and moved toward the stairway, removing his gray serge jacket as he came. Underneath, he wore a crisp white shirt, its boiled collar and cuffs neatly fastened, and a navy-and-gray striped tie.

"Well, hello," he said pleasantly, his brows rising slightly.

"Oh, uh, h-hi," said Serena, moving down a step and backing up it again. "I-I was just looking for, um, Frances."

"Were you?" he asked. "I was looking for you."

"Really?"

"Was it important, what you needed Frances for?"

"Oh, no…I was just going to ask her about…about a recipe…for—"

"That's good," he interrupted, with a smile. "Because I let all the staff off for the rest of the day. For Spring Fair, you know."

"Oh, that's right," murmured Serena. She and Constance had attended the event the night before and had unsuccessfully tried to convince Trenton to go with them. "That's why classes are out early too."

"Yes. The boys are gone too. Frances left out what she called a cold collation for our dinner," he added. "Sandwich meats and such, I guess. I hope that's all right."

"Of course. But you…said you were looking for me?"

"What?"

"Were you…looking for me?"

"Oh, yes. I, uh, thought we should have a talk. If you don't mind."

"A talk?" She blinked, then began slowly down the stairs again. "Of…of course, if you want."

"Good. Why don't we…" He motioned toward the back parlor.

Following uncertainly, Serena watched the snowy shirt play across Trenton's back and shoulders.

Smiling again, Trenton motioned toward the settee then sat down beside her, facing her, only a few inches away.

"Things simply can't go on as they have," he blurted.

Serena noticed his eyes were as red as hers must have been, and his face showed signs of fatigue.

"With us, you mean," she forced out between stiff lips.

"Yes," he sighed. "Serena, I have no appetite. I rarely sleep. My work is suffering. And I think it's pretty much the same for you."

"Yes."

"Well, we simply can't go on being so distant, yet living so close, making each other miserable."

"Do you…do you want me to leave?"

"No!" he nearly shouted. "N-not unless you want to, of course."

"Then do you have a solution?"

"Yes. Or at least a compromise." He cleared his throat. "This morning, I looked out at this glorious day and wished I could share it. Suddenly, I wondered why I was being—as you once called me—such a prig. Why should I expect you to follow 1909 mores when you're used to those of 2009? It may not be exactly what I wish," he went on purposefully, "but it's certainly better than our being apart! If you still feel the same way, I want us to be together, even if you still think you can't marry me."

Serena looked into eyes so dark with need they were nearly onyx. If Trenton were willing to make such a compromise and make himself so vulnerable by breaking the silence between them, surely she could put aside her feelings about "Tabitha," at least enough for them to be together? As long as she didn't have to make a lifelong commitment, perhaps she could just deal with the issue when it came up.

"Yes," she said. "It's what I want—more than anything."

"God," Trenton groaned, spanning the distance between them and pulling her to him with a single stroke. "Thank God! I love you so much, Serena. I've needed you so much!" He blistered her neck with scalding kisses.

"I love you too, Trenton." She sighed happily, running her hands along that perfect back. "I've always loved you. I never stopped, even for one moment, in all this miserable time!"

"Neither have I, not even for a second," Trenton assured her, lifting her into his lap. "And I know I never will!"

Serena furrowed her brow, afraid that Trenton wouldn't be able to keep the promise he made so determinedly. But he was concentrating on her neck and didn't see the look of doubt, so she tried to push away her qualms for the moment. And in no time, Trenton's kisses made her forget everything except the feel and smell and taste of him. She had dreamed of this and wished for it for so long and had thought that she would never have it again. Yet here she was in his arms. At last! Trenton! Serena turned so she could snuggle closer to his wonderful chest and gave a happy sigh, deep in her throat.

Trenton murmured appreciatively. "You curl up like a little kitten. I think I'll have to call you 'Tabby.'"

"You think…what?" gasped Serena.

"Well…that I'll call you 'Tabby,' because right now you're like a cuddly kitten," Trenton answered with a quizzical frown. "Do you mind?"

Covering her face, Serena burst into convulsive laughter.

Trenton gave her a half smile, unsure whether to be amused or offended.

"What's so hilarious? Something I said? Because I called you 'Tabby'?"

"Yes…no!" said Serena. Her laughter was fading now and her eyes showed traces of tears. "It's just, when I think of all the pain and the stupid waste of time, just because…" But if she told him, he might never say those wonderful things about her or, if he did, it might be as a result of prompting. "It's nothing," she assured him. "Just a misunderstanding. I'll tell you all about it…someday. For now, please just forgive the terrible way I've treated you. Oh, and if you still want me to, I'll marry you."

"You'll…?" Trenton sputtered. "Well, of course, I want you to. Didn't I just ask you five minutes ago?"

"No," said Serena, slanting him a wicked little smile. "You mentioned marriage, but you didn't actually propose."

"Well, Milady," he answered, with mock seriousness, "if you require it, I'll gladly beg for your hand on bended knee. Of course, you'll have to give up your place on my lap first."

"Oh no," giggled Serena, snuggling closer. "Not that! So I suppose I should go ahead and accept your gracious invitation. I'll marry you anytime, anywhere. Just don't make me move right now."

"I thought that was all I had to say." Trenton laughed. "I know my Tabby."

Serena gave the buttons on Trenton's crisp white shirt a wry smile as she buried her head against his chest. It was a silly nickname and probably not one she would have picked to have a permanent place in their romantic repertoire. But she wouldn't let Trenton know how she felt, because she knew he would use the endearment over and over, because it had marked such a momentous change in their lives, and because he thought it brought her pleasure. And Serena knew she would someday learn to love the name for the same reasons.

Trenton's fingers made little ripples along her back, filling her with contentment, and Serena thought she'd be satisfied to stay just like this for the rest of her life. But contentment was not an emotion she'd feel for long.

At first, when Trenton began to stroke her hair, Serena laughed and purred like a kitten. Then, as his movements became more sensual, she was amazed to discover how truly erotic it could be to have him dart his fingers around her hairline. The kittenish purrs became moans deep in her throat.

Trenton's groans echoed Serena's, sending a delicious chill through her veins. Forgetting contentment, Serena pulled herself up to feel the length of Trenton's torso against her and presented her mouth to him.

When his tongue darted across her lips, Serena gave a startled little gasp and answered in kind. Their tongues playing an intimate game of hide-and-seek, they somehow ended up prone on the stiff little curve-seated settee, Trenton's full weight a marvel on top of her. Even through all her petticoats, Serena could feel his need.

She wasn't really aware of how the tiny buttons on the bodice of her high-necked dress had come open, she only knew his lips and his tongue at the edge of her corset cover were driving her to desperation.

She could only helplessly repeat, "My angel, my angel," over and over again.

Trenton gave a low chuckle. "Much as I appreciate the sentiment, I'm feeling decidedly unangelic at the moment. Rather wicked, in fact!"

"In-in that case," ventured Serena, "would I be really depraved if I suggest that we spend the afternoon in an even more wicked way?"

"That's a wonderful idea," said Trenton, immediately straightening up and pulling her with him. "After all, we are alone."

"That's right," Serena realized. "Everyone's gone from the house, probably for several hours. Even from the school. It almost seems… Trenton, did you plan it this way?"

"Well, somewhat," he answered, with a mock guilty look. "I had hoped we would have something to celebrate. Though I didn't realize it would be so momentous, due to whatever it was I said." He took both her hands in his and had begun to draw her up from the settee, when he stopped and looked at her quizzically.

"Serena, that, uh, thing you did at the cabin? When you…" A dull scarlet stained Trenton's cheeks and worked toward his hairline. In all his moods and reactions, Serena had never before seen him blush.

"Yes?" said Serena. "I, uh, think I know what you mean. Was there something wrong?" Well, after all, all those manuals in the twenty-first century said you should discuss this sort of thing.

"Well, it's just that…I'm not completely inexperienced—even before my marriage—but in all my experiences, I've never—"

"I knew it!" Serena blurted out. "The romance writers make it seem like it was all the rage, even back in caveman days, but I didn't believe it!"

"I…don't think so," said Trenton, still red-faced.

"Well, it's almost run-of-the-mill in 2008. For some people, it's just about like shaking hands." By now, Serena was blushing even more vividly than Trenton. "Oh, not to me, of course! I think it's only for people in love. It's very intimate."

"Very intimate!" Trenton agreed.

"Are…are you saying you don't want me to do it?" asked Serena.

"No!" Trenton nearly shouted. "No," he amended, more mildly. "It's just that it seemed so…so…" Trenton paused. "Well, is there… uh…some way I might reciprocate?"

"Well, yes, there are…uh…things you could." Serena bit her lip. "I might be able to teach you, if you'd like."

"And I thought my education was complete!" Trenton chuckled. He pulled her up from the settee and wrapped his arm around her. "Come on, my Tabby, let's hurry to my first lesson!"

But they didn't actually hurry. They stopped several times on the stairs to kiss and caress and undo a few more buttons.

Then, on the landing, Trenton pulled Serena up short for a moment. "It wasn't really about something I said, was it? It's what I will say someday, right?" he asked, with startling insight.

"Exactly," said Serena. "And someday, we'll laugh about it, but only—"

"After I've said it?"

Serena nodded.

"Okay," he agreed. "As long as it doesn't keep us apart."

"Don't worry," Serena answered emphatically. "I've learned from this time not to ever let that sort of thing—or anything else, if I can help it—keep us apart again."

"That's definitely worth a celebration," grinned Trenton, grabbing her again.

Their celebrating lasted all afternoon and well into the night. They clung together in joy and relief, reveling in each other's touch and vowing to spend all their tomorrows, in whatever era they found themselves, in each other's arms.

As Serena had expected, Trenton proved to be an apt and eager pupil and even taught her a few things along the way.

With the strain of the past weeks behind them, both were finally able to sleep peacefully, so several times, they napped, curled up together, only to wake and make love again. They were still together, in Trenton's big mahogany-framed bed, when sounds of the household's return reverberated through the walls. Luckily, no one came looking for them.

The house had grown quiet again, when Trenton and Serena suddenly realized they were starving and sneaked, stifling giggles, downstairs for a snack. Frances had put away her "cold collation," but Trenton and Serena raided the pantry and feasted on ham and apple slices and ZuZu Wafers and kisses. Like lovers through the ages, they fed each other tidbits and drank the most sustenance from each other's eyes.

Chapter 15

June 15, 1909 was an absolutely beautiful day. The air was warm but temperate with a light breeze and fluffy white clouds dotting a blue sky. The lawns at the Longworths' and Trices's homes and at the college were lush, deep green, and immaculately manicured. Roses and rhododendron bloomed in the garden and dandelions, buttercups, Queen Anne's Lace, and red and white clover dotted the hillside. All thought of the winter's snows and the sadness that had accompanied them had passed.

It was the day before Serena's wedding to Trenton Longworth.

All through the house, there was fervent activity, since the ceremony was to take place in the front parlor.

The parlor furniture and the front stair banister glowed with an extra coat of lemony wax. In the kitchen, Frances and Neva were beginning to work on the four-tiered wedding cake. Stacks of chairs brought over from the college waited on the side porch to be decorated and arranged for the guests.

Soon, Randy McNaught was due to arrive with the flowers not available in the Longworth's gardens, which he had volunteered to deliver, with special ice-packed boxes from the florist in Belle Vieux.

But Randy's arrival would bring on another wedding tradition, for as soon as he completed the group, Trenton's bachelor party would begin.

Even Malcolm had agreed to join Trenton's "last stand" and was contributing some of his own special beer. Not that it would be the kind of raunchy party they threw in the twenty-first century, Serena thought. There were no strippers or tacky videos available in the 1909 Virginia foothills. Though she trusted Trenton, even in a situation like that, Serena was glad that that particular rite of passage wasn't the style in her current era.

Serena wouldn't be having a typical "bachelorette" party, either. Instead, she, Constance, Frances, and Alice Trice and a few others had planned to get together to finish work on the bows and flowers for tomorrow. They might have a glass of wine or two, and Serena was sure there would be a few sly comments at her expense, but nothing outlandish, like policemen barging in and turning out to be strippers, was likely to happen.

She and Trenton didn't need last celebrations of freedom, Serena mused; they felt most free when they were together.

It wasn't as if there hadn't been enough parties, either. Ever since Trenton and Serena had announced their engagement, they had been the center of a veritable social whirlwind, which seemed to have taken over the entire community. Evidently, all you must do to be accepted and to have everything forgiven in this time was to agree to become an "honest woman." In any case, there had been a barrage of fetes, quilting bees, coffee klatches, showers, and even a pig pickin' in their honor. And suddenly, instead of shunning Serena, everyone had been anxious to help with their plans. Frances and Neva had been invaluable. Malcolm and his relay of Dun boys had hustled constantly to deliver messages and supplies. The Trices had ordered everything available in wedding supplies and trinkets. Trenton and Serena had received a mountain of gifts from the sublime to the ridiculous, but often the ridiculous were more appreciated, because they had been handmade by servants or by one of the poorer residents of the community.

Instead of studiously ignoring Serena, the college boys had showered them both with silly attentions. Before their departure for the summer, the entire student body had serenaded the happy couple with "Daisy, Daisy" and "I Love You Truly." Morty Shine and his cohorts had offered some "rude" jokes (which would have been considered tame in 2009) and had presented Trenton and Serena with a huge banner (made with purloined sheets) with "Best Wishes" and the fiancées initials emblazoned across it in silver paint.

The banner was hanging over the doorway now, a cherished, if somewhat amateurish addition to the upcoming day.

It would actually be upon them soon, Serena mused. There had been times when she had thought the months would never pass.

But actually, the time had virtually flown by in a harried, delirious haze. Trenton and Serena had decided, on the night they became engaged, to marry as soon as possible after the boys left school, so that they would have the entire summer to honeymoon and to adjust to being married. So they had known that they had a short time in which to plan and arrange their wedding.

There had been so many things to do, and it wasn't as easy to arrange things in 1909, as it would have been in the twenty-first century, especially in the foothills of the Virginia mountains.

There were no fashion warehouses on the highway with thousands of ready-made wedding dresses to choose from. There wasn't even a highway. But there was a wonderful dressmaker—modiste, she called herself—who was rumored to have apprenticed with the legendary House of Worth in Paris, and, as soon as the roads were negotiable for Mergatroid and the carriage, Serena and Constance had rushed to her shop with sketches for the wedding gown.

Mille Mireux not only agreed to fashion the dress, but she was also so impressed with the girls' designs (including Serena's insistence on "shockingly" sheer sleeves and shadow panel from bustline to neck) that she asked if she could include the pictures in her sample book.

The dress had turned out just as Serena had hoped it would. Its basic style was that of the early nineteen-hundreds wedding dress, with a bell-shaped skirt, leg-o'-mutton sleeves and a tiny waistline, nipped in by dozens of tucks on the bodice. Handmade lace trimmed the neckline, sleeves, and hemline, and hundreds of seed pearls had been sewn all over the dress and veil. The dress was hanging in the sewing room, carefully covered, so that it would be a complete surprise for Trenton at the wedding.

Besides her wedding gown, Mille Mireux had helped with Serena's trousseau. Serena had insisted that she didn't need trousseau, what with all the clothes she had from Cousin Violet, but Constance had argued that Serena needed her own clothes to start out her new life, and Trenton had backed his sister up. Though Violet's bequest seemed to Serena to be more than adequate for the next year or two, the idea of having some clothes of her own design did appeal to her. Besides, since Cousin Violet was expected at the wedding, it would be nice, she agreed, to at least have her own outfit to "go away" in.

But one thing Serena had not asked the dressmaker to make for her was her lingerie. She was too shy to describe what she wanted, but she was determined to have it.

So Serena and Constance searched all the shops in Belle Vieux and even ventured as far as Charlottesville, but to no avail.

There were beautiful corsets, corset covers, petticoats, garters, and even embroidered hosiery, but nothing Serena wanted to purchase for "sleep" wear (in which she had no intention of actually sleeping). Serena bought a few lacy silk or lawn nightgowns for when company was in the house or Trenton was away, but the voluminous garments, with high necks and long sleeves did not fill the bill.

"Maybe you could find what you want in New York or Paris," offered Constance, who had only a vague idea of it herself, "but I doubt that you'll find it anywhere else."

"Actually, I'm afraid I'll have to wait fifty years to find it anywhere," Serena lamented.

Finally, Serena decided to make the lingerie herself. She purchased silk and lace, chiffon and ribbon, and even a few feathers, and, with Constance's blushing help, made herself "unmentionables" of every color and description.

"You know, it might not be so bad to have something like this for the, uh, right fellow," said Constance wistfully, holding up a red chiffon baby-doll outfit.

"Definitely," answered Serena with a giggle. She couldn't wait to see Trenton's reaction to her inventions. In fact, she was so anxious she could barely stand it.

On the night they became engaged, Serena and Trenton had reveled in being together and had enjoyed each other to the fullest. However, on that night they had come to another agreement.

"This will be our last time like this until our wedding night," they had told each other.

Because of servants and neighbors, but especially for the reputation of the school, Serena and Trenton had decided not to make love again until they were married. Serena had been just as resigned to the idea as Trenton was. One simply could not live comfortably by twenty-first century mores in 1909.

"Besides," said Serena. "It'll give us something to really look forward to after the wedding."

"As if beginning our lives officially together weren't enough." Trenton grinned.

So they had sealed the pact with a kiss, and they had stuck to it ever since.

Not that it had been easy. On several late nights in the parlor, and once even on a blackberry-picking trip up Butler's Peak, they had considered going back on their promise, but in the end, self-control had prevailed.

But enough of denial and discipline, Serena had thought as she had watched Constance lovingly wrap tissue around a lavender teddy and halter top, trimmed with ribbon forget-me-nots. In a little less than twenty-four hours, she would be free to regale Trenton with all these creations, among other things.

One of her outfits, she hadn't even shared with Constance. She'd constructed it from scraps of a gray-striped silk dress of Constance's. It was completed by combs with pointed ears attached and even a long, cotton-stuffed tail. There was also a red ribbon collar, with "Tabby" embroidered on it. The whole thing was already wrapped in several layers of tissue paper and hidden in the bottom of her suitcase. It was a silly getup, but she knew Trenton would get a kick out of it.

Serena's reverie was suddenly shattered by the sounds of dogs barking and the guttural eruption of an "Ah-oo-ga" horn. Followed by Constance, she rushed down the stairs and flung open the front door, just as Randy was bringing his big red roadster to a stop, with Lady and Cahoudalin chasing close behind.

"The flowers!" Serena and Constance chorused together, overlooking Randy in their enthusiasm.

"I hope they haven't wilted," said Serena, running toward the loaded back seat of the open car.

The surrounding gardens and grounds were aglow with blossoms; in the midst of all the activity, Serena had even insisted that her parents' special rhododendron bush (where they would eventually share their first kiss) be planted, but the cool mountain climate wasn't conducive to the gardenias, orchids, and exotic lilies Randy had with him. The florist had had them shipped to Belle Vieux from exotic climes in a refrigerated train car.

"I got here as fast as I could, Miss Serena," Randy drawled apologetically.

"Oh, of course, you did," said Serena. "And, by the way, good afternoon, Randy."

"Yes, hello, Randy," echoed Constance, reaching for the metal florist boxes.

"Here, Miss Constance. Don't strain yourself," said Randy. "That ice makes 'em heavy. And the florist said to keep the boxes level, so the flowers wouldn't bruise. Let Malcolm and me do it." He nodded toward the butler, who had quietly appeared behind them.

Malcolm commandeered the Trice boys to carry the large, beautifully wrapped gift box, which Randy said was from him and his parents, and the two oddly-shaped, awkwardly-wrapped additional presents.

"Just a couple of extras I thought y'all might like," said Randy. Serena was sure the "extras" were more of the "whatnot" shelves Randy was so fond of.

"What's all that?" Serena exclaimed, noticing the bottles, which were revealed on the floorboard when the other things had been taken out.

"That's my contribution to Trenton's party tonight. That one," said Randy, pointing to a tall fluted bottle. "Is a special liqueur my father brought back from Italy. The others." He indicated several large brown bottles. "Are good ol' Kentucky bourbon, the prime drink of every self-respecting Southern boy! Since I don't have to go back tonight," he added. "I intend to see that all the boys have a real good time!"

It had been arranged that Randy would stay in one of the guest rooms, when the bachelor party was over and then would drive Trenton and Serena to the train after the wedding the next day.

"Well. Don't you guys have too good a time," admonished Serena, following along as the bottles were carried into the house. "Remember, we don't want anyone sick for the wedding."

"Oh, no, Ma'am," Randy answered her.

At five o'clock, the ladies began to arrive, and, from the sounds from the staff dining room downstairs, they knew that Trenton's party was gearing up too.

The upstairs group included Serena and Constance, Frances and Neva, who had contributed so much to the coming day, Alice Trice, Katja Karsten, who, with her husband, had stayed on after the school closed so that she could sing at the wedding, and Lavinia Frye, who had eventually brought herself to apologize, in her brusque way, for her comments at the store.

"I just didn't want you to suffer, because of the way people would treat you," she had rationalized. "When I moved here from the north, I learned I had to change my ways, and evidently the ways in California are different too."

"I guess so," Serena had answered with arched brows.

But it was all behind them now, and all the women greeted each other with smiles and hugs. Downstairs, the men were shouting their greetings and laughing with uproarious determination.

As Serena led the women to the back parlor, the eighth member of their group broke free from her mother's hand and darted up to grab Serena. Lettie had been allowed to join the party for a few moments.

Serena held up her hand in a gesture that Lettie understood as "wait," but instead of calming down, Lettie clasped Serena's hand and turned it around.

"She just can't get enough of that ring," said Alice, as Lettie gazed into the center of the stone in Serena's engagement ring.

"Well, who can blame her," said Lavinia. "It's a stunner!"

Since Trenton had ordered the ring from Tiffany's, Serena's lessons with Lettie had been hindered by the child's fascination with the stone. It was a large oval sapphire surrounded by diamonds, and Lettie was enthralled with the world she saw within its depths.

"Maybe a glass of lemonade will distract her," said Serena, turning the stone to the back of her hand as she poured.

Lettie shrugged, obviously aware that Serena wouldn't restore the ring to its proper position for the moment, and took the lemonade. However, after a second glass, she jumped up again and began gesticulating to her mother.

"She wants to show you her wedding present," said Alice.

"But she already helped you make the napkins," said Serena.

"This is something just from her," said Mrs. Trice. She nodded to Lettie.

The child stood in the middle of the group, smoothed down her skirts and—with a proud smile—spelled out the word "love," and then immediately gave Serena a big hug.

"I worked with her for a long time, and I truly believe she knows what it means now," said Alice. "She'll do it for anyone in the family, but when we asked her to do it for a chair and other inanimate objects, she just laughed."

"You have my admiration," said Serena. "You've taught her something I had no idea how to convey to her."

"Well, that's only because you worked with me so much and I sat in on all those lessons," Alice answered. "And since you've shown us how to talk to each other, I enjoy spending that time with her so much more. Besides, I don't think you're going to have as much time to work with her from now on," she added saucily. "You might have little ones of your own soon."

"But by then, I'll bet this smart girl will be accepted by the Gallaudet School." Serena chucked Lettie under the chin.

By the time Lettie had had some sugar cookies, two lady fingers, and another glass of lemonade and had hugged everyone in the room, it was time for the Trices's maid to take her home and for the ladies to get to some adult conversation.

"I decided if the men were going to have fun, we should too," said Serena, pulling a bucket holding two bottles of iced wine, from its hiding place behind a sofa.

Downstairs, the men were singing a riotous version of "For He's a Jolly Good Fellow."

"Of course, if you'd rather continue to have lemonade, that's fine," she added. But everyone was quick to accept a wine glass. "Or you can have both. I could even teach you to make coolers."

Their chairs and settees pulled in a circle, the women settled down to sip wine coolers (which were a big hit) and tie bows and make paper orange blossoms and forget-me-nots.

Downstairs, the men erupted into occasional bout of raucous laughter.

"Vere vill you be going for your vedding trip?" asked Katja Karsten, as she accepted a second cooler.

"Well, we're taking the train to Richmond tomorrow," Serena answered. "And then in a couple of days, we'll go on to the Plaza, in New York, for almost three weeks. I can't wait to see the Plaza. It's still new now and really in its heyday." Constance flashed her a warning blink. "I mean, I know it's a couple of years old," Serena hurried on, "but I hear it hasn't lost any of its luster."

Honestly, she'd have to be careful what she said when she was drinking wine!

She hadn't made a slip like that in quite a while. However, no one seemed to notice. The women simply nodded their heads and continued to sip their coolers.

"Oh, I'll say!" said Lavinia Frye. "Some of my friends who still live up there've seen the place and said it was slap up to the mark! 'Course they didn't get to stay there just, kinda looked around."

"I'd like to go on another honeymoon," said Neva with a wicked little smile. The young widow had changed into a light blue eyelet which somehow made her look sultry. "My last one was pretty nice. Of course, we didn't go anyplace like the Plaza, but still." She raised her eyebrows.

"It would be lovely to go anywhere on a honeymoon, as long as you were with the man you loved," said Constance with her usual wistfulness on the subject.

Everyone nodded and smiled and took another sip of their coolers.

By ten thirty, when Serena's party began to break up, they had opened a third bottle of wine and had dispensed with the lemonade, but had nevertheless finished all the flowers and bows; Serena had received all sorts of marital advice and admonitions, and the married women in the group had regaled everyone with the most touching and funniest memories from their marriages. Many of the stories had begun with, "I can't believe I'm telling you this!" and there was lots of giggling and a few tears.

During these hours, the men had sung at the tops of their voices, shouted, laughed, and beaten loudly on the walls or tables. There was even one time when Serena could have sworn they were doing flamenco dances on those tables.

But, as the ladies hugged Serena good night and offered wishes for a beautiful wedding day, the men had grown strangely quiet. (Perhaps, even ominously so?) Were they all passed out on the floor?

At Serena's and Constance's urging, Frances checked downstairs in the party room, but came back shaking her head.

"There's no one down there. I guess they must be seeing each other home."

"I hope so," said Serena fervently. She climbed the stairs to her room with a heavy heart. Surely Trenton wouldn't get himself hurt or in any kind of trouble. Tomorrow would be the most important day of their lives and Serena hated to think that anything might mar it.

Distractedly, she pulled the combs from her hair in semi-darkness and started to work on the tiny buttons down her back before she caught sight of her bridal veil hanging on the door of her wardrobe. She and Constance had just completed sewing the pearls on it that morning. She decided that another look at it might help cheer her up.

She turned up the gas in her flowered table lamp and was fluffing the veil through her fingers when she heard a strange sound from outside.

Was it music? Serena hurried to her window.

All the men from the party were lined up on the lawn below her. Randy was determinedly strumming on a banjo, while Olef Karsten pumped on an ancient but colorful balalaika accordion. When they caught sight of her, all of them swept her deep, theatrical bows, and then burst into song.

Serena smiled, relief mixing with amusement. Even Trenton and Malcolm didn't sound as musical as usual and the others could make no claim to be singers. Still, it was the thought that counted, and she continued to smile and laugh during several minutes of impromptu concert. But when they launched into a mournful "After the Ball," for the second time, the Mmes. Frye, Karsten, and Trice appeared and convinced their men it was time to go, and Serena could hear Constance, Neva, and Frances calling the others from the porch. They were ignored, however, as the men huddled in a conference.

Finally, after much laughter and gesticulation, they broke apart, and Trenton sketched her another dramatic, if slightly unbalanced, bow.

"A solo for my lady," he intoned.

Randy jangled the banjo strings a couple of times, and then Trenton launched into "I Love You Truly," a song that was still new in 1909.

Unlike in his attempts at the other songs, Trenton put his whole soul into this rendition, and his voice resonated beautifully. Malcolm and even Randy, who joined in on some choruses, also managed to sound musical this time.

Serena had heard the song many times as a child at weddings and thought it rather heavy and artificial, but tonight, with Trenton singing it to her from his heart, it struck her as completely wonderful. By the time they sang the last line, with Trenton's voice soaring and Malcolm finding a cavernously low "dear" at the end, Serena had to wipe tears from her eyes.

From her perch high above, Serena repeated the last line, "For I love you truly, truly dear."

Trenton joined with her, their voices blending perfectly, just as she believed their lives would. Then Trenton tried to bow and blow a kiss at the same time and nearly fell on his face.

It was then that Serena called down theatrically, "Thank you, my wonderful troubadours. Never have I heard a more moving concert, but now, I think we should all be winding our ways toward bed."

"Well, in that case," Trenton called, with a grin. He brushed his hands together, as if in preparation for something. Then, he headed toward the side of the house, below Serena.

Serena gasped as she realized what Trenton was about to do. One of the ivy trellises attached to the house ran up directly beside Serena's window.

"No!" Serena shouted.

But despite her protests, Trenton grabbed unto the slats. Like a hero from a 1950s TV comedy, he slipped after a couple of steps and fell on his rear in the grass, pulling several vines of ivy down with him.

Serena shrieked and would have bolted toward the stairs and the outside had Trenton not looked up with a grin and started to brush himself off. Malcolm and Randy laughingly helped him up, while Frances, Neva, and Constance rushed from the porch to fawn over him.

Then, despite the protests of Serena and the other women, Trenton started for the trellis again. This time, though Serena thought her heart would stop before he did, he made it all the way to the rungs beside her window. Serena reached out and helped him over the sill. He might have had a few scrapes and bruises, and his white dress shirt and the ivy trellis would probably never be quite the same again, but Trenton was essentially none the worse for his climb.

"Hello, bride," he greeted her, with a slight lisp. Then, without another word, pulled her into a passionate kiss, to the vociferous delight of the crowd in the yard below. Trenton pulled down the shade and kissed her again. When the group cheered at their shadows on the shade, Trenton moved Serena out of range, to the wall beside the bed.

The spectators below booed and laughed.

"Just think," Serena sighed, when they briefly came up for air. "Tomorrow at this time, we'll be married, and it'll be perfectly acceptable for us to be alone in a bedroom together, anytime we want to."

Trenton grinned and traced the curve of her cheek with his finger. "Is that your subtle way of telling me we're not free to do anything we want to tonight?"

Serena turned and kissed his finger. "Maybe it is," she said regretfully. "We decided to wait so that our wedding night would be really special, and we just have one more night to go."

"Well," said Trenton, finding the partially unbuttoned back of her dress and continuing the process. "Tonight could be really special."

"With everyone downstairs knowing you're here?" Serena laughed, playing with his open shirt collar. "I thought we had to consider the reputation of the school."

"Well," said Trenton again, giving her a boyish grimace. "School is out." He began to kiss her neck. "Those people downstairs are our friends and relatives. Surely," he blew softly in her ear and along her neck. "They won't say anything."

"Oh, okay," said Serena, surrendering to his embrace. After all, what was one night, more or less? She was still a little leery of how 1909 society would react to this obvious lapse, and she wasn't comfortable with the tacit audience downstairs. Still, she loved this man more than she had ever thought possible, and what he was doing was sending chills through every pore. She moved her hands to his marvelous muscled rear and pulled him closer to her. His kiss was even more heated than the others, his tongue probing. His need was palpable and hers answered it. She heard herself moan.

Then the flower-enameled porcelain clock on her dresser chimed the three-quarter hour.

"We can't," she cried.

Pulling away only slightly, Trenton gave her a befuddled frown.

"It's almost midnight, which means it'll be our wedding day, and we absolutely can't see each other 'til I walk down the aisle. Oh, I know it's just a superstition," she hurried on, in the face of his blank stare, "but you can't expect a woman who traveled in time to be completely rational. I'll take any kind of help I can get, even magical."

Trenton shrugged. "Okay. I guess you're right." He kissed her one more time. "I didn't really expect you to go along with it, anyway," he admitted, with a devilish grin. "But you know," he went on, with only a slight slur. "You're beginning to think like a 1909 woman, and, at the moment, it's damned inconvenient."

"And you're beginning to think more like a 2009 man," said Serena, moving with Trenton toward the door. "And, at the moment, it's…damned tempting!"

Trenton made a comical move, as if to come back into the room, but Serena laughingly put up her hands to stop him. "No, no. Down, boy! Keep that thought 'til tomorrow."

"Oh, all right!" He stuck his lip out in mock childishness. "But I want you to know, I intend to thoroughly make up for this tomorrow night!"

"I'll hold you to that," Serena sighed intensely.

Trenton lifted his brows wickedly. "My sweet, Tabby, you may certainly hold me to anything you wish to. In fact, I can barely wait."

"It's less than twenty-four hours now." Serena smiled. "But it's less than fifteen minutes 'til our wedding day, and…"

"Yes, my lady," said Trenton, sketching her another deep bow. "Since you insist, I'll go—for now." With that, he turned from the doorway and began to move down the hall.

Serena watched with a grin as Trenton swayed his way down the passageway. He even managed to jump up a few inches and kick his heels together a couple of times without much threat to the tables stationed by the bedroom doors.

CHAPTER 16

IF possible, Serena's wedding day was even more beautiful than the one before. Everything would have been perfect had Serena not awoken with the fear that her groom might not feel up to attending the ceremony.

It seemed that even in 1909, a bachelor's rites of passage could cause havoc. Serena had seen those candid video shows in the twenty-first century where someone passed out or threw up at the altar because of too much partying the night before the wedding, and she had visions of that sort of thing happening today.

Not that she begrudged Trenton's having had a good time. He certainly had a right to some male bonding. Besides, she loved Trenton's silly side, and he didn't get to show it that often because of keeping up the serious image of the school.

Still, she hated to see the wedding day and night they had both planned for and looked forward to marred by last night's hijinks. Actually, Serena knew that, if it were humanly possible, Trenton wouldn't miss any of today's activities, but the idea of his dragging himself down the aisle, fighting off waves of nausea at the reception, and struggling manfully to "do his duty" on their wedding night did not cheer Serena very much.

As she watched the Trice children racing around the yard, trying to catch Lady and Cahudalin and adorn them with lacy white wedding bows, Serena thought of Trenton's falling on that same grass the night before. She wanted to make sure he was all right. Why was she insisting on not seeing her groom on the day of the wedding?

Yet as she had told Trenton the night before, a woman who had traveled in time was not prone to flaunting superstitions.

So feeling completely frustrated, Serena paced in front of her window, as she had so many times since coming here, until a knock on the door announced Constance, who breezed in carrying a huge tray of breakfast delicacies.

"Good morning, bride," she chirped cheerfully. "Frances insists you eat every bit of this, to give you strength for the day."

Serena dutifully sat down beside her little boudoir table, with the tray overlapping on both its sides, but she couldn't imagine actually eating.

"Is…Trenton…," she faltered, unable to contain her worries.

"He's fine," Constance insisted.

Serena gave her a doubtful look.

"Well, perhaps a little under the weather," Constance conceded. "But not too bad. Frances is taking charge of him now, making him eat all this too, and drink lots of coffee."

Serena managed a tentative smile.

"You must know," Constance added, "that he'd never let himself indulge enough to ruin anything for your day. He was just getting into the spirit of things last night. Some of the other fellows, I'm not sure about, but… Anyway, he says to tell you he does love you truly, and he's looking forward to the festivities with great anticipation."

Serena's smile became radiant. "Tell him I feel exactly the same!"

"It was a rather eventful night," Constance began, with an odd look crossing her face. "Oh well, I'd better go see that your bath is being run. You eat and relax and enjoy yourself. This is your day!"

With much of the weight off her mind, Serena found that she could eat, after all, and even savor most of the enormous breakfast.

Soon after that, Constance arrived to ceremoniously escort her to her bath. The huge oval tub, with its bronze-covered claw feet, had been filled almost to the rim with warm water, to which had been added some of Frances's "soothing and invigorating" bath salts. There were even rose petals floating on the water's surface and tucked between the folds of the fluffy towels laid out on the chair.

"Left over from Lettie's basket," Constance explained. "And by the way," she added at the doorway, "we put the ivy that Trenton tore down last night in the bouquets and garlands. I don't know why we didn't think of it before. It means 'loyalty,' you know."

The bath was wonderful, but when she had luxuriated in it for as long as possible, Serena returned to the isolation of her room and nothing to do.

She tried resting, with her feet higher than her head, but she was too restless to stay still for long. She buffed her nails 'til they were pink and glowing. She watched the Trice children's attempts to tie the bows around the dogs' necks. Before long, she had returned to pacing.

Serena knew that the last of the decorating was being completed downstairs, and she wished she could go down and help, but if she did, she would be certain to run into Trenton before the wedding. Besides, everyone would probably chase her upstairs because she wasn't supposed to have to work on "her day." If only "her day" included something to occupy her mind and her jangled nerves!

In the twenty-first century, Serena knew that brides often had too much to do on their wedding days. Calling photographers, florists, and caterers, to make sure they were coming as scheduled. Having their hair and nails and make-up done at some elite beauty salon. Meeting the planes of relatives who had had to wait 'til the last day to take off from their jobs. However, in the well-oiled mechanisms of the Longworth household, with its virtually irreplaceable servants, most chores were handled for her by others. After some initial guilt, she had come to appreciate this, but not today!

Serena decided to try reading her novel for a while. It was considered very risqué for this era, and Constance had found it enthralling, but today, Serena wasn't able to lose herself in it.

For the second time that day, she opened the enameled heart-shaped box that held Trenton's wedding gift to her, a pair of diamond-encircled sapphire earrings. They were a perfect match for her engagement ring and would be stunning with her Alice-blue "going away suit." (She had given Trenton a new pocket watch, with an inscription about their spanning time together.) Enclosed with the earrings had been a poem from Trenton comparing their blue to her eyes, and staring into their depths often entranced her almost as much as it did Lettie. But today, they wouldn't work their magic.

For the third time that day, Serena compared the lists of necessities for the honeymoon trip to the contents of her trunks and Gladstone bags. Everything was packed and ready.

For perhaps the tenth time, Serena admired her wedding dress and veil. She buffed her nails again and checked the edges for nicks that might catch on her wedding ensemble. She watched the Trice children retie the dog's bows again. She returned to pacing.

Finally, when she thought she could stand it no longer, Constance and two of the maids arrived to help her with her hair and dress.

Constance, Serena's only attendant besides Lettie, was already dressed in the vivid pink that was her most becoming hue, and her hair was puffed and curled elaborately and adorned with pink nasturtiums. She was all smiles, yet Serena sensed that there was something Constance wasn't telling her.

"Is it Trenton?" Serena asked when Clara Lou was across the room heating the curling iron at the lamp.

"Oh no!" Constance answered sincerely. "He's hale and hearty! Frances insisted on dosing all the guys with her special hangover concoction, even sent some of it down to the Frye's," she added, pronouncing the new slang word "hangover" with a little laugh. "And she wanted me to tell you," she whispered, with a giggle and a glance toward Clara Lou, "that she added a little something to Trenton's that you'll be glad of on your wedding night."

Serena thought, in a flush of heat, of her nights with Trenton. "My god, if Trenton were any more potent," she laughed softly, "or passionate than he already is, I don't know if I could…uh, but that's neither here nor there," she amended as she caught a sidelong glance at Constance's rosy blush. "I still want to know what's bothering you."

"Nothing's bothering me," Constance insisted. "I just need to tell you something about me—in a minute," she added, as Clara Lou approached with the curling iron.

But it wasn't until they were standing at the top of the stairs, waiting to march down for the ceremony that Constance told her.

"This morning, I told Randy I'd marry him," she abruptly confided.

"You…? But you're in love with Malcolm," said Serena, with sudden assurance.

"You're right," Constance acknowledged, giving her mouth a wry twist. "But I can never be with him. You and Trennie aren't the only ones who got together after the parties last night. I'd had just enough wine to accost Malcolm. I actually got up the nerve to tell him I love him, but I think he already knew it. I might not have gotten him to acknowledge it if he hadn't been drinking too. But he said it would never work out."

"But I think he loves you too, Connie," Serena insisted. "I think maybe that's why he avoids you sometimes. He's afraid he'll show it."

"You're right. He told me so too," Constance amazed her by saying. "He said he'd always love me, but that we're from two different worlds, and that I couldn't marry a man who'd been a servant in my house."

"He's more than a servant," Serena insisted. "He's invaluable, not only to the household, but to the school. I'm sure Trenton would be willing to change his job, probably just his title really, to some kind of college administrator position, and then it'd be all right. If he needed a little more schooling, he could get it, but he's educated himself so well, and he's so good at so many things that—"

"No, Reenie," Constance resignedly interrupted Serena's babbling. "Thanks for trying, but Malcolm would never agree to it. I tried to convince him last night we could work it out some way, but his mind is made up. Being from the Old Country, he's much more class-conscious than we are. Besides, he says he's too old for me. So this morning, I told Randy 'yes,'" she concluded.

"Oh, but Con—"

"I'm twenty-six years old, Reen," said Constance. "I want a home of my own and children. And Randy is a good man. He knows I don't care as much as he does, but he wants me anyway. And he'll take good care of me. And…and Malcolm is thinking of courting Neva."

"Neva! But—"

"No, it's all right," Constance assured her. "I know now it's for the best. Malcolm and I had our moment. I-I even convinced him to kiss me, and that will have to sustain me forever. This is the way it has to be. If Malcolm and I had met in another time and place, then maybe…"

Suddenly, as clearly as if she were speaking in her ear, Serena heard her mother say, about first stepping into the house, "It was like I'd come home."

"Con," she said, "do you believe in reincarnation?"

"Reincarnation?" said Constance. "Oh, why not? You convinced us that time travel was possible, might as well do it with reincarnation too. Why?"

"Good," answered Serena. "Because I think you and Malcolm might be my parents in another life."

"You mean, he and I might come back to this house as other people?" asked Constance, remembering Serena's account of her parents, "and meet and fall in love and marry?"

"And spend more than thirty years together," supplied Serena.

"That idea sustains me even more," said Constance huskily. "Oh, if only it's so. Even if we won't really remember this life, I know somehow we'll be aware of it. But Rena, what makes you think we're your parents?"

Serena told her what her mother had said. "And because you and Malcolm are so much like them in so many ways," answered Serena. "And because, from the first day I met you, I felt a kind of special connection with you I've never felt with anyone else but my mother."

"And I can think of no one I'd be more proud to have for a daughter than you." Constance said, her eyes swimming with tears.

Serena felt her own eyes moistening. "If we're not careful, our mascara will run."

"And then people will know we're wearing it," said Constance, with a soggy conspiratorial giggle.

Serena and Constance squared their shoulders and sighed collectively. Below them, Katja Karsten was just completing "Because," another old standard that sounded somewhat exotic in a 1909 setting, with her Norwegian accent.

All the parlor doors had been flung open, so that the back and front rooms were joined, and all the guests would have a view of Serena and Constance on the stairs. And through the screen of flowers at the top of the flight, Serena could see nearly everyone she had met since coming to this time, all decked out in their best. Many of Malcolm's Dun boys, all the household staff and their families, and just about every resident of the surrounding countryside were in attendance. There were several groups from Belle Vieux and there were friends and dignitaries from Charlottesville, Richmond, and even as far away as Washington, DC.

Thelma Privette's new baby slept in her lap, while her daughter was already showing signs of her own pregnancy. True to his plan, Malcolm was seated beside Neva, who was resplendent in yellow eyelet, though Serena couldn't help thinking it made her olive complexion a bit sallow. Frances was sporting a huge flower-decked hat. Estey Wooten, in bright turquoise, seemed to have recovered from her disappointment over Trenton and was making eyes at the Frye's oldest boy, home on leave from the Navy.

Serena noted an expectant shifting in the group, and then the pianist began Wagner's "Wedding March."

From a doorway to the side, Trenton and Lawrence Trice, in striped pants and tailed morning coats, approached the fern-and-flower-decked "altar" at the front of the parlors. Serena grinned in relief. Trenton looked breathtakingly handsome. The glossy black of the tuxedo jacket echoed the waves of his hair and deepened his sparkling pewter eyes. And not only did he appear to be over his hangover, but, as he peered up to the top of the stairway, Trenton glowed with joy and vitality. Except for the gray at his temples, he was the image of the happy exuberant twenty-two-year-old with the world at his feet that Serena had seen in the photograph on the twenty-first century tour of the house.

With a last squeeze of Serena's hand, Constance set off down the stairs.

"One day maybe my daughter," she whispered. "But in just a few moments, definitely my sister."

Serena watched as Constance came into the view of the guests, at the top of the stairs. Randy was beaming at her. Malcolm also turned around, but in just a moment, pulled his gaze away and smiled, instead, at Neva.

As Constance reached the ground floor, Alice Trice brought a very excited Lettie out on the landing and started her down. Dressed in a sky-blue frock, styled in a child's version of Constance's dress, the little girl looked angelic and almost acted that way. She performed the job of sprinkling petals in Serena's path with importance, only stopping once or twice to spell out love and hug one of the wedding guests.

At last, the pianist executed a dramatic roll on the keys and then began to play "The Wedding March" at a much slower and more regal pace, and it was Serena's turn to descend the stairs. She looked through the flowers at her wonderful husband-to-be, whom she had traveled over ten decades to meet. She looked down at her fragrant bouquet, with trails of Trenton's ivy making a graceful addition. Loyalty. Yes, loyalty forever. She moved onto the top step.

As Serena came into view and began to descend, Trenton's smile became even brighter, seeming to emanate from his whole body, and Serena thought she saw the sparkle of tears in his eyes. She knew that her own face reflected those same emotions, and that she and Trenton would share all their smiles and tears for many lifetimes to come. This was indeed her destiny.

Without a falter, Serena made it to the bottom of the stairs and marched into the parlor toward her groom. She knew she was moving not only into her own future and her children's, but also into her parents' future and, again, into her own.

Serena stepped happily forward and took Trenton's hand.

Epilogue

After finally getting a very restive and excited Lettie Trice-Jensen to sleep for the night, Martha Whitter had returned to the Longworth College hundred-tenth-year celebration. Now, she twitched impatiently while the hostess exchanged parting pleasantries with some of the other guests.

"Have you seen Serena Cassidy recently?" she asked as soon as she got a chance. "I've looked all over, but I can't find her anywhere."

"I think she must have gone back into town early with the Ingersols," said Grace Pierson. "She wasn't feeling too well, you know. But she's quite a popular young lady tonight," Miss Pierson added. "Even Senator Marshall was looking for her. Seemed really upset that Miss Cassidy had already gone back before she had a chance to talk with her."

"Well, I know how she feels," railed Martha. "There's somethin' she's just gotta see before she leaves town tomorrow." From her side, she hefted an old photo album, with her index finger marking a place between the pages. "Look at this! You won't believe it!"

The picture she pointed out was taken on the side porch of Longworth mansion. It depicted a happy group of adults and children, seated in wicker furniture and comically brandishing palm fans and banjos.

"This was taken in 1916," said Martha. "It says it's Serena and Trenton Longworth and their children and his sister Constance and her family. No wonder Mother got so upset! Look at that picture of Serena Longworth! She looks just like little Miss Cassidy. Even that broach Miss Rena's wearing looks like it could be the same one that poor lonely child found the other day, in that antique store down in Belle Vieux! Land's sakes! Miss Pierson, they could be the same person, 'cept I wish that girl could look half as happy as Serena Longworth evidently was!"

From the picture, Serena's smile was luminous.

SOURCES

Books used for research, though not directly quoted in *All Our Yesterdays*.

Bagby Harrison, Helen. *The Bagbys of Brazil*. Broadman Press, 1954.
Batterberry, David. *Fashion: The Mirror of History*. Greenwich House, 1982.
Chester, Ellen. *Woman of Valor: Margaret Sanger and the Birth Control Movement in America*. Simon and Schuster, 1992/2007.
Crouch, Barry A. and Van Cleve, John Vickrey. *A Place of Their Own: Creating the Deaf Community in America*. Gallaudet University Press, March, 1989.
Curtayne, Alice. *Twenty Tales of Irish Saints*. Sophia Institute Press, 2004.
Erbsen, Wayne. *Manners & Morals of Victorian America*. Native Ground Books and Music, 2009.
Harington, Peter D. *Christmas Treevia*. Harrington Co., pub, 1994.
Matleucci, Marco. *History of the Motor Car*. Crown Publishers, pub, 1970.
Telesco, Patricia. *A Victorian Grimoire: Enchantment, Romance, Magic*. Llewellyn Publications, 1994.
This Fabulous Century: 1900–1910. Time-Life Books, 1985.

About the Author

Lyra Lavender was born in Virginia, but now lives in Florida. She spent most of her working life as a social worker. Now that she is retired, she has much more time to engage in many of the pursuits which she enjoys the most. These include reading many different types of publications, writing, singing, traveling, making jewelry and figurines, and spending time with her husband, Charles, and her sister and her family.

CPSIA information can be obtained
at www.ICGtesting.com
Printed in the USA
FSHW021146080720
71569FS